Fire and Ice:
The Awakening

By Juliana Presto

Fire and Ice: The Awakening
Copyright © 2014 by Juliana Presto

Summary: "Marina Coralin struggles with depression after the
appearance of inexplicable powers led to a mass death. Carter
Pyric grapples with the carefully hidden secrets his mother's
death left him to face. When the two meet on an uncharted
island, their combined forces lead to a newfound trusting
relationship and shocking discoveries about their lineage."

Cover design by Littera Designs
www.litteradesigns.com

For A.J.,
Whose interest with science and
attitude that there are endless possibilities
helped inspire me to create the world
of the Serions.

Chapter One

Marina

The tide rolls into the sandy shore, foam forming on the tips of the rippling turquoise waves; a beautiful scene, day after day. I wade into the cold water and feel its icy touch froth around my ankles. I could freeze it, walk on top of it at will, but I don't. I've shed that careless use of my abilities in attempt for a normal life. And what a joke this 'normal life' is.

I peer into the swirling depths of the ocean in hopes of seeing a fish darting beneath the waves. It'll be my only hope for dinner since all the fruit is rotten by now.

The water has no effect on me. I can register the cool waves but they don't feel bitingly cold to me, simply the same temperature as my body, because they are. My skin is cold to the touch, ice cold. There are times when I still shiver, but the ocean never chills me.

I realize that by now I would've spotted fish if they were swimming anywhere near. I guess it's time to test if those spiky green plants are edible. Sighing, I notice how far I've wandered from the shore. Taking a reluctant breath, I dive into the clear water.

The splotchy film clouding my vision vanishes as my eyes instantly adjust to the underwater world. The fading light shines through the water and casts rippling reflections on the sandy sea floor. Shells dot the ground, turning over as the incoming tide disrupts them. I run my fingers over a smooth shell's surface, but decide to leave it. I already own a large enough collection of similar and exotic shells.

I kick my legs against the current and appear at the shore in seconds. I brush a piece of slick seaweed out of my long hair and fling it back into the ocean, where it disappears into the water. My lungs don't at all burn, despite the fact that I was submerged underwater for several minutes.

The realization irritates me, only reminding me of why I'm here. I want so badly to fit in, but sometimes having power over water and ice can have its advantages.

As the sun sets and transforms the sky into a mural, I walk along the shore. The water touches my feet every so often, erasing the prints in the sand that I've tracked behind me. I try to pay attention to the beautiful sky and the ocean I love, but all I can think about is what I regret. It's been six months; six months alone on this island. But it was my decision.

It's what I wanted.

Still, I wish I could reverse the past that started it all. I wish I could turn back and change history, but I know I can't. The memories haunt me and play back through my mind over and over again until I want to scream. Even now, six months later, I find myself unable to stop thinking about the awful moment when my life plummeted to change.

I walked down the steps that led from my house to the beach with a surfboard tucked under my arm. The cool breeze welcomed me to the Port Angeles beach. I ran over the soft sand and into the sparkling sea. Within seconds I paddled out far, eager to surf the tall waves.

I waited and then I saw the wave rolling towards me, powerful and roaring. I pushed upwards and balanced on my board as the wave lifted me high. I felt myself riding on the ocean as the salty water sprayed up around me. That's when it happened.

As I glided back to the shore I felt the edge of my board collide with something hard and I was thrown into the sea. I used my hands to push me up, but I found that it was hard to move them through the ocean, almost as if something was blocking me. I looked down and gasped as I saw that the water around my hands was slowly solidifying. It became colder and whiter. It became ice.

My eyes widened with shock as I realized suddenly that I was causing it. I didn't know how or why but somehow, I was. The ice spread until it coated the nearby area of ocean, freezing over the surface. I heard people frantically screaming as they were trapped under the ice, unable to free themselves, unable to breath.

A weight of regret crashed down on me as I realized that I was causing them that pain. I had put people's lives at risk. I didn't know how I'd done it, and I didn't know how to stop it, but I felt awful all the same.

My guilt was overcome with surprise when I noticed that I was trapped under the sheet of ice as well, and I didn't *need* to breathe. My lungs felt as if they were brimming with air even though my supply of oxygen should've run out long ago. Sure enough, no clear bubbles rose to the surface. It was like I was breathing under water. It was impossible, but I found it coming to me naturally.

These newfound abilities terrified and bewildered me. I was overwhelmed and suddenly felt that I had to surface due to the claustrophobia of the world crashing down on me.

I pounded on the ice above me, but the frosty surface remained intact. As I brought my hands up again with a forceful blow the water mimicked my actions and streams jetted powerfully upward, banging against the ice. At this point I was hardly shocked, only relived that the water also seemed to respond to my command.

I made a fist and hit the layer of ice as hard as I could. The water followed and I heard a tremendous crack as the ice above me shattered. I shot upward and took a refreshing gulp of air even though it wasn't necessary.

I swam to shore and saw that people stared at me, wide eyed with shock and horror. They knew that I had generated the ice somehow, that it wasn't natural. I looked back over my shoulder and at the sheet of white that still remained. Horror filled me as I saw the hazy shapes of limp bodies floating under the surface. Even with the ice blurring their images, I knew with dread that they had died from suffocation, because of *me*.

The words 'freak' and 'killer' fluttered amongst the small crowd, much to my dismay. I looked at the people, petrified as I tried to find the right words to explain the shock and terror and guilt that welled up inside me.

"Marina!" I heard someone call.

I turned towards the sound and saw that my best friend, Rain, was running towards me. Her face was filled with confusion and worry so she must have known what I had done. Rain stood in front of me and looked back at the frozen ocean. The breeze blew her blonde hair back as she took a deep breath.

"What happened, Marina?" Rain asked in bewilderment. I shook my head, at loss for an answer. "Those people *died*," she annunciated.

"I don't know what happened," I said honestly, in a hushed tone so nobody else overheard. "I was surfing and the water started to freeze and…it was my fault. I didn't know how to control it, but I could make the water move and freeze it. And I could breathe underwater." My words were slow, filled with shock and disbelief.

Rain looked at me blankly, as if she didn't know how to respond.

"I'm not lying! You saw it happen!"

"I believe you, but –but how? How could this happen?"

"I don't know."

"You killed those people!" I heard somebody yell in rage. They were getting over initial shock and becoming angry at what I'd done.

"I didn't mean to!" I protested, cringing away like a deer caught in headlights. "I don't know how it happened!"

The yells intermixed until I couldn't understand a single person's angry words, just a roar of rage. I saw tears rolling down people's faces as they sobbed for the losses of their family or friends. I couldn't take it any longer. I couldn't stand knowing that it was my fault that these people were dead.

Without another thought, I ran back into the ocean, running through the path I'd cleared of ice.

"Marina, wait!" Rain called, but I ignored her.

I dove into the churning water and felt my body completely submerged. I felt like I belonged. I swam underwater for a long distance, what must have been miles. My body seemed to cut through the water quickly and my legs never tired. I never needed to rise to the surface to take a single breath.

Eventually, I saw that the seafloor curved upward, creating shallow waters so I couldn't stay underwater any longer. I stood and saw that I was only a few yards away from an island lush with greenery. The waves washed into a clean sandy beach, but I could see trees, bushes, and bright flowers sprouting further back. I wondered why I'd never heard of the beautiful island previously.

I called up a mental map, and scanned down the coastline. Looking void of human life, it appeared this island was uncharted.

I fought against the current and walked to the shore, surveying the scene. The sky was darkening and the temperature was dropping. It would be night soon so I would be forced to stay on the island. A black shape darted down from the trees and swooped over my head. I shrieked as the bat squeaked a high pitched sound. Nightfall was near and I had to find shelter from these nocturnal animals and crawling bugs.

I batted the scratchy branches away as I stumbled through the trees. The ground was uneven with hills and I nearly tripped over the tree roots that spread over the dirt like an intricate spider web. The sky was darkening to navy and I heard crickets chirping their songs. Desperate to find somewhere to rest, I trudged through the bushes, their boughs scratching my legs as I rubbed against them.

Finally, I found a hollowed-out space in the hills. It was only about four feet deep and barely wider, but it would give me shelter for the night. I squeezed my eyes shut in disgust as I brushed away the stringy remnants of spider webs that hung from the ceiling. When it seemed clear of bugs and debris, I crawled into the opening and lay on the dirt ground.

The dirt was cool against my skin. It was compacted to feel hard underneath my head, but I would have to stand it.

As I shut my eyes, I tried to block out the rustling sounds of spindly bugs and shadowy bats that made up the night. I tried to forget the disturbing image of the helpless bodies trapped under the ice. Instead, I focused on the soothing sound of the ocean waves, repeatedly rolling into the shore.

Eventually, I fell asleep, but the memories of what had brought me here plagued my dreams.

The uncharted island is where I've resided ever since. For six months I've been stranded here, isolated in desertion. I missed my fifteenth birthday, but I try not to think about what I've lost. And I've never once attempted to return.

After so long, the days seem to blend together. They're all mostly the same. I try to build onto my shelter, making it more comfortable. I need to scavenge for edible fruit and plants and if my efforts are futile, then I must find and cook fish. With the identical days boring me more and more, I often sit on the sand and stare at the waves, or collect more seashells to add to my growing collection. Most of all, I spend my time in the water, but always refrain from using the powers that forced me to come here.

Walking along the beach, I realize that it'll be dark soon and I still need to find food. My supplies have run dry. I pluck a thick leaf off the plants that sprout beside my makeshift hut, and sniff it suspiciously. Even though it'll probably be undesirable, it doesn't look *too* poisonous. I bite into it and crinkle my nose in disgust at the grass-like taste that meets my tongue. At least it's edible. With edible being a blessing, it'll have to do.

In my time living here, I've tied sticks and logs together so that my shelter is more spacious, now sticking out of the hill a few feet. I sit in front of the opening that's covered only with flimsy banana leaves and exhale in contentment as I stare at the sunset. I watch it every night, because it's the most beautiful thing in my life. It fills me with a sense of hope.

Keeping my eyes on the scenery, I lean against my hut and breathe in deeply. The salty scent of the sea is always the aroma of the island, one thing I never tire of.

As I sit through another evening in desertion, I wonder if someday I can return to society. I suppose I theoretically could, but will I? I don't know if I can ever face those people again, the people who know that I killed their families. I always regret that day and the shroud of sorrow never lifts. I want so badly to change that day, but it's etched into history forever.

I know that my family, Rain, and my other friends must all be extremely concerned about me. Though, sometimes I think it's better for me to stay out of their lives. My powers would only bring them stress.

My powers; strange, unnatural, *inhuman*.

I still haven't figured out what triggered them, why I've become like this. For nearly fifteen years I lived an average life and nothing about me ever seemed unusual. I can only fabricate ridiculous reasons that I'll never be able to prove true. And the possibilities are endless.

Chapter Two

Carter

The boat glides over the ocean as I bring my oar through the water in smooth, strong strokes. I can feel the waves rocking the polished wooden kayak below me. The sun is still high in the sky, shining bright, unusually warm rays down.

"Where exactly are we supposed to be going?" I ask.

My dad shrugs. "Wherever the ocean takes us."

"Are there even any islands in this direction?"

"Not any charted ones, but don't worry Carter, we can go back when we need to."

I nod warily, now unsure if this is such a good idea. Even though I'm enjoying the kayak ride now, the unpredictable ocean could always change course.

My father's face is filled with reminiscence as he gazes at the horizon. His eyes glaze over with nostalgia, but it's bittersweet. It's a look he reserves only for remembering my mother. I questioned why he spontaneously pulled me along on a trip here, why he chose this city of all places to possibly pursue a new job, but now I understand.

I think I may have figured out his constant shift in holding a steady career or staying rooted in one place for too long. He always gravitates towards places that remind him of my mom, but after a while, the aching becomes unbearable.

We've paddled out so far that I can't see the land behind us any longer. All I can see is the blue-green waves of the ocean and the clear blue sky that seem to spread on forever. Not a single wispy cloud or soaring bird mars the sky's clarity.

My dad and I row the boat farther out into sea, our long oars slapping the water in unison. The motions become rhythmic and continuous. I shiver as cold wind blasts past me, realizing it must be getting late, as the weather is getting noticeably colder.

Dark gray clouds are now rushing into the sky and hiding the sun. I can feel the waves beneath the boat becoming quicker and choppier, larger. It's harder to yank my oar through the water and my arms are growing sore from the work. As I see the dark clouds forming one mass that covers the sky, I realize what's coming.

"I think there's going to be a storm," I say.

My dad looks up at the clouds and nods in agreement. "We should be getting back now."

Just as we attempt to turn the boat around, I see it coming. The waves are growing much taller and violent. Before either of us can react, a huge wave comes rolling towards us. I hear the roar of the water and my eyes are focused on the blue shadow looming above me. I'm frozen with fear as the wave comes closer and closer. Then it crashes down on us.

I grip the edge of the boat tightly until my knuckles turn white and I feel the cold water pour over me. I'm nearly thrown over the side, but I hold on firmly. I look over my shoulder and realize with a start that the seat beside me is vacant.

My dad is in the water, his arms flailing as he struggles to keep his head above the surface.

"Dad!" I yell.

"I'm fine, Carter! Turn the boat around!" he commands, spluttering over the words.

I try to oblige, but then I notice that the oars have been lost. I see them floating in the water nearby, far out of my reach. The waves keep forming, powerful, but not as high as the last. Before I can do anything, my dad is carried away in the direction of the shore. Luckily, he seems strong enough to not be dragged under by the current, and I can only hope that he'll safely return to land soon.

I'm not as lucky.

The ocean has a different plan for me. Its roiling current brings me farther out in the opposite direction. I can't do anything to stop it since my paddles are gone.

As the boat rushes over the sea with uncontrollable speed, I hang on for my life. Water sloshes over the side of the boat and begins to pool around my feet. Worries of sinking fill my head. My clothes are completely drenched by this point and I'm shaking with the cold.

Another monstrous wave peaks in front of me, and I shut my eyes as I see its shadow towering overhead. My boat surges directly into the center of the wave, but by now I hardly register the water, as I'm already soaking. I spit out the salty water that fills my mouth and nose. By now the boat is brimming with water and I don't see how it isn't being weighed down.

This is pure luck. Even though I'm caught in this unfortunate dilemma, it's a miracle that by now I haven't been thrown overboard and the kayak is still afloat. I don't even see how it's possible.

Blisters form on the tips of my fingers from gripping the wet wood so tightly for so long. I ignore the stinging since clinging on is the only chance I have at surviving.

Drops of rain pound down harshly as the clouds discard their contents. I sigh, thinking there isn't a single way this could possibly get worse. I have no idea where I'm headed and no idea when this will stop. I can only hope that when this ends, I'll still be alive.

Through the sheet of rain I make out a hazy shape coming into view on the horizon. I blink, thinking it might be only my imagination. No, there's definitely something there.

I stare at the shape as the fast speed my boat is traveling at brings me closer. It slowly comes into focus. I gasp as I realize that it's an island, an uncharted island, from what my dad claimed.

The ocean laps a beach and further back there's an array of leafy green bushes and tropical flowers growing on the sloping hills that the land leads into. Tall palm trees grow along the beach and the wind bends their narrow trunks. Their feathery tops blow to the side and all the trees curve in the same direction.

There's no sign of inhabitation that I can see on the island. Of course not; it's uncharted. It seems clean and beautiful and undisturbed. No trash litters the beach like any of the public beaches I've traveled to. If any animals live there, they all seem to be cowering from the storm.

The rough waves crash onto the tan sand as the tide gets higher and higher. I watch the water continuously washing into the shore and then forcefully pulling backward, shells and rocks spinning away and dropping underwater. If anything had previously been on the beach, it would've long since been washed away by the aggressive storm.

I come nearer to the island until it can't be more than fifty yards away. The raging waters propel me forward and I've been lucky enough to not encounter any more giant waves. Still, the sea underneath is wild and I'm becoming slightly dizzy as the water continues to rock the boat vigorously.

I'm glad that soon I'll be able to rest on the island. Then all my relief vanishes as my eyes lock on the rocks. Large and jagged, they stick out of the water like menacing spikes. They haphazardly dot the shore where the water meets the sand, but I see that there's a cluster of boulders directly in my path.

I reach my arm down and try as hard as I can to change my course, but the waves are too strong. I stare at the black rocks with dread. There's no way that I'll be able to avoid them now. And my boat is traveling with such speed that the sharp rocks will surely impale the wood; impale me. I take a deep breath and I become closer and closer to the rocks, fearing for my life.

Soon, I'm only a few feet away from the points that jut out of the ocean. I take one last look at the stormy waters and brace myself, squeezing my eyes shut as I feel the forceful impact. Then everything turns black.

Chapter Three

Marina

I instantly know that there had been a viscous storm during the night. The ground around my feet has been turned into wet mud, created by water seeping through the small cracks in my tightly woven ceiling. It's not often that this island attracts storms ranking above a light, short-lived rain.

Trying to avoid the mud, I crawl out of my hut. When I pull back the banana leaves, droplets of water fling towards me. They feel good on my skin; refreshing. No matter how much I pretend that I'm not different, I can't ignore the feeling that water and ice feel nourishing to me. Whenever I'm in the water, I feel at home.

The storm doesn't seem to have caused much damage. Nothing really appears out of place.

I make my way down to the ocean to fish, not wanting to eat another meal of those bitter, spiky plants. The sand is impeccably clean, washed and eroded by the high tide last night. The sky is now clear and blue with no leftover clouds. The only trace of the storm is the lingering cold wind that whips my hair forcefully.

I blink several times, thinking I'm imagining things, as I see a shape by the water's edge. My eyes didn't deceive me. There's definitely something laying there. I'm surprised, since not many objects usually wash up onto this beach.

As I get closer, I notice that planks of wood are spread out amongst the jagged rocks. The wood has been split apart, their ends splintered with broken edges. The severed planks lead me on a short trail to the shape that originally captured my attention. I quickly run over the sand and weave my way around the large pieces of wood. Finally, I reach it.

To my shock, it's a boy, who looks hardly older than me. Nobody ever comes onto my uncharted island, and yet he's here, flesh and blood. A nasty gash is etched across his forehead, tingeing strands of his brown hair red with blood. Scrapes run down his arms, trickling narrow lines of crimson. I assume that the wounds are inflicted by the rocks that he lays miraculously right between.

Lucky for him, his injuries don't look fatal. Even though the water reaches his feet, his head is facing upward and out of the ocean's reach. Still, for a moment I'm worried he's dead.

I lay my hand on his chest and thankfully feel it rise and fall with steady breaths. I notice something strange; his clothes are completely dry, and even *warm*, like they've just been pulled from the dryer. From the evidential wooden planks and the way he's passed out with injuries I would've guessed that he wrecked recently, meaning his clothes would be damp, or at least cold. Even though it's odd, I ignore my realization, thinking that I need to wake him.

Trying to be gentle, I shake his arm. For a moment I worry that he'll stay unconscious, as if in a coma, but then his eyes flutter open.

He stares at me, his eyes wide with surprise and confusion. His eyes are hazel with golden flecks, like bright sparks. I stare back at him, my mind racing with just as many questions as his probably is. I'm bewildered at his sudden appearance on the island I've come to claim as my own.

"Where am I? Who are you?" the boy asks in a daze.

"Marina," I answer, avoiding the first question.

He sits up, his eyes darting over the beach. "I'm alive," he mutters incredulously. He looks back at me. "My boat was shipwrecked on this island, wasn't it?"

I nod slowly. "I think so. What were you doing so far out at sea?"

"What are you doing on this island?" he asks in return.

"I think we both have a lot of explaining to do," I sigh. "I'll show you my hut and we can make a fire so you can warm up some." I say this thinking that a shipwreck would be rattling and traumatic, forgetting that his clothes were already completely dry.

I walk back to my hut and the boy follows me without further question until we reach it, when he asks, "So this is where you live?"

"Yes, why?"

"Well, why do you live on a deserted island anyway?"

Brushing off the ground with my hand, I clear a space and sit on the dirt. "Like I said, we both have a lot of explaining to do. First of all, who are you?"

"My name's Carter Pyric."

"And I'm Marina Coralin. So, why are *you* here?"

Carter shrugs. "My dad and I were in a boat, but then a storm came. He was carried back to shore, but I lost my oars and my boat crashed on those rocks." He points at the black seaside rocks warily, as if they're sharp, dangerous swords.

"You're not hurt too badly, are you?" I ask, glancing at the cut on his forehead.

"No, don't worry about me." Carter immediately changes the subject. "Why do you live here? Why would anybody live on an island all alone?"

I hesitate, knowing I can't reveal my powers to him. "I ran away and this is where I ended up," I answer limitedly.

"Didn't you ever want to go back?"

"No, I did something that I still feel awful about. I don't think I'll ever go back."

Carter nods slowly, not ambushing me with any more questions.

I notice the blue backpack slung over his shoulders and immediately wonder if he has any useful items. "What do you have in there?" I point at his backpack.

"Just a flash light, a first aid kit, some food –"

"Food?" I ask eagerly.

"Yeah." Carter reaches into his backpack and pulls out a bag of beef jerky. Even though it's hardly a meal, I've been living on badly cooked fish and strange plants, so I'm excited to see some regular food. "Do you want some?"

"Yes, thank you!" I snatch the package and almost shovel multiple pieces into my mouth, but then realize I should be rationing it. I reluctantly place it inside my hut for a later meal.

"How long have you been living here?" Carter asks.

"Six months."

He looks at me, his eyes wide with surprise. "How did you even survive here so long? Did you have any supplies?"

"No, I had to find food on my own. There's fish and there was fruit, but I've already eaten all of it."

Carter stays silent for a few moments, but then says, "I guess I'll be stuck on this island for a while, won't I? Do you think there's any way I could get back?" He looks at that shore hopefully, his eyes lingering on the shards of his demolished boat.

"How far away do you live anyway?" I wonder.

"I was just vacationing here," Carter answers. "I'm from Arizona. What about you?"

"Before I ran away, I lived about as close to this island as you can get. My house was right on the Port Angeles shore." I use past tense, assuming that I don't belong at my old home any longer. I've changed since then; developed abilities that I can't explain. I'm reminded that Carter can't know about my control over water and ice. I'll just have to leave him full of curiosity and unanswered questions.

"Even living close, there's no way off this island," Carter replies. "Neither of us has the stamina to swim that far. It'd be almost impossible for anyone."

"Yeah," I murmur, even though I know I could swim back if I really tried.

***

"Does this really stand up against storms and protect you from wild animals?" Carter asks.

"Well enough," I answer. "And I don't think there are any wild animals here. There should be room for both of us."

I enter my shelter and push against one wall. Any leftover water that leaked through the cracks in the ceiling has evaporated leaving the dry, but cool surface of dirt I'm familiar with. The ground is completely smooth, since I long ago made sure to pry away all the rocks, but still compacted and solid. I couldn't find anything to make a suitable pillow and I'm accustomed to the dirt by now.

Carter lies on his side against the other wall, turning and fidgeting in attempt to find a comfortable position. There's more than two feet of space between us, but I still feel the pink flush rising to my cheeks. I offered that he could stay in my hut since it would be rude to force him to sleep outside in the night with no shelter, especially with the chances of another raging storm. Still, the only comfort this provides is warmth. Seeing his restlessness proves my point.

"Sorry if it's uncomfortable," I apologize.

"No, it's fine," Carter replies. He arches an eyebrow and adds, "But are you sure there's no way of leaving this island?"

21

I laugh. "Not that I know of."

"You must be pretty brave to live here for six months. I can't imagine it."

"You get used to it."

With those words being said, I close my eyes and try to fall asleep. As on many nights, my thoughts keep me awake. They're mostly worries and questions about who I am, or more of what I've become. I've always wanted to test out my powers to discover how far they stretch, where they come from, but that would require using them. And that's something I promised myself I'd never do again.

The next morning, I soundlessly exit my shelter, not wanting to wake Carter. I immediately run down the beach and into ocean, drops of water splashing up around my ankles. Once the calm waves peak up to my waist I dive into the sea.

I swim a short distance until I reach the colorful coral reef that I love to explore. Bright fish dart in and out of the tendrils of coral that wave with the motions of the water. A small fish swims under my arm, the sun that shines through the waves glinting off its dark purple scales. Its feathery tail moves smoothly back and forth as it scurries away.

I drift closer to the coral reef, my eyes trained on the beautiful underwater garden. I don't notice that I slice myself on the sharp rocks that litter the floor, until a twinge of pain runs through my finger. I examine the small cut, blood blooming from the narrow, but long wound. It tints the water around red, but washes away soon after. Only small trails of crimson swirl through the ocean.

Something is moving towards me. I see its dark shadow growing on the sand. Slowly, I turn around and find myself face to face with a shark. I'm instantly immobile and my muscles clench up with fear. Even through all my years of surfing and time in the ocean, I've never encountered a shark. I've always been scared of them after hearing the attack stories, though.

It must have been attracted by the blood from my cut. It stays still, as if analyzing me, its beady eyes staring at the red lingering in the water.

Then, it suddenly turns away, ignoring me as if I'm just an insignificant part of ocean. Maybe I am. Maybe with what's become of me, and how much time I spend underwater, I've morphed into a creature that even a shark's acute sense of smell can't make out as human. Even though it saved me now, I can't help but be troubled by the fact. Any other human would've been attacked by the bloodthirsty shark, and even though I'm thankful I wasn't, it's another reminder that I'm not normal.

Maybe I'm not even human.

Bothered by the thought, I quickly swim back to shore and stagger out of the water. A clam shell lies at the water's edge amongst the remains of Carter's boat. I pick it up, turning it over in my hand. It's a common clam shell, but stripes of orange and peach are streaked across the white surface and it stands out as pretty to me. Clasping my hand around it, I walk back through the forest.

Carter's sitting outside my hut, staring into the trees. I realize as I see the blood dried in his hair and across his forehead that he never did anything about his injuries.

"Shouldn't you clean your wounds?" I ask.

He runs his hand across his forehead in confusion and then laughs at himself. "I completely forget about that! I think I have a first aid kit inside my backpack." He takes note of the water dripping from my hair and clothes and adds, "Have you been swimming?"

"Yes," I answer limitedly. "So you have a first aid kit, right?"

Carter takes a small white container out of his backpack and clicks it open. "Yeah, but it looks like I'm out of bandages."

"Then we'll just have to clean your cuts. Are you sure you don't have a concussion?"

"Do I look like I have a concussion?"

I stare into his pupils, but quickly tear my gaze away. "No."

Ten minutes later we've cleaned Carter's wounds and spread medication on them. Most of his injuries are minor, but the rocks carved a jagged gash on his forehead and even with the medicine, I'm still worried about infection setting in.

"We should try to find some fish to eat," I inform. "We need to save some of the food you brought for when we can't find anything else."

"So you just fish from the ocean?" Carter asks.

"Yes, come on." I grab his arm to lead him, but we both pull away at the same time. His skin feels unnaturally warm, contrasting with my cold temperature. "Do you have a fever?"

Carter shakes his head in bewilderment. "I feel fine, but your hands are really cold. Are you alright?"

"Oh, no, I'm fine," I say dismissively, but I want to slap myself for being so careless.

I'd already firmly decided that Carter couldn't find out about my powers for various reasons. My unusually icy cold skin would definitely give away that there was something strange about me. It's almost impossible to have a body temperature as low as mine. I cross my arms in front of my chest self-consciously under Carter's suspicious glances.

But he's not the only one with questions. Carter certainly doesn't seem sick, but after feeling the heat blazing over his skin, I can't come up with another explanation.

Carter and I stare at each other for a minute without speaking. I can sense the questions racing through his mind, just as they are through mine, but neither of us speaks a word. I doubt we'd even be willing to answer if one of us finally said what was on our minds aloud.

As we look at each other, I can't help but feel a connection between us. I can't describe it, as I can't explain many aspects of my life.

I gulp and awkwardly look down at the dirt, slowly continuing through the forest. "We should hurry before all the fish are gone."

Carter mutters in agreement, but I don't look back to see his expression.

Just yesterday I was bursting with many questions. They all revolved around what the world had stealthily hidden from me, about me. I couldn't find an explanation no matter how hard I racked my brain for a logical answer. Now Carter has been added to the mysteries imprinted in my mind and I can't fathom a way my nagging curiosity will disappear.

I realize with a start that what held me awake last night was not guilt, but thoughts of him. He consumed my mind, as he does now. I have a feeling that our lives are intertwined, and now there's no going back.

Chapter Four

Carter

Marina was right; my skin does feel strangely warm. I can sense the heat radiating off my body, but I can't explain it. Other than the pain that throbs across my forehead, I feel fine, not at all feverish. But then again, I can't explain the way her skin is so cold. It's like touching ice. It just doesn't make sense.

But a lot of things about her don't seem to make sense. I'm sure they would if she explained, but she doesn't. She never told me why she ran away to this island or how she got here. I can only guess that she had a boat that turned into the same wreck as mine when it hit those rocks, leaving her stranded.

She must have done something terrible to feel she's banned from her own home. I wouldn't hold it against her; I long to know more about her, but she keeps her mouth shut. She silently refuses to reveal a thing.

Her scenario makes me fear I can never return, either. The difference between us is that she chose to come here, or at least somewhere far away, where as I did not. My dad will never be able to track me down here and it's virtually impossible for me to make it back to the mainland. I could never swim such a great distance across the treacherous sea and make it out alive. And I definitely don't have the correct supplies to repair my boat or build a new one that wouldn't crack into pieces half way through my journey.

At least I'm not alone on this island. It would drive me to insanity to live here in isolation. Marina must use the ocean as her distracting escape from the misery of what she's gotten herself into.

As I search the island for any trace of leftover fruit, I only think about how our situation is becoming worse. Each tree and bush is bare of fruit and soon my few provisions will run out. Despite what she says, I don't think Marina likes to catch the fish, going out of her way to kill them, unless they come straight to her. Unless we stumble over a hidden grove of fruit trees, sooner or later we'll starve.

I trudge over the fallen leaves and branches that carpet the dirt and see Marina standing in the water, the waves splashing around her knees. Her eyes are trained on the horizon, so all I see is golden brown hair streaming behind her.

"Any luck?" I call.

She seems startled and I know she's forgotten her task of catching fish. "What? Oh, no, there don't seem to be many fish around anymore."

"There's not any fruit either," I reply, hiding a grin.

It's clear that Marina's reluctant to leave the ocean, but she slowly walks out of the water and up the smooth sand to where I stand. I notice the conch shell her fingers are clasped around and recall the pile of sea shells in the corner of her hut.

"I guess we'll have to eat the food I brought," I say.

"Do you have any extra?" Marina asks hopefully.

"I'm sorry, but no. Don't worry, we'll find food eventually. We won't starve." My statement contrasts with my thoughts, but I don't want to add to her worry. Although, I suppose she's used to worry after being secluded here for so long.

"How old are you anyway?" I ask suddenly.

"Fifteen," Marina answers, slightly caught off guard. "What about you?"

"I turned sixteen a few weeks ago."

"I try not to think about this, but it always makes me sad when I realize all the things I'm missing at home, like my fifteenth birthday. I know that I shouldn't focus on my problems so much, but I can't help it. Being alone so much, all I can do is think. And a lot of the time I think about what I'm missing."

"Look at it this way, not many people get to live on an uncharted island for a half a year. In fact, I bet you were the first person to ever come here. That's pretty cool, right?"

"That's one way to think of it," she says with a laugh. Marina looks at me, her aqua eyes full of curiosity and asks, "Are you actually *glad* that you were shipwrecked here? Do you just think of this all as an exciting adventure?"

I hesitate for a moment. "To be honest, of course not, but maybe this isn't as bad as it seems.

She shrugs. "I guess."

The day crawls by slowly and Marina again leaves for a swim in the ocean. It's almost like she can't stand to be separated from the water for too long. After the storm and the shipwreck, I'm jumpy around the sea. So with Marina gone, it leaves me time to explore the place that could serve as my home for years.

The island is larger than it at first seems. The wide beach curves about halfway around the perimeter, but the other edges are dominated by a slope of rocks that scare me after my encounter with even the lesser ones on the beach. A lush forest fills in the center, and I'm assuming many animals have claimed it as their home and are hiding away in the foliage of the trees and bushes.

I realize as I walk along the sand that my shoes must have been lost at sea. My bare footprints are indented into the tan beach, the granules seeming to slightly compact where I walk. It's almost like they're melting down into what would be a solid mass if more heat was applied.

Between the way Marina acted like she was burned by a scalding temperature when she touched my arm and how the sand seems to melt when I walk over it, I can feel something happening to me.

It's the same with Marina, her iciness, my heat. We seem to be opposites, yet somehow we're alike; we have an inexplicable connection. I know she feels it too, but neither of us voice it, because we can't explain it.

With me only caught up in my thoughts, I don't notice that I've walked all the way to the rock cliffs on the other side of the island, until the bottom of my foot grazes against one. I stumble backwards, more from surprise than pain.

When I see the rocky formations in black and gray jutting from the side of the otherwise tropical island, I remember the boulders along the shore. The clear picture stands out like it's the only spot of color in a dull black and white photo.

I remember that when the waves were propelling me towards those rocks, they were the only thing I was focused on. There was a storm raging on around me and large drops of rain splattering on my head. Rough waves splashed over the side of the kayak and filled the boat with water. I was in danger of sinking and drowning, yet all I could stare at were those rocks. Every time I glance at them, I'm still worried they'll pierce through my heart, skewering me.

I turn abruptly and stalk away from the rocks, not looking back. I want to leave the cliffs behind me and never venture to that side of the island again. It's simply a deserted and barren area that's maybe simply meant for ships to crash against as a mechanism to keep it secluded.

There's certainly a reason this island was never discovered. Aside from where Marina's been, the uncharted island is undisturbed, meaning that we're the only people to ever wash ashore here. I don't see how that's possible with its location being not too far off the Washington coast. It's almost like some force kept people from reaching this island for all the years that it's existed.

Ever since that shipwreck, my life is cloaked in mystery: this unknown island, Marina's past, the strange things that are happening to *me*.

I've found that after hours of searching my brain for any explanation, I can't find one. It's best to just forget about it, and instead of only confusing myself, focus on trying to survive while living on an island with no escape.

But even when I try to ignore it, this situation only gets stranger and stranger.

I make my way back to the beach, purposely not looking at the sand, but I can feel the crunch of the granules beneath my feet. When I look over my shoulder I don't just see a trail of footprints that will be erased by wind or water, but a path of shapes hardened permanently, imprinted there forever. At the moment, the island records all the steps I take.

"This is the last time we'll get any of these for a while, so enjoy it while you can," Marina tells me as she walks up.

She's holding a bunch of bananas in her hand. Their yellow surfaces are speckled with patches of brown and they look soft, but at least edible and not rotten. I can tell she's thankful to have found any food still growing here since she was clearly under the impression that she'd eaten it all. Though, we will have to wait quite a while before the prime of next growing season for fruit begins.

"I thought they were all gone," I replied.

"It was hard to find these."

When we sit down to eat, I can't help but think that a banana or two isn't much of a filling meal. But I understand a few things about survival and know that we can't have extravagant meals since our few meager provisions and any fish we can catch need to last for however long we're here.

The banana is spotted with darkened bruises, but it doesn't taste too bad so I eat it without complaints. Marina savors it almost as if it were a delicacy, but I can't blame her. She told me before this she'd been reduced to eating plants that she wasn't even positive weren't poisonous. It must be terrible, risking your life just to get your hands on a morsel of food, so you don't starve to death.

I shiver as the sky dims and a night breeze begins to blow. "It's getting pretty cold. Do you think we could start a fire?"

"Really?" Marina asks, raising an eyebrow in surprise. "You think this is cold?"

"Well, if you don't want to…"

"No, it's fine. I'm sure I can start a fire. It's just that, well, to me it's too hot if anything."

Marina reaches over to a pile of flimsy sticks that she must've gathered and tosses them to the space between us. She grabs two flat gray stones that lie beside the sticks and quickly rubs them together just above the newly made pile. I cringe at the loud, scratchy sounds that it makes. Sparks fly from the stones and land on the sticks, igniting the wood. Soon a blazing fire crackles in front of our faces.

I'm comforted by the instant heat and golden flicker of the flames. When Marina leans towards the fire I can't help but notice how the flames seem to shrink and die down. She seems uncomfortable and as a result, stands up and backs away. Marina stands solidary, a few feet away on a small sloped hill, with her arms folded, staring accusingly at the fire.

"You don't like fire?" I ask. "You seemed to at least know how to start it well."

"I've learned survival techniques after six months," she answers. "But I'm not all that fond of fire."

"There's no need to be scared of it."

"It's not that."

Marina hesitantly walks over until she stands only a few inches away from the fire. With a loud crackle, the dancing flames rapidly lessen until they vanish altogether. I stare in surprise at the nonexistent fire for a moment before either of us speak.

"What happened?" I question.

"Must have been a sudden wind," she mutters dismissively, but at the moment the air is stagnant and still.

Chapter Five

Marina

What have I been thinking? That's the first thought that enters my brain as I dump the charred firewood away into an empty hollowed pit. After he noticed how I'm always freezing and how the fire extinguished when I stepped near it, Carter must definitely have suspicions about me. But it's not just the strange abilities I've developed that make it noticeable.

It's also the fact that I spend every second I can in the sea. I can't help it. The ocean calls to me and if I don't answer, then I feel deprived, as if an important part of me is missing.

My eyes are downcast as I walk back to my hut. I don't know what Carter's thinking, but I know it must be about how I'm freakily abnormal.

Not paying attention, in the dark I stumble over a tree root that snakes out over the ground. To stop me from falling, Carter instinctively grabs my hand. His grip is tight so I luckily don't further embarrass myself by falling face-first on the dirt.

I look up and our eyes meet. I can't describe the feeling that I know we both share, until I see the gold flecks in his eyes, like sparks. The feeling is like bright sparks, full of energy, flying out from a fire. We both hold on longer than necessary, but then pull away simultaneously in embarrassment.

I realize suddenly that his hand didn't burn me and he didn't recoil as if I was an icy temperature. If our unusual body temperatures still remain, then we were oblivious.

"Thanks, I almost fell," I say finally.

Carter gives me an unreadable look. "No problem."

We don't speak for the rest of the night. Whether it's from tension or confusion, we seem to have made a silent agreement to stay quiet. I soundlessly crawl into my hut and turn towards the wall. I hear Carter pushing back the banana leaves and I don't want to endure any more tension, so I immediately shut my eyes and force myself to fall asleep.

***

I awake abruptly and feel as if I'm boiling in a volcano, only inches away from the scalding lava. I sit up straight and feel intense heat radiating off Carter. Peaceful in his sleep, he looks fine, but I know something is horribly wrong.

"Carter!" I scream in worry.

He bolts up, eyes wide. "What's wrong?"

"You're burning up!"

"What?" He gives me a confused look and analyzes his hand. "I don't know what you mean." Carter's hand brushes against his jacket and the spot where his fingers just barely touched bursts into flames. I gasp, but Carter acts quickly. He throws his jacket to the ground and stomps out the flames. "What's happening to me?" he cries.

"Don't worry," I try to reassure him, coming closer.

"No, stay away from me!" Carter commands. "I'm dangerous!" He scoots away into the corner of my hut, backing flat against the wall.

I recall the day I froze the water and shudder. "You know, I'm sure it's nothing we can't handle."

He quirks an eyebrow and asks in bewilderment, "How are you not terrified by this? It's not normal! *I'm* not normal!"

I fall silent and see how scared he is. He's terrified to discover these newfound abilities he possesses. I can clearly see the confusion and terror flashing in his eyes. I know exactly how he feels because it mirrors how I felt the day I discovered my powers over water and ice, the day I trapped people under a layer of frozen ocean. All my fear and guilt from that moment has never faded completely. It's those feelings that brought me to this island, and it's those feelings still pounding through me that make me sure I can't return home.

"No," I finally whisper. "You're just like me."

Chapter Six

Carter

"What?" I ask, perplexed. I don't understand what she can possibly mean. "So everything you touch catches on fire?" I catch her blank look. "No, I didn't think so!"

Marina sighs and says, "No, that's not what I mean." She looks thoughtful, as if debating something and then almost reluctantly adds, "Come with me, I'll show you what I mean."

She leads me to the place I most expected, the beach. We stand only a few inches from the water's edge and the cold night air makes me shiver. The moon is full and glows bright in the sky, casting reflections on the calm waves. The rippling water looks navy with pinpoints of white like diamonds, mirrored from the stars.

"Are you going to tell me what you mean?" I press for answers.

Marina takes a deep breath and shakily stretches her arm out in the direction of water. Slowly, she clenches her hand into a tight fist, her nails biting into her palm. She shuts her eyes for a moment, as if scared for what will happen, but then opens them wide with a determined expression.

I'm bewildered by her actions and stare at Marina in confusion. I notice how her blue-green eyes are trained on the ocean and never stray away. I follow her gaze to the water, and then I see it.

I almost don't believe it, but the moonlight illuminates the scene well, and I'm positive my eyes aren't misleading me. My eyes widen as I stare at the sea.

The tips of the small waves turn pale with ice and freeze in place. The ice spreads quickly over the ocean like an intricate web. The blue water turns a frosty white and is frozen in stillness. The sturdy ice has now grown to cover the ocean in a large area; a layer that's a couple inches thick. It creates a smooth, hard surface that reminds me of an ice skating rink.

I finally take my eyes off the ice and stare at Marina in awe. Not even glancing at me, she brings her arm up forcefully and a large wave rises from the shoreline, obviously not of natural forces. It's headed in the wrong direction and it's too close to shore to pick up that much height.

Marina pushes her hand outwards again and the wave races towards the layer of ice. A loud smack sounds into the still night as the wave comes crashing down on the sheet of white. Fractures snake out across the surface and the ice cracks into several pieces. The current resumes its course and pulls out to sea, guiding the pieces of ice along with it.

Her arm dropping and returning to her side, Marina turns towards me with an unreadable expression. She looks at me without speaking, as if waiting for me to say the first word.

I'm astounded and almost can't speak. "Wow," I finally say, breathlessly.

Marina laughs and replies with a smile, "That's one explanation for it."

"How did this happen?"

"How did I get powers over water and ice? I have absolutely no idea. They're the reason I came to this island and I swore to myself that I'd never use them again."

"I sorry that I made you break your promise," I apologize. My voice is soft, still stunned.

"You didn't make me do anything," Marina replies. "It's not your fault. Besides, it's nice to know that I've finally gained control of my abilities and have had some practice using them. It's also nice to have someone else know, someone that I wanted to."

"You said that's why you came here. What do you mean?"

Marina's silent for a moment and then sighs. "I think it was enough that I showed you my powers. I don't want to overwhelm you." She laughs it off, but I see the worry blossom in her eyes.

"So are you trying to say that we both have strange powers?" I ask in disbelief.

"That's what it looks like. Here, try to melt the ice."

"What?"

"Do exactly what I did before," she phrases more simply.

I mirror Marina's previous actions, making a fist and stretching my arm out in the direction of the ice that's drifting away into the distance. I'm not sure what I should be doing, so I simply focus on the ice, focus on melting the ice. Even though it sounds crazy, Marina believes I can do it and after I saw what she was just able to do, I just might believe it, too.

Lighting up the darkness, a few tiny amber flames flicker on the frost. I stare at them in awe as they engulf the ice. I realize that I'm causing this. I'm causing fire to burn on top of the powerful ocean, something nearly impossible. My gaze never wavers from the fire, as I'm too astounded to look away. The flames dance over the waves, a light in the dark of the night.

I slowly retract my arm and unclench my fist. As I do this, the fire vanquishes, but the ice has also disappeared with it. I realize that when Marina showed me what to do, I had control over my abilities. What I thought before was a curse of danger, I now understand can be a gift. The shocking truth is that I have power over heat and fire.

I see that Marina's smiling when I look back at her. "I'm not the only one."

"But how did this happen to us?" I wonder incredulously.

She shrugs and responds, "I have no idea, but it's definitely not something that happens to most people, correction, most humans."

"Are trying to say that we're not human?"

"I don't know what I'm trying to say. All I know is that we're at least not average humans. I mean, Carter, you can make fire burn on top of water and I can turn the ocean to ice. You're always unnaturally warm and I'm always extremely cold."

I reach out to touch her arm, expecting the cringe as if I'm touching freezing ice, but her temperature seems normal. "Not anymore."

"What?"

"You're not cold anymore."

Marina knits her eyebrows in confusion and gently touches my hand. "And you don't feel like you have a fever anymore!" she exclaims.

"Maybe we just don't notice that we have strange temperatures because we're alike," I suggest. "There's a reason that only we have come to this island."

"We have a connection," she whispers, but then looks embarrassed, as if she hadn't meant to voice it.

I smile and reply quietly, "I know."

"All I'm trying to say is that we're not alone in this," Marina clarifies. "We both have powers and both wonder where they come from. We're both trapped on an uncharted island that only we've ever come to. We're both in the same situation."

"Thank you." She's given me hope, so I'm not tormented by terror.

Then she does something I didn't expect. She walks towards me and wraps her arms around me in an embrace. I'm surprised at first, since I haven't known Marina long, but then I hug her back. It feels good to know there's somebody here who I can count on, somebody I can trust.

Chapter Seven

Marina

I can't believe I've finally done it, revealed my powers to Carter. I swore that I'd never tell him and never even use my powers again, but I broke both of those solemn oaths last night. I know I can trust him since he's just like me. Or is he?

Fire and ice; even though we both possess strange powers and are stranded here, fire and ice are complete opposites. Maybe we're not quite as alike as I thought. It disturbs me to know that I burned out fire simply by coming near it, and Carter could easily melt my ice even when it floated on the vast ocean. Even if our abilities come from the same source, maybe we're destined to be opposites, to counteract each other.

I trust Carter even if I've only known him for a short period of time. At this point he understands me better than anyone ever has, and I'll be forced to work with him in figuring out this enigma, rather or not I want to. But I know in my heart that I do want to; I want to get to know him the best I can as I spend more time with him.

As I walk out of my hut, I see a small puddle of water pooled in the hollow in the dirt. It must have sprinkled a light rain last night; an after-effect from the recent storm. I look over my shoulder with a small smile and then slowly point my closed fist towards it.

The clear water stands still for a second and then a thin frost forms on the surface. I can see frosty white color coming into the puddle as the water solidifies. Then it is ice. I crouch down and place the tip of my index finger on the ice. I know the hard surface is cold, but to me it seems nearly room temperature.

I stay squatted by my puddle of ice and stare intently at it. I thought I would never use my powers again. I thought that they only brought destruction, death, and danger. Now I'm beginning to change my views. I see now as I use my abilities that they're also full of wonder and promise. With such talents, I could do great things. And they're a large part of me that I shouldn't be forced to hide.

"So breaking that promise to yourself wasn't just a one-time thing?"

I jump up, startled, when I hear Carter's voice. "Haven't you ever heard of hello?" I ask turning to face him.

"Sorry," Carter replies with a chuckle. "How do you know how to use your powers with such control?"

"Instinct," I say with a shrug. "It seemed to be the same for you."

He nods, thinking for a moment. "You know, now we have to ask ourselves, how did this happen? Even though neither of us have a clue, we need to do everything it takes to find out. This might be the strangest thing that's ever happened to anyone, and it's important to figure it out."

"Where do we start?"

"I think to figure anything out we'd have to leave this island."

"No!" I exclaim immediately.

"Marina, what could have possibly happened that's so bad you can never leave this island?" Carter asks.

"I don't like to talk about it," I say firmly, even though it's held me captive almost every waking moment for the past six months.

"You're going to need to get over it eventually," Carter sighs. "And maybe confiding in someone will help you realize whatever you did isn't so bad. I'm sure what you did really isn't that bad. Maybe if you told me I could help you realize that."

"No, it's awful," I whisper.

"Did you do it on purpose?" he questions.

"Of course not!"

"Then it's not so bad." Carter lays his hand on my shoulder in attempt to comfort me, but the action seems slightly awkward. "Really, you can't live in fear."

"You wouldn't say that if you knew what happened." I stare into his kind hazel eyes, seeing the curiousness for what I might reveal about my past. Not taking my eyes off his, I finally say with dread, "Carter, people died."

Distinct surprise passes over his face for a moment, but he quickly hides it. "Marina I know that you would never kill people. You're a good person."

"I don't know. I don't know how it happened. I couldn't control it at all. It was the first time I'd ever used my powers and I didn't even try to. I had no idea I was…different. I was just surfing on the beach by my house and the ocean started turning to ice. I fell and was trapped, but I could break the ice by moving the water. Still, the other people couldn't get out before they drowned."

The words pour out of my mouth before I muffle them. I realize that I've wanted to tell someone ever since I discovered my powers. I've kept the regret brewing inside me and it feels good to let the secret out of the barred cage inside my heart.

"It was an accident," Carter says finally. "Your powers had just surfaced and you didn't know how to control them. It was only luck that I didn't cause a disaster when I discovered it."

"Thank you," I say softly. "But now you can see why I can never return. Even though it was truly an accident, those people who witnessed it are never going to believe that. I heard them calling me a freak and a killer. They'll always think I'm some abnormal murderous creature." I shudder with disgust at my own words.

"You're not any of those things, Marina. When people don't understand something, they usually assume that it's dangerous and bad."

"I am dangerous."

"That's what I said before, and you tried to tell me I was wrong."

"You *were* wrong," I reply. "You're not dangerous. You've never hurt or killed anyone with your powers, whereas I have, even if it wasn't intentional."

"I haven't *yet*," Carter responds gravely. "I don't know when things could get out of control and I won't be able to stop it. Maybe you haven't realized this, but ice and water aren't usually thought of as dangerous or destructive. Fire burns and destroys everything in its path. It reduces anything nearby into ashes and ruins it forever. I'm fire."

"You're not fire," I contradict. "You just have the ability to cause fire, but you had it under control much quicker than I did."

"You've had six months to get used to all this, but I've just discovered it."

"Like I said, before last night I never once intentionally controlled water or turned anything to ice. I tried as hard as I could to have a normal life, but I realized that I was being ridiculous. There was nothing normal about it. I spent every moment thinking about what I'd done and I was stranded on a deserted island that had never been discovered before."

"Do you really want to spend your whole life on an island?" Carter questions.

"No, but I can't go back," I answer.

"Maybe you're not ready to go back home, but you don't have to go there. We can go somewhere else where nobody knows what you did. We need answers, Marina, and this island isn't going to give us any."

"We'd basically be runaways. We'd be all alone. And what about your family? They must be so worried."

"I would go back to Arizona eventually, but we could stick together for a while. We can help each other out, since we both need some support right now."

I ponder over what Carter's just suggested for a moment. It had never even crossed my mind to leave and go somewhere else entirely, basically be on the run. But now that Carter's here, I know I'm not the only one like this, and I know I won't be alone. Still, everything has been happening so quickly and I wish the racing pace of life would just slow down.

"I'm sorry, Carter, but not yet. I still need a while to get used to all this."

I see irritation flicker in his eyes and know he must be thinking about how I've had half a year to get used to this. Though, Carter is understanding and says with a sigh, "Okay, I know this is all a lot to take in. We don't have to leave now, but we can't spend our lives trapped here."

"I know," I reply with a nod.

Looking back at my puddle of ice on the ground, I see the sun glint off the slick surface. Carter gives me a small grin and his hand clenches into a fist. Orange flames appear on the ice and dance as the air feeds them. I look at him questioningly as the fire dies down.

"It's fun to try it out when I've only just discovered it," Carter explains with a hint of excitement.

Even though he was previously terrified of what was happening to him, now he's taking it much better than I ever have. I don't know if Carter is only trying to seem like it doesn't bother him for my sake, but I know that either way, he didn't learn of his powers through a traumatic experience as I did. When he found out he could control fire, I was there to help explain. When I found out I could control water and ice, an on looking crowd was in hysterics because I'd just killed their family members.

Without another word, Carter walks into the depths of the forest, leaving me to ponder over everything. I can't handle this any longer. No matter how Carter tries to console me, I still have a guilty conscience that eats at my soul. Even if I had no idea what was going on, the dreaded word *murderer* runs through my mind as I remember the angry crowds' claims.

I can never have anything close to a normal life.

I sprint into the ocean at top speed and dive into the water. I hardly notice the refreshing touch of the cool water against my skin; I'm too angry and determined to simply get away from all the thoughts that pound in my mind. But they're trapped inside and will stay with me forever.

My speed is so fast that I seem to glide through the sea as smoothly as a dolphin. The strong current never delays me for even a few seconds. I'm swimming faster than I ever have before; faster than I even thought possible.

The coral reef and sand are a blur around me and my heart pounds with exhilaration. I don't stop my rapid pace until I reach a deep part of the ocean, barren of any fish or living sea creatures. I can tell I'm deep below the surface since the pale sun rays are dim through the dark water. I don't know how far I've gone, but I know that after my tremendously fast race through the water, I don't yet possess the strength to swim back.

I blow the air out of my nose and watch the crystalline bubbles ascend. With all air out of my lungs, I easily sink to the sand. Luckily for me, the air isn't necessary since I can somehow breathe underwater.

Sinking into the sand, I watch the rhythmic motions of the rippling tide above me. Calmed by the image, I lay on the seafloor and close my eyes in attempt to shut out all the stress and rage that previously boiled out of me. I can feel my anger lessening as I'm slowly lulled into sleep.

**

I gasp as my eyes fly open and feel my chest constricting. My lungs are tightening and a weight is being pushed down on me. I can't breathe.

My first instinct is that I need to somehow get air. I inhale deeply, but only water floods through me. Using every ounce of strength I can muster, I push off the ground and up towards the surface. Even with my powerful kicks, I don't know if I'll make it in time. I was very far underwater and with the pain coursing through my chest, I worry that I only have seconds.

As I push myself upward, my eyesight darkens and my attempts weaken. I know that I'm close to reaching the air now, but my efforts seem futile.

My hand emerges into open air and I rise up to the surface. My body goes limp with fatigue and I barely have the strength to take a small breath of air. My vision is blurred and darkened, and I can't see where I am. Slowly, the shapes around me fade and the light darkens as I lose consciousness.

"Marina?" a frantic voice cries.

I blink as my eyes adjust to the light. I must be back in the forest since I see the green foliage of trees in my peripheral view and feel the dirt underneath me. Carter leans over me, his brow furrowed with worry. I can tell that he was scared I wouldn't survive.

"Carter, what happened?" I ask, remembering the awful feeling of almost drowning.

I sit up and realize that his hand is clasped around mine. His palm is clammy with sweat and I realize that he was truly worried about me. The side of my mouth curves up in a small grin as I look up at him. Carter glances at our hands and embarrassment reddens his cheeks. He immediately let's go and opens his mouth as if in protest, but is at a loss for words.

"Sorry," Carter finally says.

"No, it's fine," I assure him. "You were just worried that I was going to die."

He nods in relief. "Exactly. How did that happen, Marina?"

"How did what happen?" I ask in confusion.

"How did you pass out?" he exclaims.

"I was being careless," I admit. "I was feeling awful again and swam out farther than I ever had before. I sank to the seafloor and fell asleep. I don't know how long I was down there, but it must have been a while because when I woke up I felt like I couldn't get enough air. I barely made it to the surface and passed out."

"I was really worried when you never came back. I went looking for you and saw a shape in the ocean. When I realized it was you, I swam and pulled you back to shore. I'm just glad the current carried you close enough so I noticed where you were."

"You were able to swim that far?"

"I couldn't just let you drown!"

"Why do you think I couldn't breathe?" I question.

"Because people need air," Carter answers, raising an eyebrow.

"I know, but I can breathe underwater," I explain.

"Really?"

I nod. "I guess it was stupid to fall asleep underwater, but I didn't think I'd ever run out of air."

Carter looks at me thoughtfully and says, "Well, we're not immortal or indestructible. We both have our limits. I'm sure that if I was trapped in a burning building for hours I'd eventually burn or suffocate to death. And even though you seem to be able to somewhat breathe underwater, you are still human. You'll eventually need to breathe air."

"But I'm not human, Carter."

"Yes, you are. I know this is all traumatic, but you're not some strange creature. You're still a person, you're just special."

"Abnormal," I protest.

"Think of it this way, you would've drowned if I hadn't saved you in time. Normal people drown if they're underwater too long."

"I just realized that I never thanked you for saving my life," I say, realizing how hard it must have been for him to swim such a long distance across the ocean, pulling my weight with him, especially when he's wary of the sea. "Thank you."

"You're welcome," Carter answers. "But it's not that big of a deal. I know you would've done the same for me. Besides, I couldn't just leave you to die. I would regret it forever."

I comprehend the meaning of his words. I can tell that Carter wouldn't only feel the remorse of letting somebody die; he'd miss me. But of course he would. Since Carter and I are each other's only company on this island and we've confided in each other, we've become close friends. The unexpected burst of excitement fluttering inside me fades, even though a small part of me wonders if it's something more…

My thoughts are interrupted as I get the unsettling feeling that somebody is watching me. My instincts are alert as I feel eyes staring at my turned back. In an instinctive motion, I quickly swivel my head around, but nobody is there.

"Is everything okay?" Carter asks in concern.

"Yes," I mumble, but then inquire, "You don't think anyone else is on this island do you?"

"How could they be? Besides, you've been here far longer than I have. You know this place much better than I do."

I nod, but remain partially unconvinced. I don't know how someone else could be here, but my instincts almost never steer me incorrectly. "Yeah, I guess it was probably just my imagination," I murmur. "I'm going to just go take a walk in the forest," I add, my curiosity getting the better of me.

"Try not to get hurt," Carter says, half joking.

I mumble an agreement and rush into the dense wall of trees, into the spot where I thought somebody was watching me. I part the scratchy branches, clearing a path for me to walk through. My steps are light and balanced as I'm careful to not make a sound. I peer into the trees and wait in silence for something to happen.

A light wind stirs in the air. It whips my wavy hair across my face and I have to brush it out of my eyes. In the second my eyes are covered, the sound of leaves crunching and delicate branches being bent and strained reaches my ears. My head snaps up as I scrutinize the area around me. Both the ground and trees above look undisturbed, so the sounds seem likely explained as caused by the wind.

Though, in my time here I've come accustomed to what such small winds can move. The noises sounded too solid to be caused from such an airy substance.

I don't know how anyone would've arrived here without Carter and me noticing. This is the only time I've doubted my solidary existence here, with the exception of Carter. I don't see how anyone could've come today, unless it was when Carter and I were fully occupied with my near-death.

Still, there's no trace of a destroyed boat like when Carter was shipwrecked and anyone lucky enough to survive the journey here without a boat would've at least passed out from lack of air in the churning sea or be deterred by the rocks. I can't formulate any other rational explanation for anybody coming here aside from the water. Nobody would have the supplies for a planned trip here since the island is uncharted.

My suspicions seem to be revealed as faulty when I find no evidence, no matter how hard I search. The detective act I'm putting on is futile when there's no clues to be found. I must have mistaken the wary gaze of a frightened animal as a human intentionally spying on me from the coverage of the trees. Of course Carter and I are still alone on this island.

When the light dims and the sky transforms to the color of a ripe peach, I'm surprised by how long I've been searching. I got too caught up in my goal of proving my theory correct. After circling the entire forest for this long period of time, I'm a bit disoriented and unsure of the way back to my hut.

The stump of a fallen tree jutting from the ground catches my eye and I sit down on it, trying to focus on the area that I now know like the back of my hand. If I concentrate, I can easily find my way back, as I know every inch of the island.

A twig snaps from behind a group of trees and catches my attention. The soft sound of what seems to be footsteps is near. With my previous idea fresh in my mind, I'm still uneasy. I quietly creep over to the trees and hide behind the large wooden trunk. Angling myself toward the other side where the sounds came from, I take a deep breath, not knowing who or what I'll find.

Not wanting it to take me by surprise, I spring out from behind the tree like a devious cheetah pouncing on its prey. I collide into somebody so quickly that I don't even have the chance to see who it is first.

I open my eyes from where I lay sprawled on the ground, and find myself face to face with Carter. We stare at each other wide-eyed with surprise. I feel like a complete idiot. Of course it would be Carter exploring as he usually does. I'd gotten too worried that a stranger really was lurking around, and my imagination had gotten the best of me.

"What in the world was that about, Marina?" Carter exclaims.

"I'm sorry," I mumble in embarrassment. "I thought somebody was spying on me and when I heard footsteps…"

Carter sits up and his eyes dart cautiously around us. "Wouldn't you have noticed if somebody else was here?"

"It was only today and I don't see how we couldn't have seen them arriving."

"So you were probably just imagining things?"

"I guess."

"You know, you've got to stop being so…nervous. You're always worrying and imagining things and thinking of ways everything could go wrong. I just want you to know, Marina, everything's okay."

I purse my lips in frustration. "You just don't understand!"

Carter sighs and lays his hand on mine in attempt to comfort me. "I know that you think you're a terrible person because you *accidently*," he emphasizes the word to show it's true, "killed people. That one event didn't wreck your life. You've just got to move on from that and not let it make you miserable all the time. You have your entire life ahead of you, so don't destroy it."

"Thank you, Carter," I say sincerely in a soft voice.

"You're welcome," he replies and his fingers twine around mine.

I wonder for a moment if it's simply a gesture to comfort me since Carter's very caring, but then I look up into his eyes. Our gazes lock and the golden sparks in his eyes are almost hypnotizing. He gives me a small, slightly embarrassed smile, but doesn't move.

My breath catches in my throat and I open my mouth to say something, but no words come out. Instead, I avert my eyes and look down at the plain ground.

Carter laughs, but it's a forced sound to conceal the awkwardness hanging between us. We stand up and I realize our hands are still clasped together. Our eyes meet again and we both end up turning away, letting go of each other's hands.

After a minute of silence Carter inquires, "Do you think you're ready to leave this island yet?"

I take a deep breath. "I'm sorry, but no, not yet. I promise I will be soon, though."

"I just really think we should find out how we have powers over fire and ice. It's not just something that happens every day."

"I know, and we've got to be the only ones in the world like this. It's pretty coincidental that we both washed up on this island. Think about it, we, the only people in the world with strange abilities, both end up on an uncharted island when I live in Washington and you're from Arizona. It can't just be a coincidence. There's an important reason for this; it's fate."

"Well, I'm glad that this happened," Carter says. "And I'm glad I met you."

"Me too," I agree, unable to stop the smile that emerges on my face.

Not another word is spoken between us after that, as we walk in silence, back to my shelter. The sun is just a small glowing orange orb just above the sea, slowly disappearing from my view. I watch until it's gone altogether and the sky begins to change from the mural of color to a solid deep blue.

I wordlessly take out the last of Carter's meager provisions and we split them equally. The air is thick with our silence and I only hear myself chewing on the tough, salty meat.

"How will we leave when you want to?" Carter finally says.

"We have some time to think about it," I say with a shrug. "I could swim the distance, but I don't think I have enough strength to carry you behind me."

"And I'm guessing if you made some sort of ice raft it would melt when I sat on it."

"Yes, even if I can't tell anymore and you can control it better now, you're still pretty hot."

I realize how I worded that just a moment too late, when his face is already tinging pink. I feel heat rushing into my cheeks as I stammer out a clarification, "I –I mean, that your skin is…uh, warm."

"I know," he says in amusement and the redness fades.

He rests his wrist on the ground so his palm is facing outwards, towards a tree. He looks to be concentrating hard and before I can react, a branch of the tree bursts into flames.

I immediately freeze the flame and they grotesquely stick out in spikes from the tree. They curve at odd angles and end in sharp points, frosty white with an orange tint beneath. I wonder if the fire still rages on beneath my sturdy case of ice.

53

"Why would you do that?" I exclaim.

Carter shrugs and replies, "Just testing this out. Besides, I knew you would freeze it before anything burned down."

"I won't always be around to fix your mistakes," I say in annoyance. "You can't be careless and burn down a whole forest just because you were curious to see what you could do!"

"I'm not that irresponsible," Carter protests. "And I'm older than you."

"Only by a year, and that doesn't mean you're more responsible!"

"Marina, I can handle this fine," he says honestly.

"I know," I sigh. "But I don't know if I can."

"You can," Carter encourages. "Everything is going to be okay," he adds in assurance.

I nod, melancholy as usual, and stare ahead at nothing, facing the sea, my back to the forest. As the night encloses around the island, I still feel someone's stare boring into my back. I know Carter must be aware of my thoughts as he narrows his eyes and looks behind us in a quick, jerky motion.

"Do you think someone's here, too?" I question.

"No, of course not," Carter says evenly. He shivers as a light breeze edges into the atmosphere, even the slightest bit of cold still having effect on him. "I'm going to go inside. Night." He looks back at me and adds, "Maybe we can think about expanding this into a real house sometime. We need something to provide shelter." With that suggestion, Carter climbs into the shack and disappears behind the banana leaves.

With no one around to distract me, my senses are alert and I'm verging on paranoia. When the wind rustles the leaves above me, I jump up in panic. A leathery bat glides from the tree and cracks a twig in the process. I'm startled and let out a high-pitched yelp.

"What's wrong?" Carter exclaims, emerging from the shelter and jumping up in a defensive stance.

An embarrassed grin reaches my lips. "Nothing," I tell him. "I just got startled by a bat."

"You sure?" Not the slightest hint of irritation is evident in Carter's tone, even though I disturbed him for no reason. The way he came to my defense so quickly and seemed so worried only adds to my suspicions that he cares about me being alright.

"Yes."

He gives a forced laugh and says, "We're both being ridiculous and too easily scared. Let's just both remember that there's obviously nobody here except us."

"Of course. I'd have to start hallucinating eventually after being trapped here so long," I laugh.

"You should get some rest. It'll be good for you."

"I guess."

Carter nods and retreats into the hut. I stand alone outside for a few moments. The wind catches the salty scent of the sea and brings it towards me. It blows the ripples of my long hair around my face and brings its cool, refreshing feel. I feel almost regenerated, but I long to swim. It would calm my nerves. But it's late and I'm still apprehensive to be alone here, especially at night.

Turning my back on the ocean, I see a shadow shift the trees out of the corner of my eye. Containing the worry that surges through me, I dismiss it as simply the shadow of a branch or bat shifting in the wind. I convince myself that I'm simply imagining things, until the feeling that I'm being watched fades to such a small amount that I can easily ignore it.

Listening to Carter's advice to get some rest, I retire into the safety of my shelter as I leave the uneasiness that previously consumed me behind.

Chapter Eight

Carter

It shakes me awake suddenly, like an electric current passing through my body. I jitter from the after-shock. The feeling wasn't painful, nor was it pleasant. Tingles still prickle down my arms.

I look around the enclosed space, but see nothing out of the ordinary, nothing that might have shocked me somehow. The small hut is the same as always: a floor, ceiling, and sloped walls all made of dry brown dirt with only a few belongings strewn beside the door.

I only now notice that Marina is awake too. She looks equally surprised as her eyes meet mine. "Did you feel that?" she asks.

"Yes. Maybe it was a poisonous spider bite." I search my arms for any trace of red marring the skin or swelling welts, but I see nothing unusual.

Marina copies my actions and answers, "It doesn't look like it."

"What could it be?"

"I feel like my whole past is a mystery," she sighs in despair. "Lots of it *is*, and yours, too. We don't know why or how we have these abilities, why we never knew about it before, or what that feeling was. Everything's just so *weird* lately."

"Hey, we've been over this. Everything's going to be alright," I reply optimistically.

Marina stares at the ground, trying to keep the disagreement from her face. After a moment, she looks up at me with a determined light in her turquoise eyes. "You know what, Carter? I'm ready to leave this island," she states firmly.

"You sure?" I stammer, surprised by her hasty decision after so long delaying it.

"Yes, I can't spend my whole life stranded here."

"Then let's find a way to leave," I suggest with a smile. "Do you know how to build a boat?"

"We don't have the supplies," Marina answers thoughtfully. "But I'm sure we'll think of something. In the meantime, we'll just have to wait here and come up with ideas, but just know that I'm ready to leave whenever you are."

I'm so glad that Marina's finally decided to depart from this uncharted island and get back to civilization. I'm determined to find out how we can possibly control fire and ice, and I'm not going to let the fact that I can hold me back from living life. Not thinking, I reach over and intertwine my fingers with hers. Marina looks at me, her eyes wide with surprise.

"Oh, I'm sorry," I say, feeling the heat rush to my face.

"No, it's…um fine," Marina says softly, and tightens her grasp on my hand.

We both smile as we sit in silence. I suddenly realize that we've slowly been gravitating closer together. Her nose is only two inches from mine. The mixture of excitement and nervousness is clear in Marina's eyes, framed by her long, dark lashes. I feel the same way. My hand is still clasped around hers and I feel slight perspiration on her palm. She slowly moves closer until we're nearly touching.

Suddenly, an enormous boom echoes through the atmosphere. We jump away from each other, startled.

"What was that?" Marina gasps.

Letting go of her hand, I push away the slick banana leaves and peer out. The sky has turned from yesterday's clear blue to a pale gray, darker in spots where waterlogged clouds reside. I assume the loud sound must've been the rage of thunder. "It looks like another storm."

"Like the one that brought you here?"

"Yeah, I think it's going to set us back a few days."

"So when I finally agree to leave, a storm comes and messes everything up. Just my luck," Marina mutters in irritation.

"I think you might want to take my advice and build a larger, sturdier shelter if we're going to be stuck here for a while."

"Well, you can't exactly build in the middle of a storm."

We spend the majority of the day idling in the hut. Boredom overcomes me and I suggest that it's a good idea to get some rest. It's not so much that I'm physically tired, but my brain can only take so many shocking realizations at once. It feels numb with knowledge, and I can't just keep attempting to solve what I know I currently have no answers to. It doesn't take long to fall asleep and I'm glad I used the time to take a break from my new life.

I see that Marina ignored my idea of resting by the way she's crouched in the corner, intent in her work. She's sorted her impressive collection of seashells into multiple piles that look to be categorized by type, color, and size. Marina must have gotten bored after so much time of waiting for the storm to pass that she did the only thing she could think of to fill time.

"I'm guessing we need more fish," I say habitually. Marina jumps, startled out of her concentration. "Sorry."

"No, you're right. I'll try to be fast."

She starts out the door, but I rest my hand on her arm to stop her. "I'll go, it's about time I make myself useful around here."

"You sure?" Marina wonders, raising an eyebrow. "I know you don't like the water."

"I'll be fine," I reply and leave without another word.

Truthfully, I'm nervous for Marina to return to the ocean after she nearly drowned last time. If I hadn't seen a shape bobbing on the horizon when I did and gotten the adrenaline to swim the distance, she couldn't have possibly survived. I shudder thinking of what would've been Marina's fate.

We both have our limits. She got too discouraged and that mixed with the thought that she was indestructible was almost her defeat. That's one of the main reasons I'm so anxious to leave this island. I know that Marina dwells on the sorrows and regrets of her past. No matter what she says, I know that beneath her act, she still hasn't forgiven herself. I can't seem to convince Marina that it wasn't her fault.

The wind is too cold for my liking and I shiver, my teeth chattering. The rain pours down as thunder continues to boom across the sky, accented by flashes of lightning. The waves by the smooth beach Marina normally spends her time at seem unforgiving and hazardous. I know I'd get swept out to sea. Grudgingly, I venture to the rocky cliffs.

Against all odds, the water by the rocks seems calmer. I stare at the sharp edges like they're my enemy, and I still feel like they are.

Trying to not stare at the jagged dark surface below me, I take the safest path over the rocks and into the ocean. The rocks are slick from the rain, as are my feet. My bare feet provide hardly any traction against the slippery boulders. An uncharacteristically large wave comes crashing down around my ankles and causes me to lose my balance.

The strong current tries to pull me away, but I cling to the jagged edges of the rocks. My knuckles turn white from trying so hard to not be taken out to sea. I've never been that great of a swimmer. I can do the basic free style decently and stay afloat in a lake, but I stand absolutely no chance against the powerful ocean, especially when the few objects I have to cling onto are slick with water.

I feel my grasp lessening against my will, but I can do nothing to stop it. Eventually just the tips of my fingers on my right hand are clenched around a piece that sticks out from the formations. The current is relentless and my arm aches. The seafloor below me dives down steeply so that I wouldn't be able to stand with my head anywhere near the surface. I know that I won't be able to hold on much longer.

Just when I feel myself starting to slip away, I hear a sound. It's drowned out by the rain and thunder, but it begins to sound clearer.

It's a voice, yelling out in panic; Marina's voice. "Carter?" she cries.

"Here!" I yell, just as I lose my hold on the rocks.

A wave crashes over my head and fills my lungs with water. I gasp for breath, but there's no air to breathe. I only see the dark blue waves churning violently above me. It only reminds me of the terrible storm that brought me here.

I struggle against the current, but it pulls me down and away. No matter how hard I try, I can't resurface. And I'm running out of the little breath I held as I feel my chest constricting.

Suddenly, a hand is in front of my face. I grab it and I'm pulled to the surface. I take a gulp of necessary air and instantly feel better.

Marina waits beside me. "Come on!" She grabs my arm and leads me to the rocks.

I pull myself out of the water, scratching my leg against a sharp peak. Even though it seems minor, pain floods through my leg. I feebly stand up and see the waves wash a line of blood away from the rocks. The cut winding down my leg is a new addition to the healing scars from my ship wreck.

"Are you okay?" Marina asks worriedly, taking my arm and guiding me onto the sand of the beach.

"Yes," I gasp breathlessly after a moment.

She gives me a halfhearted smile. "I guess you were right about leaving this island. In the past two days we've both almost drowned."

"This place almost seems cursed. Thanks for helping me."

"Well, now we're even, but of course I would've saved you anyway."

"How did you know I needed help?" I ask, realizing that Marina would've been in the hut.

"That's the strange part," Marina replies, her eyebrows knitting together in confusion. "I was organizing my shells when I suddenly felt panicked. I didn't know why, but then I heard a voice in my head asking for help. I immediately thought it must be you."

"I didn't call for help," I respond in bewilderment, remembering how I was too stunned to speak.

"I just thought that maybe you had a new...power or something."

"Not that I know of."

"Actually, looking back, I think it was a girl's voice," Marina says in realization. "At the time I didn't have the chance to think about it, but who could it be?"

I shrug, at loss for an explanation. "That's why we need answers. I'm just glad that you came in time before I drowned."

"I'm glad, too," she says softly, with a smile.

Before I can react, she hugs me. I'm taken off guard again, like the night on the beach when we found out about each other's powers. I understand why she wants to feel close to somebody, feel cared about, after living in isolation for half a year. She still feels like she's an enemy of everyone she used to know; that they all think of her as a menace now. But now, with our arms wrapped around each other, I know it's something more than simply longing company.

Marina looks up at me and her eyes lock with mine. In this one moment, the wind seems to stop. I don't register the cold temperature of my clothes, drenched from the ocean. We lean towards each other until our faces are less than an inch apart. I feel her breath on my face, smell the seawater soaking her windswept hair. I close the distance between us and kiss her.

I can't describe the feeling that overcomes me. It's like something I've craved forever. We stand that way for a moment, our lips pressed together, but then she withdraws.

"I'm sorry," I say quietly.

"You don't need to apologize," she replies softly. I see the redness of a blush rise into Marina's cheeks and she smiles. "I have to admit, Carter, I've wanted to do that for a while."

"So have I," I respond, finally sharing my feelings with her.

I take her hand and we wordlessly walk across the shore. We're oblivious to the rain that pours down, adding to the soaking state of our clothes and the thunder that booms in the sky. Nothing penetrates our happiness and I'm glad that for once we've both forgotten the worry and sorrow that seems to relentlessly plague us.

"So…" I say, the word ringing with tension.

Marina laughs and for once I don't see any hidden regret in her bright eyes. "This is nice," she says, glancing at our clasped hands.

I nod, thinking how in one moment our conversation changed from how we were so relieved each other were safe…to this. That shows that we really are concerned about each other. And for me at least, that worry is magnified because of how much danger this island seems to cause. I wouldn't be surprised if it really was cursed after I almost died in a ship wreck and we both nearly drowned.

Suddenly, I'm aware of the cold after standing out here in the rain for so long. Marina must be immune to it because cold, icy, and wet seems to describe the perfect climate for her. I shiver, despite my attempts to resist the frigid air.

"We should probably go back inside the hut," Marina says sympathetically.

"I don't mind if you want to stay outside."

"No, it might not be good for you to be in cold temperatures for too long. And I probably shouldn't be around extreme heat very often."

We enter our shelter and I immediately feel claustrophobic. After being outside in the open air, even with the cold and rain, this seems confined and stagnant. But I know Marina was right to return here. We still have so much more to discover about what's happened to us, and we shouldn't take any risks before we know everything for sure.

"You're right," Marina says.

"What?" I ask.

"It wasn't my fault. It was an accident. I didn't mean to kill all those people," Marina responds matter-of-factly.

"I'm glad you finally realized that," I say in relief. The regret that previously haunted her eyes has died.

"I'm glad, too. Thank you for helping me realize it."

"No problem."

We sit side by side in silence for a moment, our backs pressed against the sloped dirt walls. Marina rests her head on my shoulder and for once the gesture doesn't seem awkward. I twine my fingers around hers and we just stay that way, listening to the rain pound just outside. A slight cold penetrates the hut, but I ignore it. It seems that now the cold is being pushed away, as if heat is counteracting it.

"You know, maybe it won't be so bad being stuck on this island," Marina reasons. "At least you're here with me."

I smile. "When you think about it, it's a good thing that you ran away and I got shipwrecked here. If that hadn't happened we never would've met each other. And we both overcame hardships together and didn't have to face our powers alone."

Marina mirrors my expression. "That's true. I guess it is a good thing that we both got stuck on this island."

Our eyes lock again and she slowly leans closer towards me. Then the moment halts as a sudden gunshot rings through the air.

Chapter Nine

Marina

"What was that?" I gasp in terror.

Carter is just as startled as I am, his eyes wide with fear. "I think it was…"

"A gunshot," we both finish in unison.

"That means that I was right," I whisper in understanding. "Somebody was here."

"But how?" Carter asks.

"I don't know," I say, barely choking out the words. I try to keep my voice calm and not let it rise to the note of panic that it wants to take. I gulp down the fear that floods through me and add, "But they're here now." I wish whoever's here hadn't arrived, not only because of our safety, but because they destroyed the moment. "What should we do?"

"We need to get out of here before they find us," Carter declares.

"What do they want?" I wonder.

If they've taken the precaution to be armed with a gun, that can't be a good sign. The fact that they fired it, probably only to scare us, is even worse.

"I don't know...just stay close."

Carter departs from the shelter and creeps around the trees, sticking to the shadows. Darkness has fallen and it only adds to my worry. We won't be able to see if a bullet is coming towards us, ready to pierce our hearts...I shake the awful thought from my mind and take Carter's hand. I'm glad to have him by my side and know I'm not alone. He gratefully wraps his fingers around mine and pulls me behind a cluster of trees.

"We have to be quiet, and keep your eyes open," he warns in a soft whisper.

I nod and peer into the darkness, but nothing moves in my line of view. "Where do you think they are?" I ask, careful to keep my voice almost inaudible.

"I don't know."

The night is still, aside from the rain that still falls. The thunder has subsided and is nonexistent at the moment. I stand still, lurking close to the looming trees and trying to keep my breathing even. Carter squeezes my hand, letting me know everything will be okay.

Even though I know it's only been minutes, it seems we've stood here for hours. We can't leave, because if the people in possession of the guns detect any movement, and we don't even know where they reside at the moment, we'll be as good as dead.

"I'm beginning to think this place really is cursed," Carter says half-jokingly.

"Or *we* are."

"No, forget I ever said anything about curses. They're not real."

I say nothing.

A rustle of movement sounds through the night and Carter and I both jump out of the trees in unison. Figures clothed in black stand before us. Their faces are obscured in shadows created by the hoods draped over their heads, so I can't see their features. They stand in a line: six of them. They all hold lethal-looking weapons. One stands in front of the others, with a stature of confidence and is clearly the figure of authority. Its hands are grasped around a silver gun that looks scarily powerful and unlike anything I've ever seen.

Carter and I stand still, not sure what to do. Any sudden movements and I'm sure that silver gun would fire straight at us with precise aim.

"What do you want?" Carter asks calmly.

The leading figure advances a few steps towards us, tapping the barrel of his gun in the palm of his hand thoughtfully. "What do you think?" It's a man's voice, deep and filled with menace and scheming.

We both look at him quizzically and Carter replies, "Are you bandits? Convicts?"

He laughs. "I know that you're not stupid. Maybe…do you really not know?" When Carter and I both stare at him blankly he adds, "Then why would you be hiding on this island?"

"We're not hiding here," I speak up.

"You really don't know, do you?" he asks incredulously.

"Just leave us alone," Carter commands. "We haven't done anything, we don't even know you!"

"Maybe you don't realize it, but your very existence is a threat to me."

Before we can react, the gun is facing towards us, the pale moonlight glinting off its silver surface. The rain has stopped, leaving my focus only on the gun. Terror courses through me and my eyes don't move from the metal. He moves his hand to the trigger and laughs cruelly.

"Run, Marina," Carter whispers. "Run!"

I dart away in the direction of the ocean and Carter is right behind me. I hear the deafening boom of the gun shooting and Carter shoves me to the ground as he dives to the space beside me. The wind is knocked out of me as I hit the dirt, and I spit the debris from my mouth.

A silver bullet streaks only a few feet above my head with indomitable speed. If Carter hadn't pushed me to the ground, then I would've been dead by now.

"Come on, Marina!" Carter instructs and pulls me to my feet.

I stabilize myself and we sprint down to the shore. The soft sand makes it noticeably harder to run and our speed reduces as our bare feet sink into the granules. Trying to trek through the sand at a fast pace is grueling and my legs ache before we've even reached the ocean. Finally, the waves lap around our feet as we stand by the water.

"How can we get away?" I ask desperately.

"I don't know, but it has to be fast!" Carter says in panic. "And I don't think I can swim fast enough."

It's hard to think with all the pressure weighing me down. Fear fills me as I rack my brain for any solution to a way of transportation that would safely get us back to Port Angeles, as quickly as possible. Suddenly, an idea glows golden. I whistle sharply, the shrill sound high-pitched and alerting. I really hope this won't fail us. It has to work.

Carter looks at me anxiously. I know he's perplexed, but he trusts me.

The black clothed figures emerge from the forest, wielding their weapons threateningly. The leader's head turns towards us, and I worry that my plan will fall through. I gulp down the anxiety and close my hand into a tight fist, my arm stretched in his direction. Their clothes are still damp from the rain and that helps my powers thrive.

I'm rushed, so my actions aren't completed, but a thin layer of white ice forms around their bodies, paralyzing them below the neck. I've trapped them momentarily. Carter smiles in approval as we look at them, helplessly frozen in place, their weapons enclosed in the frost.

"Serions!" the leader hisses. The word triggers a slight recognition at the back of my mind, but I don't have time to dwell on it.

I hear squeaking emanating from the water and see their slick gray fins appear, followed by their heads.

"Dolphins?" Carter asks quizzically.

"Yes," I answer. "Come on!"

I grab the dolphin's dorsal fin and clamp my knees firmly around its sides so I'm won't be shaken away. Carter does the same and mounts the other dolphin. I whistle loudly and the dolphins take off, splashing through the waves as they jump up into the air with us hanging on tightly.

"How did you think of this?" Carter wonders.

"Dolphins seem to respond to me, and they're fast," I answer.

Carter nods, slightly amused.

I look back over my shoulder and see our enemies standing by the water's edge. Even though I can't see their faces, I can simply tell by their stances that they're outraged. The leader points his unique gun at us and fires, but the bullet is lost at sea, since it's impossible to hit either of us with the dolphins' quick and unpredictable movements. They're powerless against us now.

The island that I've spent the last half year on fades until it's just a small speck on the dark horizon. I'm leaving behind the beach and coral reef that I spent my days on, the lush green forest, the menacing cliff of sharp rocks, and the makeshift hut. I left behind my pile of exotic shells, but it was hardly a loss since I can always gather new ones. Some things about the uncharted island I might miss after I've resided there so long, but most of me is glad to be free. I feel like I've finally been released from a confining cage, and I'm glad that Carter is by my side.

It feels like we've been riding over the waves for ages, and I assume we don't have much longer until we reach our destination. Even though we're surrounded by only dark water and a velvety blue sky on all sides with no hint of land, it didn't take me very long to swim to the island. And I'm sure that even with my abilities, these dolphins are undoubtedly quicker and more agile than I am.

I notice that Carter's face has a green tint to it and a sheen of sweat glistens on his forehead.

"Are you feeling okay?" I ask.

"Just a little nauseous," he replies weakly.

The dolphins' rapid leaps and dives through the sea would have that effect on most people. "Don't worry, we should see land soon."

"Where do you think we should start?"

"What?"

"Well, we need to find answers. We need to know what happened to us and how this happened. I doubt it'll be easy to find information, but do you think there's anyone that will know anything about this?"

I shrug. "I don't know."

"Are you going to go back home?" Carter asks.

"No," I say firmly. "Not yet," I add in a whisper.

Suddenly, the sorrow starts to slither through me again. Maybe it was wrong to run away. I can imagine my family stressing all the time as they searched everywhere for me. Rain probably convinced herself it was somehow her fault that I disappeared since she was the last one who talked to me. All along, I'd been thinking that I was helping everyone I cared about by leaving, but in reality, I wasn't.

Deep inside, I must have known that.

They wouldn't have cared that I was different from other people; that I had powers over water and ice. They only cared about my well-being and that I was safe, even if others claimed I was some sort of freak. But I know I can't return home now, and face everyone after I vanished for six months, causing them so much anguish. It was difficult enough to disembark from the island.

"Marina, what's wrong?" Carter asks, reading my expression.

"No matter what I do, my life will never be back to normal," I respond softly. "Even when I return, even if I see my family again, there will always be something wrong. Nothing can erase what I did that day, or how I was gone for half a year."

"We've been over this. I thought you'd forgiven yourself."

I shake my head, at a loss for words.

Carter stretches his arm out and takes my hand. "Don't worry, I'm not going to let anything happen to you. Everything's going to be okay. I care about you."

I smile weakly. I don't know what I'd do without Carter.

"I think I see land!" Carter exclaims, squinting into the distance.

' "Really?"

I look ahead and sure enough, I spot the outline of a beach on the horizon. Buildings with a few lights glowing in the windows are barely visible further back. It's hard to see the land with only the silver light of the moon and stars above, but I can make out the outline of my previous home.

"This is the beach where I lived," I say, sure of my statement even though I can't see the land's detail.

"I take it you're not going back home. So where do you think we should go?"

"I guess we'll be living like runaways."

"At least we'll be in civilization."

"Carter, are you sure you don't want to return home? You didn't choose to run away like I did. Your family's probably really worried about you, and you don't have any reason not to go back."

"Yes, I do," Carter contradicts. "I'm not going to abandon you. Eventually, I'll go back to Arizona, but not until we've figured everything out. Besides, it's only me and my dad. I don't have any siblings and my mom died when I was a baby. My dad will be recovering from the storm, so I think he'll be busy enough."

"I'm sorry about your mom," I say softly.

"It's fine," Carter replies, his words void of pain. "Sometimes I wish she was still here, but I don't remember her, since I was so young when she died. Dad doesn't talk about her much. I respect that, though, because I understand it must make him sad to think about her."

This is the first time Carter's shared anything about his life with me. It's strange that I never asked before, but we must have been so worried about survival and our powers back on the island that I never thought to ask him about himself. I know I've wondered.

"We moved a lot," Carter continues. "I'm not really sure why, but I guess my dad just preferred the change of scenery. I never really got to stay anywhere long enough to make close friends and any relatives I have are distant. You're the first person I've really felt…close to." I smile, and after a moment of silence, Carter asks, "Do you mind if I ask about your life before you ran away?"

"No, I don't mind. I've lived in Washington my whole life with my parents and my two younger brothers. We had some family nearby, and I have some friends. My best friend's name is Rain. She was the last person I talked to before I left. She saw what happened, but she didn't understand how I froze that water like that. I didn't understand either."

"It sounds like you left more behind than I did."

"I guess," I say faintly.

We move closer and closer to the land until I can make out the shore cloaked in shadows of the night. Even with the feathery palm trees and seaside houses tinted in gray and black, I can still make out the scene of my home. A pang of strong emotion floods through me, but I can't quite tell what it is: remorse, relief, sentimentality?

Before I can change my mind and turn back, the dolphins halt in the shallow, calm water by the shore. Taking a deep breath, I step into the water which reaches only to my mid-thighs. As Carter does the same, our dolphins chortle playfully and speed out to sea. Their tails splash a spray of sea water in my face as I watch them fade out of sight.

"It looks like we're here," Carter states plainly, with a shiver that he tries to hide.

"Yes," I answer, just as limitedly.

I recognize the beach so well; it hasn't changed at all since I left. The moonlight casts a silvery glow on the soft sand and blue water. Wooden stairs accented with slim palm trees reach up the sloping hill that leads to the houses. I can pinpoint mine in a second. Its pale tan walls, windows curtained in blue, and gathered sand dollars mounted by the door seem familiar and welcoming, but I know I can't yet walk through the clean, white front door.

Tearing my gaze from my former home, I grin nervously at Carter and wade through the rippling ocean, onto the beach. The smooth sand massages my bare feet, but I don't dwell on the familiarity any longer.

"We're finally here," Carter says, almost as if in disbelief.

"Where should we go?" I inquire.

"You're the one that knows the way around the city, but I guess we'll just camp out on the beach for the rest of the night."

"But it's so…public. Someone might recognize me and I really don't want anyone to know I'm back right now. I don't feel like explaining myself to anyone."

"I promise I'll wake you up early," Carter reasons.

"Okay, I guess it's our only option."

I lead Carter to a more sheltered area amongst the dunes. The sloping hill has almost concaved, but a solid layer of sand hangs above us, held together with the tangled roots of the dunes. The spiky plants and palm trees are all around us, delivering some shelter.

"I reminds me a little of the shelter back on the island," I say, taking a seat.

Carter sits beside me so that our shoulders are touching and shifts uncomfortably as sand scratches his legs. "I'm starting to miss the dirt, even if there was rocks in it."

I start to laugh, but then notice how he's still slightly shaking. "You don't do very well in cold temperatures, do you?" I ask, feeling the cool night breeze blow across my face. "Maybe you should start a fire." I throw down a few sticks and leaves that I pluck from the surrounding plants.

"Good idea," Carter says, grateful for my suggestion.

The fire flickers, its golden glow around us, contrasting with the previous silver light of the moon. Carter's face is illuminated by the golden light of the flames. He wraps his arm around my shoulders and feeling on top of the world, I lean my head against his shoulder. Not a word is spoken between us, because at the moment words aren't necessary.

Suddenly, fatigue overcomes me. I only now realize how exhausting the day has been; how exhausting my life has been since I met Carter. In such a short period we both nearly drowned, both revealed our newfound powers, and narrowly escaped enemies shooting at us. Our lives really have twisted into a dangerous mystery that never allows us a break.

My eyelids are weighed down heavily, and slowly I drift to sleep with Carter's arm encircling me.

***

"Marina, wake up," Carter says.

I groggily lift my eyelids and the pale morning light filters through. The pastel morning sun brightens the sky to periwinkle and lights the teal sea. The scent of the salty sea and the ocean breeze against my face is familiar and reviving.

Looking up, I realize that neither Carter nor I have moved from our position last night. His arm still rests comfortingly around my shoulders. It's so peaceful sitting here with him on the sand, on the beach of my home that I don't want to move, but I know I have to. I can already see the faint silhouettes of joggers coming closer through the mist.

"So where do we go?" I ask with a yawn.

Carter looks thoughtful. "Well, information is most easily accessed through the internet. And since we don't have any phones or computers, the only place I can think of with public internet access is the library. Do you know of any nearby?"

"Yes, I think I remember where it is," I respond.

We bury the remains of the fire with sand and head down the beach. I feel strange wandering through my hometown as if nothing is unusual. Every weathered building, blossoming tree, and road sign that dots the streets looks exactly like the picture stored in my mind of the city before I left.

Suddenly, I realize why this plan is faulty. "We left the beach early so nobody would recognize me, but this library is *public*. I might see somebody I know there!"

Carter looks at me doubtfully. "I don't think libraries are very crowed this early in the morning. And we'll be fast anyway."

We arrive at the large building quickly. Its pale gray walls are a mixture of slightly uneven tones of paint from the salty sea spray blowing past it for decades. The large set of stone stairs leads to double glass doors. Peering through the glass, I can see that the library is open with the bright lights on, but from this view I don't see anyone browsing through the books.

Carter holds open the door for me. I slip through and murmur, "Thank you."

I haven't been in here for at least two years, but everything is just as I remember, with bookcases piled high all around the room, filled with books of every size and condition. The only inhabitant I currently see is the librarian, sitting behind her tall desk and engrossed in a thick, tattered book. She has short, curly silver hair and glasses perched on her long, thin nose. She doesn't glance up at us once.

By the wall sits a table holding several computers that are slightly out-of-date, but seem to be holding up fine from their glowing screens and nearly unblemished black surfaces.

"That's what we'll need," Carter says in a hushed tone, pointing to the computers.

Once we've both pulled up the internet, I ask, "What exactly are we supposed to search for?"

Carter shrugs and whispers in my ear, "I guess just look up people with unusual powers. There's probably nothing relevant to what we want to find out, but it's a start."

I nod, and my fingers flying over the keyboard, type in the words. I scroll down the list of search results until a site catches my eye. When the page finishes reloading, my eyes hungrily scan the black typed words. I gasp as I comprehend the meaning of this, incredulous at my luck of instantly finding this site.

Chapter Ten

Carter

When I hear her gasp I nearly pounce on Marina's computer. She must have discovered some of the useful information that we've been craving. I hesitate for a moment, my stomach jumping with nerves at what I might find, but push down the feeling and lean over Marina's shoulder to see the screen.

The headline, *Woman Burns Down Mall*, is bold in large black print. My eyes are immediately drawn to the picture before I even glance over the article. It's of a young woman, probably in her late twenties, smiling towards the camera, and sparks recognition in my mind. Her strawberry blonde hair is choppily layered and her smile looks full of enthusiasm. But it's her hazel eyes that confirm my thought. They're identical to mine. Sure enough, the caption reads, *Katrina Pyric*.

"Mom," I whisper.

Marina turns towards me and replies, "I thought so!" Then worry eases into her expression and she adds, "I'm sorry…maybe we shouldn't read this."

"No!" I exclaim too sharply, too loudly. It's fortunate that the library is nearly deserted. "My dad would never talk about her. I've always thought it just depressed him, but now I think he was hiding something, too. This is my one chance to find out who she really was and what really happened to her."

Marina nods and we both turn to the screen, our eyes glued to the words as we comprehend the article.

Nobody understands how she did it. There was no evidence of matches or lighters, and she wasn't seen sneaking around anywhere beforehand. Yet, somehow, Katrina Pyric burned down a mall in Florida. It was so sudden, and the raging inferno spread so quickly that firefighters weren't able to put out the fire before the entire mall was reduced to ashes. Over a dozen people perished in the tragic event and many others were injured. The only person standing in the remains unharmed afterwards was twenty-nine year old Katrina Pyric. Even though there was no video footage, some witnesses claim they saw her suspiciously lingering around with her hand in a fist, possibly hiding something. Katrina denied that she started the fire repeatedly, but hasn't answered why she was unharmed by the fire. Since then, Katrina Pyric has vanished and nothing has been heard from her. Though it's only been two days, and the police are following this mysterious woman.

"This happened sixteen years ago, just after I was born," I say softly, glancing over the date.

"So this is about the time she supposedly died?" Marina asks.

"Yeah, my dad said she died giving birth to me, but this was a few days after. That alone already shows that he was lying."

"Then what do you think happened to her?" Marina wonders.

"Well, she disappeared after this, but I don't know if she ran away or not..." A new thought brightens in my mind. "What if she's still alive?"

"Carter, don't get your hopes up," she cautions. "We both know that's probably not true. You would've heard something from her by now. Maybe she did run away from the fire and was killed somehow soon after." She speaks the words gently.

"It could've been anything," I say with a sorrowful sigh. "She could've gotten in a car crash or fell to her death. Or…somebody could have killed her."

"But why?"

"I don't know. This article isn't very explanatory."

Without another word, Marina types *Katrina Pyric* into the search bar and quickly scrolls through the results. "The only other website with any mention of her is this," she says, bringing up another page with minimal text.

To my disappointment, it holds no useful information. It's simply a profile of my mom, listing only my dad as her husband and me as her son. The other categories: birth, death, address, and parents are listed as unknown. It appears to me that my mom's background wasn't only kept secret from me, but that she was a mystery to everyone…except my dad. I'm nearly positive he must know everything about her.

And I'm sure that pain and longing isn't the only reason he doesn't share it with me. That must be one of the factors, but there's something he's deliberately hiding from me. I just know it.

Marina sighs in exasperation. "I bet every website will be like this, never giving us the necessary information to find out how this happened to us!" I cringe as she raises her voice an octave too loud, thankful for the deserted library.

Then I notice the old librarian hobbling towards us, an unreadable expression on her creased face. Marina and I both stare at her worriedly, but before we can say anything, she speaks up, "I think I might have some materials on what you're looking for in the back."

Marina and I share a worried look, but then both our expressions turn to bewilderment. How could the librarian possibly know what we're looking for? Even if she'd heard the snippets of our conversation when our voices rose, there's no way she could've made any sense of it. She might have been curious and asked questions, rather than seeming knowledgeable, as if *she* knew more about it than we did.

"What do you think she means?" Marina whispers in my ear.

"I'm not sure…but she *must* have simply misheard what we were saying and thought it actually was something she could help with."

"That makes more sense."

Failed hearing is as good an explanation as any, especially when dealing with an elderly person, but is that all it really is?

The short woman leads us to the back of the library and enters what seems to be a storage room; filled with stacks of books not yet shelved. "So what have you found out about it so far?" she asks abruptly, turning to face us.

"What?" we ask in unison, fabricating innocent expressions.

The old woman gives a small laugh and her eyes crinkle with good-natured amusement. "I'm not clueless, you know."

"Who are you?" Marina asks cautiously, narrowing her eyes.

"You can trust me."

"That doesn't answer my question."

She looks at us for a moment, as if deciding how to react. Then, in a split-second, she's gone. In the space the woman was standing only a minute ago, there is now only air, nothingness. I gawk at the hollow space, and neither Marina nor I know what to do. Before we can even say a word, the woman is back, breathing hard from exhaustion.

"That's much harder than it used to be," she says wearily.

"You have…powers!" Marina gasps.

She replies, as if it's obvious, "You see, that's how I knew about you."

"You almost seem prepared," I say in realization. "How did you know about us? How did you even know we were coming?"

"The thoughts were simply placed into my mind, but I don't think they were my own." Marina looks at her quizzically and then asks, "Can you at least help us understand what's going on?"

"Me?" the woman replies. "I'm not the best person to ask. Age makes one forgetful." She sighs and shakes her head, as if already losing her train of thought. "I'm simply acting as a messenger. The one who can really provide you with information is Dr. Corry."

"And how are we supposed to find him?" she asks in exasperation. "Can't you just tell us what in the world is going on right now? And you never even answered my question! Who are you?"

"I don't have much time left," she says sadly. "I've used my powers far too often, and they'll come for me. They don't know I'm here, but they will soon. That's why you need to leave!" she informs urgently. "Go find Dr. Corry before they get you, too!"

Since the poor old woman clearly has no intention of being any less confusing, I simply ask, "Where is Dr. Corry?"

She scribbles down a few words on a piece of paper and thrusts it at me, her expression suddenly becoming panicked. "Hurry, run, now!" Without another question, I grab Marina's hand and we bolt out of the library. The streets fly past my vision without me really comprehending where we're going or where we plan to arrive. Though, at the same time, Marina and I seem to be in synch with each other's thoughts, never veering in opposite directions. Our pace is rapid and worry has edged into my mind.

Marina comes to an abrupt stop and I nearly fall forward at the sudden halt. Her eyes scan our surroundings warily. The atmosphere has taken on a dreary feel as if fore-telling something terrible will soon occur. Run-down houses with shattered window panes and holes punched in the thin walls line the faded street on both sides of us. The sun has vanished behind dark clouds and an awful feeling hangs heavily in the air.

"We need to leave," I say, my voice commanding.

"I don't know where to go," Marina replies.

I unclench my fist and reveal the now crumpled scrap of paper that the old woman handed me. The cursive scrawled across it is messy and almost unreadable. *1330 Expert Ave.* I read the address and question, "Do you know where that is?"

"I think it's a lab, for scientists to experiment," she says. "But it's pretty far away. Aberdeen."

"And we don't have money to pay for transportation," I sigh.

"I guess we're just going to have to leave and find shelter tonight." She turns in the opposite direction, the wind making her long hair fly behind her. "I'll lead the way," Marina says and begins walking. I follow aimlessly, with not a clue to where we need to go.

We walk nonstop, over the civilized terrain of Port Angeles and into the bordering cities. The farther we distance ourselves from the area around Marina's house, the more the dark feel to the atmosphere seems to lift. Eventually, there is no danger lurking around us, and the sky is clear of any unnaturally dark clouds, revealing a vast sheet of pale blue. The sun begins to set in a lightshow of orange and pink, indicating how long we've traveled –nearly an entire day. Still, our slow pace hasn't carried us very far.

My legs ache dully from never stopping, but I ignore the minor exhaustion since Marina keeps going. I notice sweat glistening on her forehead and the red hue of heat exhaustion on her cheeks, but she perseveres in determination, so I don't even suggest resting.

Finally, she stops at a wooden bench along the sidewalk and takes a seat. I sit down beside her and she breathes deeply, almost as if in defeat. "I feel like no matter what I do, I'm never any closer to figuring anything out. Not only is my whole life destroyed, not only have I became some abnormal creature that everyone in my old life fears, but everything that makes up my existence now is kept a secret from me."

"You know that I feel the same way," I say.

"Yeah," Marina mutters. "But now, even when we're back in civilization, how will we survive? We know somebody's after us and even if you forget that, we have no money to pay for food, shelter, or transportation."

"And we can't contact anyone who'd help us," I add, voicing more her feelings than mine.

"Exactly. This just keeps getting worse and worse."

"I'm sure that when we find this person." I point to the piece of paper. "That some of our questions will be answered and we'll find some sort of food and shelter. Until then, we're just going to have to keep walking."

"Aren't you tired at all?"

I hesitate, not wanting to slow down the pace if she doesn't mind continuing. Honestly, my legs ache from the day's nonstop walking, and my stomach is knotted into fists from the ravenous hunger of not eating for nearly two days. My throat feels scratchy like sandpaper when I swallow, because it's been just as long since I've drank water. "A little," is all I reply.

"We can't just keep walking all night."

"Maybe we could get a ride on a train," I suggest, the idea suddenly forming.

"Or a truck," Marina says deviously. "It seems as if fate is in our favor." She points to an idling white truck that workers are hauling boxes into. It's stopped nearby on the curb and the trunk is open, almost as if inviting us to hitch a ride.

"I guess it's our only option of transportation," I say.

"Hurry, the workers are done. It'll leave soon."

"How do we even know where it's going?"

Marina listens intently, motioning for me to wait. "1330 Expert Avenue?" the driver questions to the other worker.

Marina beams at me. "It seems as if my bad luck is ending!" She creeps forward stealthily, careful to stay out of sight of the workers.

I glance over at the building the boxes have been carried from. It's a hardware supply store, so I assume the scientists working at the building we've been directed to have ordered some materials for their experiments. Despite our previous streak of misfortune, the fact that we'd stop to rest right where this truck was heading towards the experimental labs is almost *too* coincidental.

The workers seem to be paying little attention, so Marina climbs into the back, signaling for me to follow. She wrinkles her nose at the gritty smell of smoke from the engine, but is careful not to make a sound as she conceals herself amongst the boxes.

I jump up into the back of the truck just as the door slides down, but I twist out of the way before it slams down on my legs. Luckily, a wall of metal separates us from the drivers. That combined with the roar of the engine will help hide Marina and my conversations from the drivers. I really hope that we aren't caught for hitching rides. We could get charges pressed against us and that would only add to the constant stress.

"This was actually a good idea," I say quietly.

Marina looks pleased with herself. "Thanks. I just really feel that we have to know what's going on. Now in addition to everything else, those people from the island are chasing us."

"That librarian said they would find her and that she didn't have much longer to live," I reply. "She seemed really scared, so we know they're powerful. I just feel bad for her. I mean, she helped us, and somehow that resulted in her possible death."

Marina nods, melancholy. "But now we know there are others like us: the librarian...your mom."

"What really happened to her?" I ask softly.

"Carter, I'm really sorry," Marina consoles, putting her hand on mine. "Even the website said she disappeared and you know that probably means she –"

"I know," I cut her off, not wanting to hear the last dreaded word.

Not only do I miss my mom, who I never even knew, but I know that her fate is the key to this mystery. Whatever happened to her is tied into what's currently happening to Marina and me. My mom was just like me. From the little information I was provided with, I can piece together that she had power over fire, fire that couldn't harm her, just like I do.

My strange abilities were passed down from her, but it wasn't just a family secret. Even though not involving fire or heat, Marina has similar abilities, as did the librarian. But I doubt there are others, or they would've been heard from by now.

"Carter, when we were on the island, the man with the gun called us Serions," Marina says with a frown. "What does that mean?"

"I've never heard of that before," I reply curiously.

"Is it some sort of a cult?" she wonders.

"Maybe. I guess that makes sense."

"But we don't even know what's going on!"

"You know, I feel like we shouldn't ask any more questions about this until we at least have some idea of what's happening. It only makes us worry more. We can wait a little longer until we find that Dr. Corry. In the meantime, let's try to talk about other things."

"Like what? I already told you about my past."

"Was there ever...anyone special?" I can't help but ask with a hint of jealousy.

Her mouth curves into a small smile. "No, not like you." Marina reaches over to hug me.

We stay with our arms around each other while the truck rumbles down the road, bumping over the gravelly roads and jostling around the boxes so they bump into us. Marina yelps as the top box slides down, just above her head. I push the cardboard box away just before it hits her. Marina clamps a hand over her mouth to muffle the yelp that escaped in her surprise. We wait for a moment, motionless, and laugh in relief as nobody realizes we've snuck onto the truck. The ride continues, only causing more anticipation to what I'll soon discover.

Chapter Eleven

Marina

The truck ride takes longer than I'd expected. I knew the lab was far from my old home, but it takes us at least a good two hours to get there, in addition to our day of walking. But I guess our pace had been pretty slow. Finally, the breaks squeak as the truck comes to a halt.

"Did you ever think about how we're going to get out unnoticed?" Carter asks.

"No," I groan, wanting to slap myself.

The only way we can exit is when the workers open the trunk, when they'll be unloading the boxes. Surely they would see us. But we're saved from being picked up by the police as the workers open the trunk from a button in the interior and linger inside.

"Come on!" Carter whispers urgently as the trunk slowly lifts.

We scramble outside and rush through the motion activated sliding glass doors before I can even take in my surroundings. Once we're inside, I can take my time since this area seems welcome to visitors. The building is clean, sterile, and empty; too cold and blank, but how else would a scientist's lab's atmosphere be?

The bright white walls reach high in the large, open space. To my left is a long hall filled with silver metal doors leading to rooms that I presume are locked with secret projects brewing inside. A desk crafted of pale wood is stationed beside two white chairs, but nobody is behind it. The floor is made of impeccably clean white tiles that must make loud echoing noises when shoes walk on it. I only now self-consciously remember that both Carter's and my feet are bare.

It's strange that since I got off the island, I haven't given a thought to my appearance. I suppose that my mind has been too preoccupied with worries. I can only imagine how I must look now with clothes I've been wearing for six months, only washed by the sea, and no shoes. The clothing has suffered wear and gained tears, stains, and faded color. My hair must be ratty and tangled, unhealthy from growing long with no trims. I'm sure my face is scratched from my chaotic escape from the island. I can already see red scrapes line my arms and Carter's wounds haven't healed.

I find it strange that neither Carter nor I have thought that the other's appearance looked ragged, and I don't think he looks bad even now. But I guess that I always see him as handsome, no matter how rugged. Though I'm sure everyone else will view us as homeless vagrants or even runaway criminals. And we are runaways, or at least I am.

The loud clack of heels on the polished tile floor interrupts my thoughts. A professionally dressed woman is walking down the hall, her black hair pulled into an elegant bun. Her business suit is beige and the clipboard in her hands is holding down color-coded papers. She looks us up and down, seeming surprised that we're here.

"Hello, how may I help you?" she asks politely.

"We'd like to see Dr. Corry," Carter replies.

"May I ask why?"

"We have our reasons," I say evasively.

The woman raises an eyebrow, but nods. "Okay, I'll see if he's available."

"Are we supposed to tell him that we have powers?" Carter asks me quietly.

"I don't know. I guess we'll just have to see what he tells us first," I reply in a whisper.

Carter nods and takes my hand. I smile in response.

"Right this way," the woman says as she returns. She motions for us to follow her down the hall as she briskly walks to a silver door and opens it quickly, ushering Carter and me inside. She leaves and the door shuts behind us.

The room looks to be an office, with the more welcoming atmosphere, personalized décor of shelves filled with pictures, and a blue and green carpet. Behind a large wooden desk with an engraved name tag reading *Dr. Dave Corry* sits a middle-aged man.

He has brown hair flecked with strands of silver and oval-shaped glasses cover brown eyes. I would've expected him to wear a lab coat, but his clothes are simply a regular polo shirt and tie. "How can I help you?" he asks.

"Um...we were sent here by the librarian..." I say.

I expect Dr. Corry to be bewildered, but my words spark interest in his expression. "Oh! I didn't think there were any more of you."

"Any more of us?" Carter asks quizzically. "What do you mean?"

"Sorry, let me introduce myself first. I'm Dr. Corry."

"I'm Carter Pyric."

"Marina Coralin."

He nods and says immediately, "You probably have a lot of questions. Let me start by saying that beginning a couple decades ago, strange things started happening. There were people who could do strange things that were humanly impossible. I had just become a scientist when I heard about this, and began studying what was going on. It's become a large part of my work now."

"What have you found out?" Carter wonders.

"Why don't you have a seat?" Dr. Corry suggests, gesturing to several chairs. "I probably have a lot to explain." We sit down simultaneously and he continues, "What are you willing to admit?"

Carter and I share a worried look and both only say, "Um..."

"I know that it's hard to say, but that you both probably have powers."

"How did you know?" I exclaim.

"You said the librarian sent you here, and she's just like you. Ever since those people starting coming here, I've been researching how they came to be like that. But what happened started becoming public. They couldn't all keep their identities hidden, and they often lost control. Fires started and there were unnatural floods. People vanished and buildings crashed. Innocent bystanders were killed, even though it was all an accident. The police started tracking down these people, thinking they were dangerous. They all began to vanish."

"Were they killed?" I ask, afraid of the answer.

Dr. Corry pauses for a second, but then nods regretfully.

"My mom," Carter whispers.

"I'm sorry," the doctor says sincerely. "Many people see what they don't understand as dangerous."

"Why did this happen to us? Who are those people chasing us?" I ask, to distract Carter from sorrow.

"This is a lot to take in, so it's best to not tell you everything at the moment. It'll be too much to understand all at once. I'm sure you're already having a hard time with this. But I *can* tell you that their leader is like you. He can feel when you use your powers, because you're all connected."

"Is that what the librarian meant when she said he'd find her?" Carter wonders. "That they'd kill her?"

"I'm sorry to say this, but they've probably gotten her by now."

At that moment, I feel an awful stab of pain course through me. I gasp and scream as the agony racks my body. A wave of misery pierces through my heart. I don't know what is happening to me; nothing was around to hurt me. Then, the pain suddenly stops and leaves me feeling horribly weak. I have to gulp down the sickness that nearly comes up, burning my throat.

I can see that Carter is having the same reactions as his hands tremble and his face begins to pale. We stay feeling awful, on the verge of sickness, for a moment, until it passes, only leaving an awful, hollow feeling consuming me.

"What just happened?" I gasp.

"Strange," Dr. Corry comments. "I think that would be the connection between everyone like you. She must have just died," he adds gravely.

I frown and ask, after the wave of sorrow for the dead woman has mostly vanished, "Does that mean that Carter and I are the only ones like us left? Aside from the one who wants to shoot us?"

"Most likely; as far as I know. Most of the others have long since been killed. It's tragic."

"Can you tell us why we're like this?" I press.

"No, not at the moment," he replies. "I'm sorry, but like I said, this is already a lot for you to process. You might even go into shock or possibly temporarily not be able to control your powers if I tell you everything right now."

I glare slightly, but resort to a sigh when I realize he's being reasonable. "So, for some reason, this enemy is tracking us. Then we can't just leave. They'll find us…kill us."

"So you have nowhere to go?" Dr. Corry questions.

"Well…" Carter begins.

"No, we don't," I say firmly.

"Well, if you're that desperate, then I have some extra rooms in my house. It's attached to the back of the lab. I'm sure my wife and son won't mind you staying here for a little while."

"Thank you," Carter and I both say gratefully.

"Do they know about...your work?" I ask, unsure if it's safe to reveal my powers to them.

Dr. Corry nods and replies, "Don't worry, I'll tell them and they'll understand."

I feel so relieved. We've found exactly what we were in search of: a source of complete information and shelter. Even if it's just for a little while, Carter and I now have protection from the armed men on the island and food so we won't starve. And I'm sure that eventually Dr. Corry will reveal everything he knows about our past and what happened to us. Life can't get better, unless the pang of sorrow inside me from missing my family disappears, which I know it won't until we're reunited. And when that event occurs is entirely up to me.

***

The guest room isn't all white like the lab was. I'm glad; if every surface was covered in the pristine color, I'd feel like more of a prisoner or a lab experiment than a guest. This room is fairly large, but with minimal furnishings. A mahogany bed, dresser, and desk make up the interior. The walls are painted pale blue and the bedspread is a similar shade, in contrast with the tan carpet.

The closet and drawers are bare, left empty for my belongings, but I have none. Though I assume eventually I'll need some new clothes, since mine have basically been reduced to tatters.

Dr. Corry said that I could stay in this room and gave Carter a guest room down the hall. His house is rather large and the comforting feel reminds me of my old home.

Without further thought, I simply collapse on the bed. For six months I've been sleeping on dirt speckled with pebbles and debris. Since I've gotten used to those meager accommodations, the bed beneath me feels heavenly. I sink into the soft covers immediately as fatigue pulls me away.

"Would you like dinner?" a voice wakes me up. The woman is unfamiliar, but seems kind, like a motherly figure. When I look at her quizzically, she adds, "I'm Dr. Corry's wife, Ellen. We're having dinner, and I'm assuming you're pretty hungry."

"Yes, thanks," I mumble.

"But before that, would you like some new clothes to change into?" Ellen's gaze sweeps over my rags of clothing and hands me a stack of clothing before I can even respond. "Meet us at dinner in a few minutes," she says, leaving.

"Thank you," I say again.

I can see that Ellen took pity on me, and probably Carter, too. But I know that's exactly the way my mom would feel in this situation. When mothers see other kids similar in age to theirs who have been in unfortunate situations, they can't help but offer aid. And I'm glad that Ellen was so kind; I was worried that Dr. Corry's family might consider us strange, despite his reassurances.

After I change into a pair of dark jeans and an only slightly baggy blue top, I head down the long hall until I discover the dining room. Carter, Dr. Corry, Ellen, and a boy I don't recognize are seated at a smooth table, lit by the chandelier above. I wordlessly take the open seat by Carter and give him a fleeting smile. Carter looks like he's cleaned up, too.

The remnants of blood have been washed from his now neatly combed hair and his wounds are bandaged. His ripped clothes have been replaced with new clean clothing, making him much neater than before. Carter looks somewhat different. Even the first time I saw him he'd just been shipwrecked and cut by the edges of rocks. It's a new look from his previous disheveled appearance, but I like it. And his warm eyes and smile are just as I've always loved.

"So, I hear you've been living on an island," the boy says awkwardly to break the silence.

He's actually more of a young man than a boy, probably nineteen or twenty. He has neatly combed wavy light brown hair and bright blue eyes. In his face and tall, lean frame I can see the resemblance to both Dr. Corry and Ellen, his parents.

"Yeah, it's nice to be back," I say with a nod.

"I'm Luke," he replies in introduction.

"Carter."

"Marina," I say. "Nice to meet you."

"Luke is my son," Dr. Corry explains, confirming my thoughts.

When Luke and I speak, I see the slight flicker of worry flash across Carter's eyes, as if he's concerned that I like Luke, in a way that would cause jealousy. The brief expression is concealed well, but I know Carter too well to overlook it. I almost laugh, but instead result to a small grin. I squeeze Carter's hand as if to say wordlessly that he doesn't need to be jealous or feel that I'm attracted to Luke. I would never do that to Carter. My feelings towards him are too strong.

"So, would you mind telling us how you came to live on an island?" Ellen asks in concern.

I immediately tense, not wanting to share the awful experience with anyone else. "Um…"

"She doesn't like telling people about it," Carter speaks up for me.

I nod in agreement.

"I understand that," Ellen says, but they all look at me with undying curiosity.

I look down at my plate, only now noticing the chicken that we're eating for dinner. The scratch of the knife on the plate as I cut a bite is shrill in the otherwise silence. Keeping my eyes downcast, I lift the chicken to my mouth and can't help but devour the food. It helps the hunger that claws at my stomach. "This is really good," I say between mouthfuls.

I'm sure that my manners aren't the best at the moment, but I don't mind. I greedily gulp my cold water empty and soon my plate doesn't have a speck of food left on it. Carter does the same as I did; we've both been starving for at least two days now. And it seems like the island was so long ago.

"Thank you for the food," I say at the end of the meal.

Dr. Corry and Ellen nod and both respond, "You're welcome."

"Do you mind if we leave?" Carter asks. "I need to talk to Marina."

"Of course," Dr. Corry replies.

Carter and I immediately exit, and I'm thankful he has come up with a reason for us to depart from the pounding tension. I'm not sure if he really has anything urgent to say, or if he just wants some time to speak alone. Either way, I follow him down the hall until we reach the back door. He pulls it open, letting in the cool night air, and motions for me to go outside.

Once we're alone, standing with only the night around us, Carter asks, "Do you think we should trust them?"

"They seem nice and helpful enough, but I don't know," I respond.

"It's just that, I don't know, it seems hard to believe that a scientist wouldn't just want to use us as an experiment. It's his work, and I just don't know if he's tricking us into trusting him."

Carter's sounding more like me. I was always the one who was guarded and untrusting, who never revealed my secrets, never believed what others said, but I guess I only became that way after the deaths. And Carter could always brighten my mood and bring me comfort when I felt miserable. Now he's begun to develop a harder edge, which seems like mine.

"Since when were you like this?" I wonder.

"Like what?" Carter replies in confusion.

"You would always look on the bright side and tell *me* to not worry. I liked that about you. I don't want you to lose that."

"I guess I've been around you too much," he says with a teasing grin. "But I just want to make sure that you're not in danger."

"What about you?"

"I'll do what I can to keep *you* safe. My life isn't nearly as important to me."

"But you can't just die because of me!" I exclaim in horror.

Carter shakes his head. "I won't die unless it's absolutely necessary."

"You won't need to," I promise.

"Good, but I just don't want you to be in danger."

I smile as he leans towards me and puts his lips to mine. The flutters in my stomach are no less than the first time as I curl my arms around his neck. When I'm with Carter I feel weightless. He's right in saying that some good came from being stranded on the island.

When the kiss ends, our arms are still around each other and I lay my head on his shoulder. The moment is interrupted by the wooden creak of the door being opened. I jerk my head up in surprise.

Luke stands in the doorway, his bright blue eyes slightly embarrassed. "I'm sorry…I didn't mean to interrupt you, just to warn you."

"What?" I ask, fear edging into my tone.

"Look, I don't know much about my dad's work. He doesn't share much about it with me for whatever reason, and I'm sure you know more about all this than I do. But I do know that when the government killed them and my dad tried to help the few survivors, the enemy was set on hunting them down. The same man who tried to kill you would always find them, and quickly, too. No matter how smart they were, he would find them. And soon they were all gone, all…dead." He whispers the last word gravely.

"You think he'll find us?" Carter asks.

"I think you're safe now, but you need to be careful," Luke replies. "It's imperative that you don't use your powers. Please don't do anything careless. It might not even be the best idea to be outside right now."

"They all died?" I ask softly.

Luke nods sadly. "It was awful. They were all gone so quickly and the way he kills them so mercilessly –"

"You saw them die?" I gulp.

"Yes, once." He grimaces at the horror of the memory. "Dad was helping to hide them so the killer came there. He tracked them down to where we lived, but we've moved since then. My mom and I were there, but that didn't make him hesitate for a second, and my dad could do little to stop him. He simply walked into the room and in one movement, broke their necks. It was so quick and his expression was so plain that it almost seemed like it hadn't happened at all, but it had."

"There was blood and their heads hung lifelessly." Luke's face remains revolted as he recalls the experience. "Without another word, he simply left. I was only five, and I've never forgotten it. It was so horrible and I was so young."

"That's terrible," Carter says quietly.

I nod in agreement, disgusted by his description. But I feel even worse for Luke, who had to actually witness that when he was just a little kid. "How old are you now?"

"Nineteen," Luke replies. "Fourteen years ago and the memory is just as vivid as when it happened."

"I'm sorry," I say.

"Thanks, but you don't need to be. They weren't anyone close to me, but it was just awful to witness. All I'm trying to say is that you don't know what he's capable of. He's extremely powerful and won't stop until he gets what he wants. And he wants you dead."

"Do you know who he is?" Carter questions.

"Just a name: Kairo." Luke says the single word with such disgust that it seems like a curse of doom.

"Kairo," Carter repeats the name. "I won't let this Kairo hurt you, Marina."

"If you want to survive then you both better get inside," Luke warns. "I don't know if he has spies, but whatever he does, Kairo doesn't let anything stop him until he achieves what he wants. You need to be smart and cautious, because it's nearly impossible to beat him."

"Thank you for warning us, Luke," I say in gratitude as we retreat and the door shuts.

"You're welcome. I just didn't want you to have to go through what the others did; to have to die in such a painful way. And Kairo doesn't deserve to achieve whatever he's attempting."

With that being stated, Luke leaves Carter and me standing in the hall, contemplating his worrisome words.

Chapter Twelve

Carter

The voice is hushed and barely audible, but it shocks me from a peaceful sleep. Even with its distance and soft tone, I can clearly make out the single word that the female voice is urgently saying: "Help!" I immediately think of Marina.

I'm running down the hall before I even remember standing up. When I reach Marina's door, I throw it open and pause in bewilderment. She appears completely fine, calm in deep sleep, nothing seeming disturbed. But she's laying very still…I cringe at the horrid thought that enters my mind, and I have to check to make sure it's wrong.

"Marina," I say, barely keeping my voice in a whisper as I stand beside her. "Marina!"

"What?" she asks worriedly, her eyes flying open.

"Are you okay?" I ask.

"Yes…" She knits her eyebrows and adds, "Why wouldn't I be?"

"You didn't call for help?"

"No…"

"That's strange," I mutter. When Marina looks at me quizzically I explain, "I heard a girl's voice asking for help. I thought it was you."

"Maybe it was somebody outside," she suggests.

"I doubt it. The area's pretty deserted and I don't think it would wake me up if it wasn't somewhere in the house, but it did sound distant."

"So you heard it in the house?"

"Actually, I'm not really sure. I think the voice was either in the house or…in my head."

"What?" Marina wonders. "Are you okay Carter?"

"Yes, I'm not going crazy," I promise. "Didn't you say that when I needed help back on the island, when I was almost drowning in the storm, that you heard someone calling for help. And didn't you only afterwards realize it had been a girl's voice?"

"Yeah," Marina replies, realization beginning to come into her expression.

"Did it sound distant and far away, yet you could hear it clearly?"

"Yes, so you're thinking that we heard the same person, whoever it was, in our *heads*? A girl, always asking for help? Does that even make sense, Carter?" The questions come rapid fire as Marina's face twists in confusion.

"I'm not sure…but if we're right, then she's somehow communicating with us, through our minds."

"Who would she be? Does the voice sound familiar to *you*?"

I shake my head. It seems that we both only afterwards remember the details of the voice, since we were both in panic when we first heard it. The faint echo of the word I previously heard was high-pitched and soft with a strange tone to it that I can't describe. There was something about her that seemed unordinary. She seemed…and that's when it dawns on me.

"She's like us," I exclaim.

Marina's eyes widen. "But Dr. Corry said we were the last ones left."

"Maybe he was wrong."

"Or maybe he was lying," she says with a hint of anger.

"We should ask him at least."

"But can we even be sure that she's like us? How would she know about us? Why would we she contact us? My entire life I've lived in Port Angeles with my *normal* family. Despite the disappearance of your mom, you'd never heard anything of this either. Your dad never told you. We definitely never knew anybody that fit this description."

"Maybe she recently developed her powers, like we did?" I suggest.

"Rain," Marina gasps.

"Who?"

"My best friend, Rain," she explains quietly. "I don't know, I kind of doubt it, but it does make sense. She's the only one who at least partially fits the description. She would immediately contact me if she needed help, and she's the only one close to me who saw what happened to me."

"The voice did sound around our age. Did you recognize it?"

"No, but I was worried about you; I didn't have time to focus."

"Do you really think it's Rain?"

"I don't know," Marina sighs miserably. "But it's the only piece of slightly rational information we have to follow."

"Sometimes it's better to not have information at all if it leads to false answers and to just more suffering. We should at least ask Dr. Corry."

"In my opinion, it's better to have any lead, even if it's false," Marina contradicts firmly. "And I don't want to be fooled by what might just be more hopeless lies."

Without waiting for me to argue, Marina rushes away, as if suddenly very determined to accomplish something. The wild look in her eyes makes me think this won't end well. I race after her as she runs down the hall and slams open the kitchen door with building fury.

"I knew we couldn't trust you!" Marina yells.

Dr. Corry, Luke, and Ellen's faces all hold the identical expression of bewilderment as they sit at the wooden table, at what was probably a formerly calm breakfast.

"What, Marina?" Luke asks worriedly.

"You lied about it!" she continues to rant, but directs her statements at Dr. Corry rather than Luke, who she might still trust. "You said we were the only ones with powers left, but you lied! My best friend Rain is just like me and you never even told me that!"

"I have absolutely no idea what you're talking about," Dr. Corry says sincerely.

Marina glares, not believing him. "She spoke to Carter and I through our heads, asking for help."

"If your friend lives in Washington, then I'm sure I wouldn't have overlooked her as one of your kind. And think, did she ever seem at all unusual, like she didn't quite belong?"

She shakes her head in a small, almost unnoticeable motion.

"I admit that I can't be completely positive that you're the only ones left, but I'm pretty sure," Dr. Corry explains steadily. "Everything I told you is what I believe to be true. I never lied to you. And I can assure you that your friend does not have powers. But I would like you to tell me about this voice you heard. Are you sure it wasn't just your imagination?"

"I heard it this morning," I speak up. "It was a girl and she only said 'help'."

"The same thing happened when Carter almost drowned on the island," Marina adds, her tone still tense and letting on traces of lingering anger.

"It doesn't necessarily mean that there's someone else with powers, does it?" Luke inquires. "Maybe it's in your abilities to hear someone else's thoughts. Is that possible, Dad?"

"I suppose…" Dr. Corry replies absentmindedly. "I'll have to do some research about this, but it's difficult when you two are the only ones left that I know of." He stands up casually and walks in the direction of his lab, the plate of buttery waffles in front of him left untouched.

"I should go talk to him. When he wants to learn more about something –" Ellen shakes her head, cutting off mid-sentence, and hurrying after her husband.

"You know, it's not good to lose control like that," Luke says sympathetically. "You're already worried enough and you've just got to believe that some people want to help you. Who do you trust right now?"

"Carter," Marina says firmly and takes my hand defensively.

"You should trust us and your family, too," Luke advises. "Not everyone wants to destroy you."

Marina frowns and I tell her, "Luke's right, this is what I've been trying to tell you."

"I just want *something* to make sense for once," she sighs.

"How much is your dad keeping from us?" I ask. "He admitted that he wouldn't tell us everything right away; something about going into shock and losing control of our powers. Is the truth really that awful?"

Luke shrugs helplessly. "Like I said, he doesn't share much with me either. I prefer not to know."

"Do you promise you told us everything?" Marina presses.

"Yes, I promise."

At this point, my curiosity to discover all the answers has subsided. It seems the truth really is something terrible and shocking; something that I might rather not know. After finding Marina, I'm happy with life and if Dr. Corry telling us what caused our powers makes us believe we're monstrous creatures, I'd rather be oblivious forever.

***

The orderly room that was before comforting now seems confining. After the island, I'm used to the outdoors and now that I'm not allowed to leave the house, claustrophobia is starting to weigh me down. I never thought I'd miss the island once Marina and I finally escaped. I was always telling her how we needed to leave and find information, but now I realize maybe the island wasn't so bad.

We had complete freedom and it was a special place: where Marina and I met. I know that we're only unable to leave to protect ourselves from Kairo, but I now almost wish we'd never learned of him.

Even if it means that we had doubts and multiplying questions, we seemed happier when we were clueless about what was going on. Maybe I'd been wrong to go searching for answers. But ultimately it wasn't my choice. Kairo appeared on the island and tried to shoot us, so our only chance of survival was escape.

And Marina coming back to Washington probably had more positive effects than negative. She needs to turn her life around and go see her family. Even though her moods have improved, I know she still feels responsible for the deaths and like she can never return.

Someone knocks on the door and I immediately unlock it, hoping for Marina. I'm surprised to see Luke.

"Are you ever worried about Marina?" he asks instantly.

I nod hesitantly.

"I just feel like something's making her unhappy and she might not care about hurting herself in order to make things right in her mind. Do you know what's going on?"

"Yes, she's been like this ever since I met her," I sigh.

"When she newly discovered her powers, she accidently drowned several people and that's why she ran away to the island. She feels like she can never return to her family and has never completely forgiven herself."

His face only shows a little surprise. "Have you tried to help her?"

"Of course! And I don't think she's as mad at herself anymore, but, I don't know…"

"I just wanted to warn you again that if Marina's this careless and doesn't care about her life when she doesn't even know enough yet to fight Kairo, when he comes, it won't end well."

"That's what I'm worried about," I reply.

"You need to protect her," Luke instructs.

"I always will."

"And you should make sure to be there for her so she doesn't feel worthless; so she doesn't end up like some of the others who committed…suicide." Luke says the last word so softly that I barely hear it. He looks slightly guilty, as if he purposely kept this from me.

"Suicide!" I exclaim in horror.

"I didn't want Marina to get any ideas. Sometimes I worry that she'll just give up on life."

"I will make sure that *never* happens!" I vow.

"Good, it was awful to see all the others end up dead," he exhales.

Luke has clearly seen many tragedies in the past, and I can't let Marina become one of those. I understand now more than ever that I need to convince Marina none of the unfortunate past is her fault, and that she doesn't need to worry. I have to be there for her, but more than anything, she needs protection from Kairo.

***

I discovered a terrace on the back of the building that I know Marina would love. It overlooks the lights of the city and in the distance, highlights the sea. The vast sheet of stars against the velvety blue is all around and the full moon glows from high above. I know this is the perfect place for Marina and me to spend time together, away from the lab yet without technically going outside.

A table now stands directly in the center with two chairs, one on either side. A plate of salmon sits before each, a meal I know as one of Marina's favorites. I place a small bouquet of two roses –one red, one pale pink –next to her plate. Now I just need for Marina to arrive, like I instructed Luke to tell her.

There's a soft knock on the sliding glass door and I immediately pull it open. Marina's eyes scan the setting and she exclaims, "Carter, this is so sweet!"

I smile. "I'm glad you like it."

She takes the seat I pull out for her and says with a laugh as she squints to see my face, "One thing, isn't it a little dark?"

"I can fix that."

Focusing on the candles I forgot to light, I close my hand into a fist and slowly orange flames tipped with yellow grow on the black wicks. Marina watches with interest as a flame flickers in the palm of my hand and then dies out.

"Doesn't that burn?" she wonders.

"Not at all. And I didn't even know I could do that," I reply, sitting in the other chair.

"Then I can do this," she says and stares at her outreached palm.

Along with a small crackling sound, a blue tinted icicle forms in her hand, jutting towards the sky in a sharp point. Marina giggles as the icicle melts and water drips between her fingers and splatters to the ground. "That's pretty cool!"

"Yeah, it is. You know, I never thought I'd say this, but I really do actually miss the island."

"I know exactly what you mean."

"And it's not really that deserted island that I miss, but I think it's the idea that we had an adventure together."

Marina smiles. "I think that's exactly it." She takes a bite of the salmon and says, "This tastes really good."

"I hoped you would like it."

We eat the meal that she affirms delicious and talk more about our experiences on the island. I've felt too sheltered, almost locked away, recently and this is so nice. Marina's eyes drift to the candles during our conversation, watching the twisting flames that never go out. I think that she's intrigued by them, for the first time seeing the beauty of fire instead of the danger.

After we've finished eating, we stand against the sturdy railing, staring at the landscape around us. Marina squints into the distance, into the vaguely visible swells of the ocean.

"You miss the water, don't you," I say, more statement than question.

"Yes," she sighs. "Back on the island it was like I *had* to be in the ocean. Now that I'm away, the need isn't as strong, but I still miss it."

"Maybe we can go back sometime," I suggest.

"Sometime…not for a while."

"Are you ready to go back home?" I ask softly.

"Not yet," she responds, as I knew she would. "Especially not if you don't come with me."

"I would, if you want me to."

I take my arm off the railing and intertwine my fingers with hers. Both smiling, we stare out at the endless stars, not having to say a single word.

Chapter Thirteen

Marina

I tear my gaze from the glowing white stars and look at Carter. "Thank you for doing all this. You're the best."

"You're welcome," Carter replies, tilting his head towards me.

I lean in and stare into his eyes, the firelight illuminating the gold in them. Carter puts his other arm around me and smiles as he leans towards me. His lips have barely brushed mine when the perfect moment is shattered. The door bangs open and Ellen walks out, her face panicked. Carter and I instantly stand still, concerned by her expression, and wait for an explanation.

"Kairo's found you. He's coming!" Ellen exclaims.

"What?" Carter cries, moving his arm again so it's protectively around my shoulders.

"Dave set up some kind of tracking system that will notify him if Kairo's in a certain distance," Ellen explains hurriedly.

"I don't know how he's found you, but he's close! We need to do something about this, and quickly!"

Carter's eyes widen with dread and then he grimaces. "It's all my fault," he whispers.

"What?" I ask.

"I was so careless and stupid!" he accuses himself, putting his head in his hands. "The candles that I lit and then we were both experimenting with our power…it's all my fault that Kairo's coming!"

"Carter, don't blame this on yourself. You forgot and –"

"Marina, I failed to protect you. If I don't do something, Kairo will come here and kill both of us. I have to get him off your trail –"

"So we're leaving then? I'm fine with that."

"No," Carter says, his voice soft with sorrow and reluctance as walks towards the open door. "*I'm* leaving."

At the moment the world seems to stop. The previously amazing night has been completely destroyed as if someone stomped all over it until there was only crushed, pitiful pieces left. My heart sinks into my stomach and for nearly a full minute I forget to breathe. My voice catches in my throat as my eyes began to water. I stare at Carter disbelievingly, finally able to speak.

"You're leaving, without me?" My voice sounds so hurt that Carter flinches, and I think I see the firelight glint off tears barely forming in his eyes.

"It's the only way to protect you. I have to. You mean everything to me."

With those last words, Carter sprints down the hall, his pace nearly impossible because he knows I'll follow. I race after him and in what seems like only a second, we're outside the lab in the parking lot, the tall street lamps providing the only strips of light.

"Marina, please don't follow me," Carter begs.

"I have to –you said you wouldn't leave…" I answer, the words cracking.

"I don't want to leave, but if I don't then Kairo will kill you! I have to lead him away with my power so he'll track me instead of you!"

"Then he'll kill *you*!"

Carter pauses, his face twisted with regret. "Your life is more important than mine."

"No, Carter, you can't!"

I run towards him, but his arm darts forward and a fiery wall rises up between us. I recoil from the writhing flames and feel the hot tears running down my cheeks. Carter stands with his hand outreached, controlling the fire. His face only shows misery and guilt and I can see that he's choking back tears, not at all wanting to leave.

"I'm so sorry, Marina," Carter says sincerely. "But your life is more important than anything."

"No, no," I say, the words high-pitched through my crying.

"I promise that if I ever can, I'll find you again, but please don't come looking for me. I'm just doing this to save you, Marina."

Before I can object, Carter turns on his heel and runs off into the distance. I stare after him, immobilized as I watch the wall of fire vanquish, but he's already too far away. I can't even see Carter behind the trees any longer through the dark night atmosphere. But then I see the burst of bright orange flames jet up, in contrast with the dark shadows, and know that he's already trying to get Kairo to follow him rather than kill me.

I can't even think of the words to describe just how empty I feel. Carter was the only person I had who cared about me. He's the reason I partially forgave myself for the deaths, and he's the reason I finally worked up the courage to leave the island. Carter was always there for me and now with him gone, it's as if someone has broken my world. The wounds of sadness that had healed from when I discovered my powers have been ripped open again, but now there's more pain.

The only thing that keeps me from breaking down is that I know Carter didn't want to leave me. He only did this to save my life and I guess that's heroically selfless in a way. But still, I feel like Carter was the only person there for me, the only one I could trust, and now I have nobody.

Now, I'm cooped up in a lab with nobody here close to me, nobody to confide in about the misery that constantly rages inside me as I remember how many people I killed. I'm worried that without Carter to confide everything to, I'll eventually just explode.

He said he'd come back if he ever could, but I know that could very well be impossible. Kairo is murderous, powerful, and doesn't give up. Just like Luke said, if he wants somebody dead, they'll end up that way sooner or later. And now, especially since he bought me time, I don't fear for my life, only Carter's. His abilities over fire that could very well be destructive give me hope that he'll survive, but I don't know what Kairo can do. If his power overcomes Carter's, then all he has to depend on is his courage, and hopefully he'll remember I'm depending on him to survive.

But sooner or later Kairo will realize I'm not with Carter and he'll come back here looking for me. I can't stay here forever. In the meantime while Kairo's preoccupied, I can't think of my future survival. As tears splatter my red face, I can only think about missing Carter, and now I have nobody to share my feelings with.

Slowly and sorrowfully, I retreat inside, knowing there's nothing I can do now. Luke immediately rushes up to me and exclaims, "Marina, what happened?"

"Carter left," I choke out.

"What? I told him to protect you! He can't just let you die!"

"He was protecting me! He said that's the only way Kairo wouldn't come, if he left and led him away by using his power. He thought it was his fault because before Kairo came, he forgot and used his powers." The words are soft and barely audible.

Luke frowns. "I'm so sorry Marina, but I can see why Carter did this. You know, he only did this because he cares about you. He couldn't let you die."

"I know, but now I have nobody, nobody there for me, nobody to confide in," I spill out my feelings thoughtlessly.

"Don't worry, whenever you need to you can talk to me."

"Thank you," I say, realizing Luke is a good friend.

"No problem, but you might need some rest now."

"Yeah, I guess."

I walk down the hall to my room and slide under the covers of the bed without even removing my shoes. The enclosing safety of the covers is comforting, but it doesn't ease my sadness. My throat burns from crying and my eyes are still wet with tears. It feels as if there's an empty chasm in my heart that aches from the nothingness. Rest is the only way that I'll feel any better, even though I know it won't help much.

I turn over on my side and close my eyes, trying to even out my breathing. Eventually, sleep starts to tug me away and the last thing I see before I fall completely unconscious is Carter's smiling face, an image saved from the moment right after our first kiss. And I know that if I wasn't so close to sleep, it would've brought on a fresh round of unstoppable tears.

When I wake up I feel exhausted and depleted. It's only four in the morning, but I can't shut down my brain long enough to go back to sleep. I feel miserable, but then I realize that Carter wouldn't want me to be sad, and that I've been selfish. Leaving was just as hard for him as it is for me.

I know that Carter is in terrible danger right now and the only way to not render his sacrifice worthless is for me to do what he wanted: protect myself from Kairo, live a decent life, and eventually return to my family. I can't just stay depressed forever.

Now determined to banish all the misery that's haunted me for months, I wipe the tear stains from my face and lifting my head high, walk out the door.

The house is completely deserted and eerily soundless. I assume that everyone is in the lab, probably obsessing over where Kairo is now. Walking outside alone at night doesn't bother me after being accustomed to the island, but then I enter the unlocked lab.

It's creepy walking through the lab in the hours before sunrise. The blinding lights glint off the surfaces of the completely white interior. My shoes against the floor are the only sounds in the barren space. I constantly look over my shoulder as I walk down the hall, feeling as if someone is going to jump out at me at any moment. It's even worse that I have no idea which room to enter.

I stand in the middle of the hall with all the uniform metal doors staring back at me. I jump as a car's horn outside cuts through the silence.

"Marina?" I recognize Dr. Corry's voice as a door opens down the hall.

I rush inside and see that the whole family is clustered around a high-tech computer with worried expressions.

"What's wrong?" I exclaim.

Dr. Corry looks up, his brow furrowed in stress. "Well, Kairo's out of the range where I can track him now, but last I saw…he was right behind Carter."

Chapter Fourteen

Carter

I know he's right behind me. I can't see him or hear him, but I can sense that he's close. I'm exhausted from running for several hours straight, but I know that I must keep going or I'll end up dead. Periodically, I shoot fire a couple feet high so Kairo won't return to Marina.

I'm not sure how he doesn't deem this some sort of trick. Why would I purposely lead him on a trail when I know he wants to kill me? Maybe he does see through me, but he thinks following me could result in at least my death anyway. But one thing I'm sure of is that he thinks Marina's with me; he doesn't think I'd ever leave her behind.

I feel terrible about running away and not allowing her to come with me. I didn't want to be away from her, and I know that she's probably feeling very alone and even more miserable, just when she had finally stopped blaming herself for the deaths. I already miss Marina and I promised I would come back if I could, but honestly I don't think my chances of surviving long enough are very high.

Kairo has been right behind me since I left. He's clever, making sure to never show himself, maybe to make me think he's left so I'll let my guard down. I don't know why Kairo wants so badly to kill me, what his powers are, or what caused us all to be like this. I'm not sure how much my cluelessness hurts my chances of living.

There's nowhere I can hide, but I can't keep up running forever. But at this rate, wherever I go, I'm sure Kairo will track me down. And that's better than having him return to murder Marina.

The area around me is completely unfamiliar, but I expected that since my experience with Washington is only recent. The street lamps are dim against the night sky and few buildings have lights on. This place seems nearly deserted with the dark allies that run in between the run-down shops and houses. It's probably a bad area of town that I would've been hesitant to pass through in different circumstances.

Now, I hardly think of the other dangers around, such as gangs or robbers, since Kairo is chasing me. I don't look back since I'm sure it would slow me down. It seems impossible that he hasn't already caught me. My legs ache and I can barely breathe, but I keep persevering forward. Maybe Kairo's waiting for the moment when I have no energy left, so he can kill me without even a fight.

I know that any time now, my energy will be drained. I need time to rest, to sleep. I don't understand how I keep up this pace so long; it must have something to do with my power. Maybe I have slightly increased strength or endurance. Nobody who hadn't trained intensely for running would be able to last this. I certainly wouldn't have been able to just a couple of weeks ago.

The night is still and quiet. Wherever Kairo is, he doesn't make a sound, but something inside me triggers paranoia. I don't know what his abilities are, but just after his ruthlessness and Luke's description, I can tell even Marina and me put together are no match for him.

Luke's horrific description plays out in my mind as I imagine Kairo's hooded figure strolling into the lab and easily snapping an innocent person's neck. I shudder at the pool of blood that my mind fabricates, hoping that my fate won't be the same.

But I don't see how I can escape from something similar. Even if I somehow lose Kairo and stop to rest, where will I go? The only buildings in sight are rundown with shattered windowpanes and broken shingles lined with spider webs. If I stop to sleep in one for the night, the possibilities of danger are endless, even aside from Kairo.

I could get bitten by a poisonous spider or attacked by a rabid animal. Abusive criminals could be waiting in the shadows for their next victim to mug. It definitely isn't safe to stop until I'm in a more populated area.

Barely able to conjure more fire, I send a burning flare up, but it sinks into my hand after only a few seconds. I'm losing energy and sooner or later something bad is going to happen. I just know it.

A nauseous headache starts to blur my vision and I know that if I run any longer I'll simply collapse. Slowing my pace, I come to a reluctant halt and turn to the direction I think Kairo's in, standing defensively and gathering all my strength. I wait, trying to hide my fear, as the menacing silence continues, but I know he's there, somewhere in the shadows.

Suddenly, Kairo stands directly in front of me, in his black cloak. I don't know if I blinked or looked away for a spilt-second, but it seems as if he's just materialized.

"So you finally gave up?" he asks mockingly.

"Never," I say, narrowing my eyes.

"Where's the girl? What's her name…Maria? Marine?" Kairo asks tauntingly.

"You won't find her."

"I'm sure she must be somewhere nearby."

I keep my expression stony so Kairo won't get any hints about Marina's whereabouts. I stare at Kairo, waiting for him to attack before I fight. I still can't see his face, hidden in the shadows of the hooded cloak he wears. But I can tell that his build is tall and muscular, strong enough to even break a neck, like Luke described. Only his hands are visible, pale in contrast with the black fabric of the cloak. One is clenched around what I think is the silver gun, even though most of it is hidden in the folds of his robe.

"So you won't tell me where she is?" Kairo says. When I stay silent, glaring, he adds, "Then I'll find out myself."

Suddenly, a horrible pain shoots through my head. I double over as my vision blurs and the world around me spins. I look at Kairo as the pain subsides and he laughs wickedly.

"Changed your mind?"

"Of course not," I reply firmly.

The pain returns in my head, but now it runs all through my body. It feels as if I'm being burned with scorching flames, stabbed with an extremely sharp blade, and being torn apart from the inside all at once. The pain is horrible and drains all the energy out of me until I pathetically collapse to the ground, writhing helplessly.

I get the sudden urge to tell Kairo exactly where Marina is right now and to even help him find her. Something in my brain persuades me that it's the right thing to do, that it will cause me to gain great things. The small part of me still able to think through the agony feels disgusted that those thoughts of betrayal to Marina even occurred to me. How could I ever even think of doing something so terrible to Marina? Then I realize that Kairo implanted those thoughts. They weren't my own.

Using every ounce of strength and will power I have left, I stagger to my feet and stammer, "You're t –trying to control my thoughts! You –you think that the pain will make me tell you?"

"Won't it?" Kairo persuades.

"I wouldn't ever betray Marina!"

The rage that fills me seems to make the pain lessen and a slight bit of my strength returns. In my pure anger I'm able to gather just enough power that I blast fire right toward Kairo's heart. He jumps back and curses, avoiding the fire before it causes any real harm. Almost instantly, I'm back to normal as the pain vanishes entirely. It seems as if I've even been replenished with new stamina to fight, or run.

"You're powerful, boy," he says accusingly. "You know, fire can be very destructive. It can be much more dangerous and harmful than your girlfriend's little freezing tricks."

"You think we wanted to be this way?" I exclaim. "I don't want to be powerful! Power only caused people to die, including my own mom! The only use for my fire is to protect us against you!"

He laughs as if what I say is stupid. "Even so, I'm still much more powerful."

"Why do you even want to kill us?"

"Hmm…I'd say it's easier to accomplish if I don't tell you." He pulls out his unique gun and says menacingly, "Time's up," as he points it straight at my heart and pulls the trigger.

I dive out of the way just in time, but I know that this won't be the end as Kairo rapidly fires. I'm barely able to dodge each lithe bullet and I know that eventually my luck will run out. Focusing on the metal, I try to melt the weapon but he only cackles as the rifle stays intact.

"You don't think I thought of that?"

Knowing that my only chance is fleeing, I dash down the street as Kairo runs after me. I look over my shoulder and he shoots his gun repeatedly, the loud explosions racking the atmosphere. His cloak billows out behind him and the wind blows his ever-present hood back from his face.

Like the cloak, Kairo's hair is inky black, opposing the pale color of his skin. His eyes look slightly sunken in, shaded with rings of gray from lack of sleep or health. His eyes shine unnaturally golden, like luminous suns, but they hold a vicious edge. I notice that he's careful to still keep half of his face hidden from my view and irritably throws the hood back over his head, pulling it down so it hangs over his eyes. I'm not sure what he's trying so hard to hide.

The gun keeps firing and I'm not sure how I continue to avoid every bullet. I don't have time to light more than little sparks of fire on the trailing ends of Kairo's clothing and they're not every effective.

He pulls the trigger again, but this time the following blast isn't nearly as explosive. I realize that he ran out of ammunition and I turn to face him, not as scared of him anymore.

"Damn!" Kairo exclaims in anger at first, but sees my defiant expressions and grins. "You think this mere gun is all I have to harm you? Sure it may be the quickest and simplest death, but earlier I wasn't even using *all* of my power!"

I know that if I don't act quickly, Kairo will do something to stop me. Trying to not let my fear block my plan, I carefully keep my hand close to my side and clench it into a fist. His eyes narrow with suspicion when he notices me staring at the fabric of his sleeve, but because of his bragging, he reacts just a second too late. Just as Kairo's about to yell something, his sleeve bursts into a fire that quickly spreads.

A wall of fire that matches the one I used to block Marina from following me raises with the motions of my hand. I know that the flames are simply a distraction that Kairo will soon extinguish so I spin on my heel and bolt down the paved sidewalk. Fear courses through me, and somehow propels me to run faster. I have to get away before Kairo's able to attack again.

No longer caring about anything other than escaping, I take a series of unknown dark allies filled with litter and sewage clogged gutters. They reek of a rank smell that makes me want to hold my breath. The narrow streets are filled with ramshackle houses and signs displaying the street names painted over with bright graffiti. I twist down so many paths that I'm completely lost, so I doubt Kairo will be able to track me, unless of course, I use fire.

Eventually, after what seems to be hours, I come to a street that's slightly more welcoming and spot a house with a 'for sale' sign mounted on the front lawn. To my relief, the front door of the vacant property is unlocked.

A quick scavenge of the house tells me that it's completely emptied of food or supplies, but at least it will give me a place to sleep.

Because the air conditioning and heater have been disabled, the rooms capture the cold edge to the night and I shiver as I curl up in a corner. I have to refrain from creating a fire. I know it will be my immediate death. So I wrap my tattered, burned jacket form the island around me and try to get some rest.

Disturbing images flash before my eyes as I dream: the article about my mom's disappearance, the storm that sent me into the rocks, Marina's tear-stained face as I ran away, the mystery girl's voice calling for help, but this time it's only from memory, not another message. Then my dreams change to horrific things I've never seen, but that I think might have happened, or that I fear will occur.

The scene is blurred, but I can clearly see Marina running in terror. A cloaked figure is right behind her. She turns to fight, but Kairo pulls out his awful gun and she falls to the ground.

The image shifts and I see my mom hiding as she listens to the yells of a crowd in the distance. She shuts her eyes as they run past and she thinks she's safe, but then she turns around. Someone is standing right behind her and she freezes as I hear the explosion of a gun.

My mom's face fades until I see the outline of a girl, but no features or color are visible. She screams for help over and over again and I try to reach her in time. Before I can react, another figure strides towards her and it's clear that a blade like a knife is pierced through her heart. The girl doubles over in pain and I can only stand there, watching and knowing that I couldn't save her in time.

She died and I didn't even know her, but it makes me feel awful all the same. She died just like Marina and my mom… and it was my fault…

I wake up in a cold sweat, misery like a weight on my chest, the nightmares of deaths still clear in my head.

"That wasn't real," I repeat to myself in a whisper, over and over. "They're not really dead. They're not –" But then I stop myself as the words catch in my throat.

What I saw happen to my mom could've been almost exactly what happened. I know for sure that she *is* dead. And it wasn't at all my fault, but there's nothing I can ever do to bring her back.

And the girl that contacted both Marina and I for help, I know nothing about her. I don't know her name, where she is, why she needs our help, or if she's even still alive. I reassure myself that even if she did get killed, it wasn't my fault either, because I didn't even know where she was so I could save her in time. I don't even know anything about her identity.

As for Marina, it's not the same. I can't say it wasn't my fault, because if Kairo murdered her, it *would be* my fault. But she can't be dead. Kairo was just here…but he could have found her. I quickly shake my head and stop thinking of that horrible dream, that awful gunshot, because I know that Marina's still alive. I can feel it. If she were dead, then I wouldn't still be so determined to keep going, to keep fighting against Kairo.

Even though it's still dark outside, I'm scared to go back to sleep. I don't want to dream of death and misery again. It's unbearable enough to always be worried when I'm awake, so can't I at least have a peaceful sleep?

It appears that nothing has changed in the house, so I decide to explore and make sure that I didn't overlook any useful belongings left behind. Soon I'll be hungry and thirsty and the nights here are very cold, reflecting the moody temperatures of the daytime. I don't know why I didn't ask to borrow one of Luke's jackets and instead kept my old one that's torn and burned through in places.

It must be the memories since it symbolizes when I first discovered I could control fire; when I set this on flames.

This room looks like it would've been a bedroom since there's only a closet and walls painted pale blue with plain carpet. A quick peek in the closet shows it's completely empty and all the other bedrooms are in the same condition. The wooden kitchen cupboards don't even hold crumbs.

There's not a single piece of furniture or any lost things. The entire place seems irritatingly sterile; there doesn't even seem to be dust. This is probably one of the few houses on the street that isn't either run down, inhabited by criminals, or kept disorganized and dirty.

Without any other choice, I leave the safety of the empty house and trek down the street. I have nowhere to go, but I do have a purpose.

I must make sure Kairo doesn't find Marina, but for now, I'm going to stay hidden, too. After earlier, I'm not ready for another fight. I don't want to be hurt or forced to leak information about where Marina is. And I want to be able to stop thinking about the terrible things that could happen. Still, no matter how hard I try, I know that nothing will stay the way I want forever.

Even if I postpone everything bad from occurring, someday it will, and soon. My future is clear now, ever since I discovered my powers, and I know one thing for sure: It involves a large amount fighting and danger, which are things I can never escape.

Chapter Fifteen

Marina

The days blur together, all seeming the same. Sometimes I can't distinguish night from day or hours from minutes. I can only register two things: that Carter's gone and that Kairo could kill me at any moment. I go through each day in a daze, pretending to not be depressed, so nobody will worry. But I know Luke can see the glaze over my eyes and tell I'm hiding something.

Sometimes he'll ask, "Are you okay, Marina? I know times are hard and if you need someone to talk to…"

But I always respond with the same simple answer, "I'm fine."

I'm not trying to be rude; Luke is the closest thing I have to a friend right now and he's always so kind, but I don't feel like having to relive everything, having to cry again. It's like my wounds scabbed over, but they never really healed. There's still poison brewing inside and the wounds could easily be reopened.

I keep thinking of Dr. Corry informing me that last he saw, Kairo was right behind Carter. Still, I force myself to believe Carter's still alive. Then I realize he must be.

If he were really dead then I would feel empty. Of course I feel awful now, but not completely empty…more like longing. And Carter has fire, literally *and* in his personality. He has something to live for; he was always the one that motivated me to keep moving forward and would never stay dejected. He has a father to return to and hopefully he thinks it's very important to see me again.

The room's changed from becoming prison-like to again seeming comforting. I spend a lot of my time sleeping since it seems all there is to do. I long for the ocean, but at the same time I don't want to leave the safety of the house.

The Corrys are as supportive as they can be, but they luckily give me space. Dr. Corry constantly checks his radar for signs of Kairo or Carter and Ellen is always considerate. Luke sometimes seems like a brother to me, and it makes me miss my little brothers back home.

I can only imagine someday my parents telling them that I have powers.

That I'm unnatural, *inhuman.*

Of course being kids they might think it's cool at first, but then they'll get older and realize how strange it is, and they might even be scared of me. I can't imagine ever telling mom, dad, my brothers, or Rain, but I know I'll have to someday.

I wonder if my parents already know. How could they not? If I'm like this, they must be, too. Carter's mom had powers, but maybe it skips a generation. Still, they must know something about this; a secret they kept from me.

I've been locked in my room for too long that my head is swimming with questions. It's so nagging that I walk down to the lab to finally learn more about who I am, to face reality.

"How did you even track Kairo?" I question instantly.

Dr. Corry looks up, startled. "When he came here many years ago, I got some of his DNA and programmed a system

124

to track him, but it only works within a certain radius because of his power.

"How did you know where Carter was?"

"I set it up to track you and Carter, too, incase Kairo was following you and we had to help."

"I just have one more question for now. Do my parents have powers?"

His face freezes, as if not wanting to answer.

"What is it?" I demand. "Tell me!"

He inhales deeply and explains, "This might be a little hard to take in, but I did some research on your backgrounds and Marina...you're adopted."

"*What*?" I exclaim. This can't be possible.

All my life I've felt so close to my family. My parents and my little brothers have always been a part of me. I never even thought to question that I was a true part of the family. I even resemble them a bit. I've always had features that were my own, like my unique eyes, but my mom's hair is almost the same shade as mine and people say my dad and I have similar personalities. I guess that was all sheer coincidence.

"But –but –are you sure?" I stutter in disbelief.

"I'm sorry," he says with a serious nod.

This is only getting worse. I'm not like other people. I killed other people. Kairo wants to kill *me*. Carter left and now he might be dead. My family isn't my real family. I don't know anything about my life except lies and regret.

"Why me?" I whisper.

At least Carter had a real dad, his own birth dad. His mom died, but at least he knew her identity. It seems that with each new piece of information, my past unravels even more, until I know nearly nothing about myself.

"And my real parents are dead," I state. I already know the answer.

"Yes, again I'm sorry. Would you like me to find out more about them?"

"No, there's no point in learning about them and thinking 'what if' when they're already gone." I stand up and walk away with new anger boiling inside me.

My eyes are downcast and I'm walking so fast that I collide with Luke. I sprawl to the ground, but quickly pick myself up and turn to walk away, but he grabs my arm to stop me.

"What happened?"

"Each day I stay here longer, I learn more about my past. And then I realize I don't *want* to know."

"What?" Luke asks, raising an eyebrow.

"I'm adopted."

"Oh, and…"

"And what?"

"Uh, nothing," Luke says, but I can see that there's definitely something very important by the look in his bright eyes.

"Luke, what is it?" I demand.

"I promise that I only just found out. I swear that I really didn't know any more than I told you before. I just –I don't know if I'm supposed to tell you right now. Promise that if I do, it won't make you do something crazy. Promise."

I nod hesitantly. "Yeah, okay, what is it? Wait, it doesn't matter. It'll just be something that makes me seem less human."

"Marina, that's the thing," Luke says softly, with a grimace that almost looks sympathetic. "You're not quite human. You're Serion."

Serion. There's that word again. The same word Kairo yelled at Carter and I as we left the island. The same word that's often ran through my head, filled with questions and mystery. *Serion.* I still don't know what it means, but I know that it somehow contributes to me being 'not quite human.' Maybe it's a race or a cult as Carter and I wondered. Or is it something much bigger? I almost don't want to find out.

I know that when Luke tells me, it'll change my life. But I can't hide from my real identity forever.

"What's Serion?" I murmur.

Luke just stares at me for a moment as if debating whether to answer. Finally he whispers, "It's a different planet. Serion, you're from there. Carter's from there. It was destroyed years ago, and the Serions migrated to Earth because they'd been warned that their home planet would explode. All the Serions have powers."

My eyes widen in shock as I stare at Luke, unable to speak or move. My heart is racing and my blood is pounding in my ears. I almost feel like my body sensed I knew who I am and is more than ready to accept that. I can't believe it. I've been thinking of myself as not quite human, but never *inhuman*. I never even guessed I was from another planet.

Those people on the beach were right. I am a freak.

A strange creature.

Dangerous.

Unnatural.

Inhuman.

Alien.

Still in shock, I begin to tear down the hall as fast as I can.

"Marina!" Luke yells and within a few seconds, he catches up and stops me. "What are you doing?"

"Leaving!" I exclaim.

"Where?"

"Home."

"Really?" he says in surprise. Carter must've told him how I never wanted to return.

"Well, to my best friend Rain. Honestly the only people I can trust are friends. My family wasn't even my real family. The only people I feel like I can trust are Carter, Rain, and you."

"You can trust us, but you can trust your family, too. They were only trying to protect you. Just because you were adopted doesn't mean they weren't your real family. They raised you and cared for you all your life. You can't forget that."

"Maybe, but I'm still only going back to see Rain right now."

"Do you promise you won't go anywhere else? You won't look for danger?"

"No, I won't." I start down the corridor.

"You're leaving now?"

"Yes, are you gonna help me pack or not?"

"Just so you know, you might have to sneak away," Luke warns as we hurry back towards the house. "My dad might not want you to go."

"Why, does he want to do experiments on me?" I ask sarcastically.

"He wants more information about what he's been studying for years, but he's a good person. He also doesn't want Kairo to kill you."

Whenever I think of Kairo killing me, I think of Carter. And I wonder if he got away in time.

"What did you tell Carter before he left?" I press.

"That he needed to protect you. But I also said he needed to be there for you. I didn't want this to happen."

Suddenly, I realize why Luke understands me so well and always prompts Carter to protect me. He was once like me in a way, sometimes not caring about life, wishing he were dead. He felt like there was nobody there for him, nobody to talk to.

"What did you do after you saw Kairo murder those...Serions?"

"What?" Luke asks in surprise.

"I mean, it messed you up pretty badly, didn't it? What was your life like?"

Luke sighs. "Constantly being scared is one of my earliest memories. Afterwards, I always felt like *I* wasn't normal. Who else's family protects runaways and only to see a psychopath come and kill them right in front of you? I know that at school people would think I was weird. I was always known as the scientist's son and somehow they knew that he researched unusual things.

"It scared me, seeing those people die. I couldn't forget it. For years I felt like it was my dad's fault. He didn't understand how awful it was for me to see that when I was only five. And my mom tried to be sympathetic, but she was always so stressed and I didn't want to worry her more.

"I was always scared that Kairo would come back and kill me. After what I saw him do to those people, in my house, I was always worried and felt like *I* was strange. Sometimes I felt like you, like it wasn't worth living. I didn't really have any friends, anyone to talk to. Then I realized there was no point in that. *I* never did anything. It wasn't worth being terrified all the time, even if Kairo was coming back."

"So you stopped being…like me?" I wonder.

"You have to stop worrying about the past, Marina," Luke tells me, nodding. "Nothing that happened was your fault, and Carter will come back."

"You and Carter are right. I'm trying hard to stop blaming myself for the deaths. That's part of why I'm going to see Rain."

"Are you going to tell her everything?"

"Yes…everything," I promise myself. "It's time that I turn my life around no matter what I've discovered."

But even as I say the words, I fear that just as I've learned of my past, I'll discover secrets of the people I used to think I knew. I'm not human. My parents lied to me all those years, my adoptive parents. What will I realize next? My little brothers work for Kairo? Rain is some deadly demon? At this point it seems anything is possible.

Chapter Sixteen

Carter

The sun peers over the horizon, glowing with the start of a new day. I've been aimlessly walking further and further for a whole day, and I still don't know where I am. But the purpose of leaving wasn't to find a destination, but to lead Kairo away.

I know just how Marina felt on the island when she was convinced somebody was following her. For the past hour I've felt like eyes are boring into my back, but when I turn around there's nobody there. Of course that doesn't stop me from thinking somebody is hiding, but I'm not incredibly worried. As I venture into the more populated city, I'm not at risk of having to fight alone.

When I hear a rustling behind me I don't even look. I figure it's just the wind in the leaves. That was a mistake.

The pain spreads through my leg before I know what's going on. I register the low whistle that cuts through the air just before something hits me, and I look down. An arrow juts out of my leg, blood trickling from the injury. It's more painful than I would have expected, but the shot was powerful and the arrow is buried deep.

Spinning around on my unharmed leg, I turn to see a figure pressed against the side of the building. He's dressed in all black, but pants and a jacket rather than a cloak. His hood is pulled over his face, but I recognize him to be one Kairo's followers from the island. His black metal crossbow is pointed straight at me.

"Who are you?" I demand.

"Definitely not your friend!" he spats.

"Not much information, but it's enough," I reply as fire flickers in my palm.

I shape it into a hasty sphere and hurl it at the boy before he shoots another arrow. Pain erupts in my leg when I put weight on it, but I downplay the wound with just a twisted grimace. He easily ducks underneath the fire.

"What's this arrow made of?" I mutter.

"I'd think you'd be smart enough to recognize poison," he laughs.

Of course: poison. I grit my teeth and pull the arrow out of my leg. I let it fall to the ground, trailing red.

He notches another arrow, but I make a fist and fire races up the leg of his pants. Ignoring my burning injury, I grab the arrow while the boy furiously tries to bat away the fire. The end of his pants begins to disintegrate and angry blisters form on his legs as he lets out a scream of pain. I feel bad about torturing him, about planning to kill him, but it seems the only way.

I'm injured so I can't escape, and I promised Marina I'd try to survive. Besides, since he works for Kairo I'm saving at least several others by killing him.

While the boy is distracted with the fire, I sneak up and taking a deep breath, push the arrow into his heart. He gasps and turns towards me as he falls to the ground. The fire flickers away as I lose my concentration. The blood is already soaking through his dark jacket.

He looks so pathetic sprawled on the ground that I begin to regret this even more. His pants have been reduced to tattered shorts and his jacket has holes burned through it. Welts and blisters erupt where the fire made contact with his skin, turning it flaming red. The long arrow sticks out from his chest and blood surrounds the wound. His face is still hidden by his hood, but I know it's filled with horrible pain.

"Kairo will find you and kill you," he chokes out. "No matter how many of us you and your girlfriend kill, you will die in the end. We will find you and we will make sure your death is painful! We will get there before you do! We will find it first! You will never –"

His last threatening words are cut off in a final breath. I stare at his limp body, but my regret recedes after hearing his last words. He still only wanted Marina and me dead.

Even in his very last moments, no shame, not even a glimpse of a good heart, shone through. The last words he could manage weren't even angry about his own death, but vengeful threats. He seems so young, but he was fully corrupted.

I carefully peel back his hood to see who I killed. The boy looks to be a little younger than I am. His features are sharp and angular, blackened with ash. His still open eyes stare straight at me, their gaze piercing and menacing. I shudder and turn away from his body.

The ground is spattered with drops of blood, both mine and his. I turn my attention to my leg and see that beneath my shorts, dark veins form a web around the wound. The poison makes my leg feel as if it's slowly and painfully burning. Fire doesn't affect me, but now I know what it feels like to others to slowly have your skin boiled and burned away.

I limp down the street and eventually have to sit on the ground to rest. I examine the arrow wound carefully and try to think of a way to heal it. I don't know a cure; I don't even know what kind of poison was used. I can't be sure if it's just a common poison or something that Kairo unnaturally conjured.

The injuries from my shipwreck on the island healed and have only left faded scars, but this can't be as easily mended. Simple bandages won't cure it.

The only thing I can think of is to keep going until I come across somewhere with access to at least search what kind of poison this is. But as I stare at the dark veins quickly spreading and developing a greenish color, my hopes aren't high for finding an easy medicinal cure.

I haul myself off the ground and hobble down the sidewalk. Soon I realize that I'll have to figure this out on my own. If I go to a hospital, they will somehow get information out of me or realize this isn't a regular poison and probably learn of my powers, or at least Kairo's. I might end up getting killed. And by now I'm almost sure this isn't a natural poison.

I take an uneasy look down and see that the damage is spreading fast. Now the red and blue veins have darkened in color and the area seems to be darkened with green and purple bruises.

The strange and extreme effects scare me, but maybe it isn't fatal. If I'm lucky, maybe the injury will fade away. I highly doubt that, but it's possible that it's just meant to cause pain and eventually, if I return, Dr. Corry will know a cure. For now, I just have to keep going and wait to see what happens.

In case somebody sees the disgusting wound and questions it, I rip a strip from my jacket and tightly tie it around my leg. I only now notice that strangely the arrow didn't cause me to bleed excessively, only leaving some dried blood around the edges. I hope that the poison isn't cutting off blood circulation, and I'm careful to loosen the knot.

After walking for many more long hours, I've bypassed another city and circled around so I'm near a stretch of rocky beach. I keep my distance from the boulders, the memories of my shipwreck still haunting me.

By now the pain searing through my leg is agonizing. Even if I'm able to survive it, I can't keep walking like this. My pace has been greatly slowed and I've been breathless and light-headed all day. The more weight I put on the injury, the worse it gets. I stop to sit on the dunes above the beach and let out a breath of relief as I finally get some rest.

Grimacing at the even darker colors of the poisoned arrow mark, I decide that I have to do something about it. I can see the future effects clearly: slow, painful death or awful amputation.

Even as I rack my brain for an answer, I don't see a solution. Discovering my fire power has brought nothing but trouble. Fire –that's it.

I know that I've heard before that in desperate situations fire has been used to help heal, either to stop blood loss or to help clean infection. I know that there will be lots of damage and pain, but maybe it'll save me. And cauterizing is the only option I've got.

I peel the sweaty make-shift bandage away and make sure nobody is anywhere in sight. When I've determined the area clear, I create small controlled flames on my fingertips. I stare at the veins snaking over my skin and hope that my immunity to fire will minimize the damage and the awful pain. Inhaling sharply, I bring my fiery hand to my leg.

At first I feel nothing and for a brief moment think that I actually got lucky enough to not feel the fire. Then a sharp stab burns through my calf, like the arrow is piercing my leg all over again. I stifle the scream that I almost let out and cringe.

The fire meeting the poison must be counteracting and have a burning effect that even my fire-proof skin can't ignore.

I squeeze my eyes shut and force myself to not move as the fire hopefully destroys the poison. A horrible sizzling sound begins as the fire crackles. I can't feel the heat in my hand, but the pain in my leg just gets worse and worse. Finally, once I feel like I'm about to explode, I can't take it any longer. I tear my hand away and immediately make the fire vanish.

My leg looks horrific, in a different way than before. The patch of discolored skin webbed with veins has been replaced with raw, bubbling blisters. The skin is mottled and ridged with red and dark pink. The pain has shifted from unbearable to stinging and tender, but from the looks of it, I'm sure anyone else would've felt much worse.

The burn is nasty, so awful I know it'll never fully heal. I stand, testing out the damage. I frown in discomfort since the pain hasn't really subsided. But at least it feels temporary instead of fatal, and not quite as intense.

I can already imagine what Marina will do when she sees this. I know she'll freak out and demand what happened. I'm getting so caught up in my thoughts of Marina that it just dawns on me, what if she gets hurt, too?

Sure, I left her in Dr. Corry's care, but I know that she won't stay there forever. She can't stay there forever. Kairo would eventually find her if she did. I can't imagine she would go back to her parents, but at least she knows her way around Washington better than I do. She did live here for almost fifteen years so I'm assuming she'd think of somewhere to go, hopefully before it's too late.

But my chances of survival are much worse than hers. Even though I've traveled far, the fact that Kairo had the boy with the arrow waiting to kill me shows he has at least a decent idea of where I am. And because of that, and since there's no one around to help me, he would probably go after me before Marina.

It's ridiculous that I'm still just wandering around. I really need to find a hotel to stay in, but I don't know how I'll gather enough money. I didn't even think to ask for any at Dr. Corry's. I only now realize that was stupid.

I end up just continuing to walk until it's completely dark. I veer away from the shore and back into an expanse of trees, somewhat like a forest. The varying types of close-grown trees provide some protection and only a few tiny houses are pushed between the clusters of plants. Each building is spread far apart, barely illuminated by the dim glow in the darkening sky.

Most of the windows are brightened with light, showing that none are empty, none are a place I could stay. Finally, when I'm about to collapse, I come across a tiny, battered wooden house. Well, it's more of a shack and looks to be infested with rats and crawling spiders, but it's better than nothing.

Just to be sure it isn't inhabited, or even the home of some rabid animal, I creep silently to the window and peer inside cautiously. It's so dark that I can hardly see the insides, but then a shift in movement catches my attention. As my eyes adjust to the darkness and see a very small light that looks to be a tiny candle, the inside of the house is better revealed.

There are the shapes of several people, whispering as if telling deep secrets. But their voices rise louder with exasperation. Still, I'm the only one in the distance to hear their words.

"So you found him dead?" a voice asks in disbelief. I immediately recognize it: Kairo.

"I just told you that!" a man responds, probably someone from the island.

"Well, he was young and stupid," Kairo replies dismissively.

"Then where's the boy, Carter? You said he'd be around here."

I tense at the mention of my name and shrink back into the shadows.

"I'm sure he is, but he's smart. He'll be hiding well, so we'll just have to wait until he's too hurt to move on. That arrow looked used and there was more blood on the ground than just the dead boy's, wasn't there? I'm nearly positive Carter was hit with an arrow and that poison is deadly."

"Why are you so worried about killing them both now anyway?" another man asks tiredly. "Aren't they necessary for later when…?"

"I have to kill them all, you idiot! I've explained this to you before!" Kairo hisses. "Soon enough, they'll figure out what's going on and fight back. Why do you think I went to all this work, even blowing up my own home? It's definitely not going to be for nothing! *Everyone* needs to pay!"

"Even your own kind? What did they do to you?"

"Clearly!" Kairo exclaims in exasperation. "You're all such idiots that if you're not careful, I might have to kill you and find some new followers." Everyone in the room immediately freezes and shuts up. "Anyway, the sacrifices must be made."

"What exactly is it for, though?" a woman inquires.

Kairo chuckles. "Well, you can't know everything! I keep my secrets just in case anyone ever changes sides."

"And what are we supposed to do now?" a man snaps irritably.

"Find the boy of course!" Kairo exclaims in exasperation. When there's silence he adds in a yell, "Now!"

From the shuffle of movement, I realize that they're coming after me, right away. I dive around the back of the house just before they flood from the doorway. After the commotion has died down, I stick to the shadows as quietly as I can, running in the opposite direction of Kairo's followers. I ignore the throbbing in my leg and keep moving stealthily.

One wrong step, one crackle of leaves and they'll find me.

One stumble and I'll be dead.

Voices are starting to get closer. I don't think they've heard me, but soon they will. With my leg, I won't be able to escape from this forest in time. The only place to hide is one of the few houses, the ones with lights on and people inside.

I have no other choice so I bang on the door of the nearest house. It looks old and probably self-built from the faded wood walls, but the lights are on, showing that somebody lives here. Nobody answers the door for at least a minute, even through my constant knocking.

Finally, a squeak indicates the lock being slid open and the door opens, just a crack. A woman in a robe narrows her eyes at me in an irritated expression.

"Can I please come in?" I beg.

"Why?" she asks suspiciously.

"It's important!" I glance over my shoulder and think I see movement amongst the trees. "Please!"

She sighs in exasperation, never letting go of the deep frown. "Only for a moment, to explain what's happening." I rush in as she opens the door wider and hear her mutter, "Those other people seemed strange, too."

"What other people?" I demand.

"Well, you're nosy aren't you?"

"Sorry, just –who were they?"

"Some group of people dressed in black, saying they were looking for a teenage boy. And their description seems to match you. They said something about him being dangerous."

"Would you more likely believe a group of strange adults in black or a boy, by himself, with a hurt leg?" I gesture to my burn and her frown deepens.

"Well, that's why I'm letting you explain right now. Who were they?"

"Bandits," I say hastily. "With guns."

"Why are they after you?" she questions.

"I don't know!" I reply. "Why are they even bandits in the first place?"

She stares at me as if weighing the truth to my answers. "What are you doing here, alone?"

"I...uh...ran away. And burnt my leg trying to use matches."

"So you're some delinquent kid?"

"No," I say, probably unconvincingly. "But do you have any extra room I could stay in for the night? I don't feel like having to run any longer when I can barely even walk. I'll end up dead by morning if I have to keep hiding from them all night long and –"

"Fine! If you'll just stop bugging me!" She shuffles through the cupboards for a moment and then shoves a few boxes in my hands along with small wad of cash. "You look like you're starving," she explains, pitying me. "Just take the last door down the hall."

"Thank you!" I say and quickly follow her directions before she changes her mind.

The small hallway means that the last door is the third door. It's a small extra bedroom with only a bed and dresser on the bare wood floor. A layer of dust is gray on the furniture, but the plain white bedspread looks clean and untouched. I set the items on the ground by the bed after looking through them. I think she knew that I was planning to leave in the morning and didn't want me starving to death.

Luckily, the box of crackers, bag of trail mix, and granola bars won't spoil. If I go in the opposite direction of Kairo and his allies, then I should be able to survive. I have money for emergencies and for the night, shelter. The comfortable bed seems like a luxury, so I instantly sink beneath the covers and fall asleep after only a few minutes. My last conscious thought is that I will make sure Marina lives, and that I will return to her.

Chapter Seventeen

Marina

I can tell by the pale light penetrating the sides of the curtains that it's early in the morning, exactly what I wanted. After quickly getting dressed, I quietly open the door and tip-toe to the kitchen where Luke is waiting for me.

"I thought you'd need some things to survive," Luke explains as he hands me a bag.

One glance through shows me there's food, water, a first aid kit, and a sharp knife. "To protect myself?" I question, holding up the weapon.

"Yeah, be careful. And there's money so you don't have to walk all the way home. I'd say a subway is your best option. And remember to never use your powers. If you do, it'll make everything much harder."

"Thank you, Luke," I say and hug him.

"You're welcome," he answers. "If you ever need help again, I'll be here. And if Carter comes back, I'll tell you."

Luke gives me a flip phone. "This is probably a good idea to have."

"Don't you need your phone?"

"No, this one's old. I have another one and my number's in the contact list if you need to call."

We both know that he leaves out the part about why I'd need to call: if I was in danger, if Kairo had found me. I'm nervous about departing and being alone, a vulnerable target, where Kairo could attack me, but I know I have to leave. I've been avoiding facing my past life for months and it's time that I set things right, especially with Carter gone. I know that he wants me to return, to stop drowning in my own misery.

And I'm not miserable any longer. Of course I miss Carter all the time, but I've changed. I've learned who I really am, and I'm not going to let that hold me back any longer. I'm going to let it build me up to be braver and stronger. And since I became friends with Carter and Luke I'll know that I'm never really alone.

"Well, I guess I should get going before your parents wake up."

Luke nods. "Just remember that Carter's alive, Marina. I know you'll find him again."

I give him a melancholy smile as I open the door. "I hope so. Thanks again for everything. Bye, Luke."

"Good luck!" he calls as I set off from the lab.

This is the turning point of my new life, one where I won't hide from my identity any longer. I won't hide from being Serion.

***

Smoke fills my lungs and makes me cough as I stand, pressed against strangers in the foul-smelling station. I've never liked traveling in subways, but Luke's suggestion makes sense. It's an easy way of transportation where Kairo's less likely to find me. I just hope the ride will be over with soon, because the fumes from the vehicle are giving me a headache.

As the arriving crowd pours into the station, a man ushers my group through the doors, grabbing each of our tickets. I immediately claim a seat, knowing that space fills up fast on these rides. I try not to avoid eye-contact with the other passengers, knowing that many are strange or even possibly dangerous.

I catch sight of a heavy-set man covered in offensive tattoos and a girl with spiky neon pink hair and dozens of piercings. A woman with her husband angrily swings her purse at strangers as she tries to crowd into a seat. A string of slurred cuss words is aimed at her.

I look down at my feet and sigh, hoping the awful subway ride will be quick.

I can tell we're moving when I feel a small lurch and hear the engine rumble. The only pleasant factor is the vehicle's speed, because everything else only gets worse. The stench of rotten food, cigarette smoke, and body odor makes me result to breathing through my mouth. I'm careful to keep to myself and not get involved in the arguments erupting around me. The tightly-packed bodies create claustrophobic humidity, which only adds to my sweat and building headache.

A teenage boy is staring at me when I take one quick look up, but I immediately look down again. He's not the kind of person I would associate with. His shaggy, purple-streaked hair, sweatshirt with a morbidly bloody image, and defiant expression tell me he's someone who probably spent time in juvie or at least thinks nothing of breaking the law frequently.

I can feel that he's still watching me, and it only makes me more uncomfortable. I position myself towards the window so my back is turned to the other people, and stare at the symmetrical walls of the dark tunnel as I wait for this to end.

After what seems like an eternity, the subway train screeches to a stop and I'm one of the first people to stand up and dash out the door. I clutch my bag to my chest and walk away as fast as I can.

The welcoming sunlight fills me with relief as I emerge in a familiar area. I can smell the salty sea and know that I'm very close to home. I hurry through the streets until I reach the beachside road where mine and Rain's houses stand. I force myself to block out any second thoughts as I walk to my best friend's house.

The scene around is beautiful: perfect paradise. The air carries the scent of the ocean and is exactly the right temperature. A light breeze ruffles the bright palm trees and a glint of sun peeking through a part in the clouds sparkles off the waves. I fight the urge to run down the sandy hill and dive into the water, promising myself that soon I'll be able to spend time in the ocean again.

Rain's pale gray house is an image etched into my mind. I walk up her cement driveway, but venture from the white front door and instead sneak around the side of the house. Her parents can't know I'm here or they'll immediately tell my mom and dad, who I'm not yet ready to face.

She always forgets to lock her window, so I easily slide back the glass and silently climb through the window. Creeping around in stealth has had its benefits. Rain is sorting through her closet with her back to me. I quietly walk behind her and clamp my hand over her mouth, stifling her scream.

She swivels around to face me and I hold a finger to my lips as I take my hand away.

Rain's light blue eyes widen in shock and she whispers incredulously, "Marina?"

"Hi, Rain," I say with a wide smile.

We throw our arms around each other in a tight embrace. When she finally lets go, Rain takes a step back and analyzes me.

"You're taller," she comments.

I laugh. "So are you."

Rains stands closer in height to me than I remembered, but other than that she looks almost exactly the same. Her bright blonde hair is still long down her slim back and I recognize the silvery blue denim jacket that she loved.

"I thought you were dead!" she exclaims.

"Almost," I admit.

"What happened?" Rain asks worriedly.

"I'll tell you everything soon," I promise. "Are your parents home?"

"No, they're at some concert today. Do you want me to call them?"

"No! Not yet. I don't want anyone else to know I'm back yet. I'm sure that'll be very…chaotic and I'm not ready yet."

"So you've been alone all this time?" Rain asks.

"Not quite," I reply, badly concealing the mix of emotions in my expression.

Rain knows me well, and one look at my face makes her grin and say, "You met a guy!"

"Yeah…" I know that there's no point in trying to keep anything from her.

"What happened?" she presses in concern, seeing the sadness in my eyes.

"It's hard to explain," I sigh. "But Carter left to protect me. He promised to come back if he could, but I'm worried that he'll be killed."

"What?" Rain exclaims in bewilderment and horror. "Killed? Marina, what in the world happened while you were gone?"

"Do you promise you'll believe me if I tell you?"

"Of course!"

I take a deep breath and begin, "When I left, I found an uncharted island." Through my detailed explanation, Rain listens intently. Through parts of it, I see the astonishment on her face, but I know that she believes me. And I know that she trusts me. She won't see me as some dangerous creature, even if I am technically inhuman. She'll be understanding and try to help me.

But it's still shocking. It's still shocking to me.

"You're…*Serion*?" Rain whispers. Her face is blank; she probably doesn't know how to react.

"Yeah," I answer.

She nods slowly and swallows. "Okay…cool."

I laugh. "Rain, you don't have to pretend to think this isn't weird."

She smiles and replies, "But you can't use your powers, right? Because then Kairo will find you?"

"Exactly, but what I want to know is what happened after I left."

"The police searched for you, but found nothing," Rain sighs. "Over time the people become convinced that the deaths couldn't have been caused by some powers you had, but I guess they were wrong. Sorry," she adds when she sees my face tense. "But your family hasn't been doing the best…"

"What?" I exclaim.

"Your brothers have had to come over here a lot," she says with a sympathetic frown. "Your mom's always depressed and your dad sort of developed a drinking problem."

I freeze, incredulous at what she tells me. My dad would previously hardly ever even touch a glass of red wine at dinner. Now he's turned into some sort of alcoholic? And my mom was always the kind of bubbly person who hardly ever got trapped in a bad mood. She was always extremely positive. I feel horrible for what I've done to my family, and that my little brothers have had to experience that environment.

"We should tell them that you're back," Rain urges.

"I −I can't. Just not quite yet. But I know I should soon; you all think so: you, Luke, *Carter*."

"Carter. It sounds like you two are really close."

"I really miss him," I admit forlornly. "I did everything I could to stop him from leaving, but if he hadn't, then I'd probably be dead right now."

"Don't worry, I'm sure that he'll come back."

"I feel that he's still alive...but you weren't there when Luke described what Kairo did."

"Luke, Carter –your life has changed so much since you left."

"What about you?"

"I have to admit, I was really worried when you disappeared. But I was convinced you weren't coming back and I had to set a good example for your brothers. I've had to take care of them, but I can't blame your parents. Everyone thought you were dead."

"I'll go see them soon," I promise, but my unvoiced thought is, *so you blame me?*

"But what do you do in the mean time?"

"Could I stay here, in the basement?"

"That's going to be a bit hard if you don't want my parents to know you're back, but we can try –"

Rain is interrupted when a piercing ringing sounds from my bag. I sift through the items and flip open the phone. "Hello?" I answer.

"Marina!" Luke's voice is relieved. "Did you find Rain?"

"Yes, and I told her everything."

"See, it wasn't that hard. Nothing happened on the way there, right?"

"No, have you heard anything from Carter?"

Our answers are clipped and rapid as we rush to fire out impending questions.

"I'm sorry, but no. My dad's been looking for any trace of him, but there's nothing. We haven't seen any of Kairo's followers around either, but I promise I'll keep looking."

"Thanks, I'll talk to you later," I end the conversation.

"Okay, bye," Luke responds as I close the phone.

"Luke?" Rain guesses curiously.

"Yes, he gave me this phone in case of emergency. He's looking for Carter, but neither of us have any idea where he's gone. I'm pretty sure he was just trying to lead Kairo away. But he didn't really have anywhere specific to go. And Carter doesn't even know we're Serion."

"Wow, that'll be a surprise," Rain replies, her eyebrows arching.

"But at least his dad can talk to him about it," I sigh. "Carter's mom was Serion, but I'm adopted."

Rain shakes her head and says, "I still can't believe that. And another thing, who do you think that girl is, the one you thought might be me?"

"I'm not sure. I haven't heard from her since, so maybe I won't anymore."

The high pitched doorbell rings through the house and Rain's eyes widen. "My parents are back early! Go to the basement and try to be quiet!"

I know the layout of Rain's house like the back of my hand, so it only takes me seconds to enter the basement and lock the door behind me. I flip on the dim light, providing a dreary glow to the familiar objects of the underground room.

Her house is one of the few with basements and aside from the near darkness, it doesn't match the preset thoughts of most dirty basements. Carpet is laid across the floor and on one of the white plaster walls hangs a large picture of the ocean. Beneath it sits a long, comfortable brown couch which has perfect view of a wide flat-screen TV. A towering bookcase stretches along the wall to the left. Its wooden shelves are filled with collectables and keepsakes. On the last wall, there's a storage closet and beside it a stack of neatly packed plastic boxes. A staircase leads up to the first floor.

I know it's a bad idea to project sound from the TV, but it seems the only thing to do down here while I wait. And I've missed the electronics I was so accustomed to in the past months.

So I sit down on the couch and turn the TV to mute, playing the most recent episode of my favorite drama mystery. The pictures flashing across the screen are confusing. The fact that I've missed a couple dozen episodes only adds to the befuddlement of the lack of hearing explanations with words.

Even though it seems amazing to finally be able to watch TV again, my attention veers from the show. I can't help but think about the last part of Rain's and my conversation: the mystery girl that spoke through Carter's and my minds. But I can't be sure if she was actually communicating with us at that moment. I'm oblivious to anything involved with Serion.

It could have been preset messages playing through our heads.

It could have been something we remembered from when we were little.

It could have been Kairo somehow trying to trick us.

Whatever it is, I don't feel like worrying about that right now. I'm back home and soon I need to return to my depressed family. At the same time, Kairo could be chasing Carter at this very second. And if he doesn't find him, he might return to Dr. Corry's lab and somehow blame them for our escape. Luke could get hurt in the process...or worse.

And if I accidently lose control of my powers, Kairo will track me down and not only possibly kill me, but maybe Rain and her parents to flick them out of the way.

I could so easily end up dead tomorrow. At the moment Carter could be being tortured or chased by Kairo and his workers. Rain, Luke, Dave, Ellen, and Rain's parents are puppets at Kairo's mercy because of our actions. My parents are on the verge of becoming miserable alcoholics beyond repair, which would cause my brothers to grow up in a bad environment. I need to do something quick. But at the moment I'm powerless.

Funny, that I'd think that since I actually have real powers. But at least I've solved one problem. I am inhuman. And I've come to terms with that. I'm okay with it.

Being Serion could cause many problems in my life, but there's nothing wrong with *me*.

Meanwhile, I can only hope that Carter's alright. I can only pray that he's still fighting for his life and not making stupid choices. Because if something happened to Carter, the person I care about most, that would set me over the edge. And *I'd* be damaged beyond repair.

"Marina, a friend of yours is here," Rain calls. Her voice rises with curiosity and hints a message.

I force myself to think it's Luke to hold back the excitement that floods through me. Maybe it's Carter.

Chapter Eighteen

Carter

I sneak off early in the morning, shoving my rations into a makeshift bag created from my jacket. That tattered thing seems to have a lot of purposes.

When I open the door, I half expect Kairo or somebody working for him to be camped out by the door, wielding a gun or knife, and ready to pounce. Cautiously taking one step outside, my eyes dart back and forth, but the area seems to be clear.

I'm still quick to depart. I locate a car rental place and use up all my money to borrow a used car on the old side. I don't know how I was fortunate enough to still have my new driver's license clinging to the briny pocket inside of my jacket.

Before I drive away, I feel slightly guilty, knowing I'll never return the car. But I figure that this car was in the worst condition of all the ones available, with its peeling paint edged with rust and growling engine. And it did use up all my money, so it's basically a fair deal.

The speed gauge is broken and stuck in one spot, so I feel like I'm racing past the speed limit, but it might be as fast as this beat-up car can accelerate.

The deserted streets of the early morning slowly grow more and more populated as I see other cars moving along the road and people pacing in and out of buildings. It's surprising that I'm able to navigate my way back to Marina's neighborhood. I guess I was paying more attention than I realized as she showed me what used to be her home, and as I ran away, I was always thinking about her; only her.

My leg isn't throbbing any longer; I only now realize that. The dull ache refuses to leave me and there's occasional bursts of pain, but it improved greatly overnight. I left the burn uncovered, even though it hardly looks any better.

The blisters have shrunk and the red, mottled skin has lightened, but it still has a raw bright pink color. I'm afraid to touch it.

It takes hours to reach Marina's street. Even though I never left Washington, for several days my only transportation was walking, slowly stretched out because of my leg impediment. I'm actually pretty impressed with myself that I made it as far as I did in that condition.

Finally, when the sun is low in the sky and I can see the glittering ocean again, I very clearly recognize where I am. It's one of the streets that Marina showed me when we went to the library. From here I'm easily able to traverse my way to her street. I see her seashell accented house as I park the rental car on the street, but I know it's not where I'll find her.

She'll be at Rain's house, a place she never showed me.

But as I walk along the sidewalk, something points me in a certain direction, and I have a strong feeling that it's that house: the one towering with several stories. It's painted a gray, faded and washed out from standing by the abrasive sea for years. Some instinct inside me knows that the unfamiliar house is Rain's, but it's not the place itself that sets off the notification inside me. I know because Marina's there.

I practically run up the drive and have stop myself from banging the door down. Instead, I press the doorbell, just once, and wait.

A girl with bright blonde hair wearing a jacket with a silver sheen opens the door and looks surprised to see me. "Hello?" It comes out as a question, not a greeting.

"Are you Rain?" I ask.

"Maybe…who are you?" she questions, narrowing her eyes.

"Carter. I'm a friend of Marina's…"

Her eyes sparkle as her expression brightens and she calls for Marina. I knew she was here, I just had a feeling. I'm ecstatic that I can finally see her again. It will repair me in ways I can't explain, beyond the burns branded into my leg. I feel terrible for leaving her, but it saved her life. We both know that.

"And I am Rain by the way," the blonde girl adds. "Nice to meet you."

I smile. "You too."

Then I see Marina slowly walking to the door. The sun shining through the door highlights her long hair with gold and her beautiful aqua eyes sparkle as her lips widen into a beaming smile. "Carter!" she exclaims, running up to me.

"Marina!"

We embrace for a long time, like we never want to let go. And I don't. I've missed Marina so much and she seems exactly the same as I left her, except for two things. She seems much less depressed, and there's another thing I never really realized because I became so accustomed to it. She always smelled like the ocean, it was sort of a salty scent, but it fit her. Now that she hasn't been in the water, it's gone.

When we stand back, Marina looks me over and gasps as her gaze falls on my burn. "What happened?" she cries and Rain grimaces.

"It's a long story…" I reply sheepishly.

"Are you okay?" she asks.

"Yeah, now anyway."

"Oh, I was so worried that Kairo found you!"

"He did."

Marina freezes. "What?"

"That's why this happened to my leg. I'll explain more later. You've been okay, right?"

"Physically," she sighs.

I frown. "I'm really sorry, Marina, but I had to leave. You know that you wouldn't be here now if I hadn't. But I'm really –"

"Carter, it's okay," she cuts me off. "I know."

I nod. "So Luke didn't come."

"No and I kind of miss him being around." Marina sees my quizzical expression and laughs in amusement. "He's sort of like a brother to me now."

"And you plan on staying here for a while?"

"I'm not sure. It all depends on what happens."

Rain has stood by awkwardly the entire time, just watching us. "Are we all in danger?" she worries. After our silence she mutters, "I'll take that as a yes."

"But we still don't know what Kairo wants," Marina replies.

"We're getting closer to finding out," I tell them. "Here's what happened…" I begin as I start explaining how I fought Kairo, the boy that shot my leg with the poison arrow, and what I heard when I waited outside the house in the forest.

Even after my explanation, Marina still looks unfazed. Her eyes blaze with intensity, her thoughts consumed elsewhere. "I just remembered something I have to tell you, something *really* important."

"What?" I ask, anxious at her tone.

"When Kairo said we were Serions, he didn't mean what we thought," Marina says, taking a deep breath. "Serion isn't a cult or a religion or anything like that. It's a race of…people," she falters and then continues, "From another planet."

"Another planet?" I exclaim incredulously. "But that means…"

"That we're technically *not* human. We're Serion."

I'm stunned into silence. Marina would make comments on the island about thinking she wasn't even human, but neither of us really believed it. I knew there was something different about us, with our inexplicable powers and Kairo's sudden obsession with killing us, but I never expected *this*, ever.

It seems unbelievable. It seems improbable. It seems impossible.

Then I realize, it doesn't. It explains everything. It makes sense that Marina and I are from another planet. That's why we have powers. That's why we have strange abilities. I still don't know what Kairo wants, but he must be Serion, too.

"So we're from the planet Serion," I say, straining to keep my voice calm.

Marina nods. "Yeah, I know it's hard to believe. Another planet, that according to what you heard, *Kairo* apparently destroyed. Luke found out after you left."

"So what, we were sent here?"

"I don't know all the details, and I'm sure there's a lot, but I know I'm adopted."

"Am I…?"

"No," she answers quickly. "Remember, your mom, Katrina, was Serion, but the government killed her. And your dad is human, but I think he knew everything."

"And, of course, never told me," I reply grudgingly.

"But how could you tell your son that?" Marina counters. "So I just wanted to let you know that you and your mom are aliens…" She laughs at the idea, even though it isn't amusing in the situation, though it does seem pretty far-fetched.

"It's so true that everything we learn just brings more questions," I sigh.

"Everything," she agrees.

"So, Serion, huh?" I say.

"Serion," she choruses.

Then we just both burst out laughing. I'm not sure why, and it's uncalled for, but it feels good to laugh together. It must be some sort of amusement at how ridiculous this seems, how many questions we have, and how much danger we could be in at any second. Two months ago if anyone had told me I wasn't human and kept a straight face for more than five minutes, I would've directed them to a psychologist.

Now, hardly anything would get a decently surprised reaction from me. After this, I have a hard time thinking of many things that are more shocking.

"Sorry for interrupting, but since we're *all* in danger, shouldn't we do something instead of just waiting around?" Rain presses.

"Well, as long as we don't use our powers I don't think Kairo will be able to find us," Marina replies.

"You two act way too calmly about this!" Rain exclaims. "You're not even trying to figure out what *is* going on!"

Marina and I both chuckle and I answer, "Trust me, we've tried and it's impossible to find any answers."

"So we just do nothing?"

"I think we need a break!" Marina suggests. "Carter's spent days getting hurt, poisoned, and nearly killed while I've been sad and miserable and only just returned home after being away for over half a year! So we should all just relax, and you don't need to be worried about us."

Rain nods slowly, but looks completely unconvinced.

"And do you mind if we both stay here for a while, in the basement?" Marina wonders.

"Sure…" she says hesitantly. "I mean I'm sure they won't mind if they found out you were here, but Carter… I'm sorry, but they'd probably be creeped out that some boy they've never heard of is secretly living in their house. Just try to be quiet and let's hope they won't realize."

"Of course," I agree.

There's a metallic jingling on the other side of the door and Rain hastily motions for us to go the basement. Marina grabs my arm and leads me there, since I don't know where to go. As I quietly walk down the staircase, Marina locks the door and joins me in the middle of the room.

"We have to be quiet," she reminds me.

"Yeah, I know."

Looking at her, it seems like an eternity that we were separated. I miss the island where we could be alone and never worry about running from Kairo or living secretly in a basement without making noise. It's ironic that I look at being stuck on an uncharted island with a very limited supply of food and no way to leave as 'the good old days'.

"Marina, I promise I will never leave again," I vow. "And now it'll probably be safer if we stick together so we have better chances of fighting back. And I'll be much more careful."

"You were just trying to be sweet," she protests.

"But I was stupid."

"It doesn't matter. It only matters that you're back and safe and alive."

We simultaneously reach forward and hug each other. With our arms around each other, it reminds me that I'm safe, for now. Even back when she was always miserable with herself, just being around her somehow always lifts my spirits.

"I feel bad that your friend's caught up in all this," I say, almost laughing as I remember Rain's expression when she pretended to think this was all no big deal.

"Oh, she'll be fine," Marina says dismissively.

"And now we just wait?"

"The only thing down here to do without making noise is watching the TV on mute, which I realized isn't very entertaining."

"We probably have a lot to tell each other anyway. I still just can't believe that we're not…not human."

"You know, I was just being sarcastic when I said that before, on the island. I never actually thought it was true. But what other explanation would there really be? I'm surprised we didn't already think of it."

I know that we're both thinking the unspoken words. *Maybe we just didn't want to believe it.*

"But now it's real and we have to live with it," Marina continues. "But answers seem like another word for questions. Luke didn't know much and I don't know what Dr. Corry knew; I kind of left before getting a truly decent explanation. But I doubt that anyone really knows the entire truth of what happened to Serion, except Kairo, and of course he won't tell us anything."

"But do you think there are other Serions?"

"Dr. Corry doesn't think so, but I'm beginning to think he's wrong. I just keep coming back to that girl."

"Have you heard her again?"

"No, but I never forget her."

"Rain, honestly what's wrong?" a woman asks in exasperation.

Marina holds a finger to her lips as we stand apart, facing the door. Rain and her parents are probably right near the basement door. I just hope she can keep our secret. Marina and I stay silent as we eavesdrop on the conversation.

"Nothing!" Rain insists.

"I can tell when you're acting strange!" her mom protests. "What are you hiding from us?"

"What happened while we were gone?" her dad demands. "Did you throw a party or something?"

"No, of course not! I don't get why you both think something's wrong! Sometimes I just remember things from the past…and it makes me sad thinking about it."

"Oh, honey, I know it's hard," her mom comforts. "But it's not just you. Oh, I feel so bad for the Coralins," she adds sympathetically. "Marina disappearing was so hard on them. They've changed so much. I do everything I can for those boys, but I don't see how it can't affect them at some point."

"But you can't blame them," her dad defends. "Imagine how we'd feel if something happened to Rain."

"I don't blame them. I just feel sorry for them."

"Nobody even knows what happened to Marina. They never even found the body, but she's been gone for so long that –"

"Dad!" Rain exclaims. "Marina might not be dead! Exactly, they *never found her body.*"

"I –I know, I'm sorry," he apologizes.

I glance over at Marina and see the pain plainly etched into her face, even in the dim lighting. It must be awful knowing what her disappearance has done to her family. I can see the guilt in her eyes as she fully blames herself for this. But how can she not? There's not really any way I can talk her out of thinking this was her fault. I can only be there for her, try to make her feel better.

"It's okay, Marina," I console. "They'll be okay again." I put my arm around her shoulders.

She gives me a half-hearted smile. "I really hope so."

***

"It's your shelter on the island all over again," I joke as I lay down in my make-shift bed of blankets.

Marina laughs. "But I think it's a bit more comfortable." She throws a few blankets down about a foot away from me and lays down. "It was actually hard for us to get used to beds again after living on the island."

"The island," I repeat. "Do you think *the island* has a name?"

"I don't know, it *is* uncharted."

"But do you think it has something to do with Serion? The only people who found it were us and Kairo."

"Of course it does! It must." Marina yawns. "Well, I think that we both need a good rest. Night, Carter."

"Good night," I murmur.

Even in in the dark room with warm blankets, I still can't sleep. What seems like hours have passed until all I can hear echoing through my head is the mystery girl pleading for help and I wonder what it means that I heard her, why she needed help.

I'm lonely in the night. The silence, only interrupted by Marina's small breaths, is unsettling. Unable to help it, I shift myself a little closer to her. It's just enough so that our wrists are touching, beneath layers of cloth. When I stretch my arm beneath the blankets, I can feel her hand brush mine.

***

The darkness seems to fade into light until I can make out a hue of green around me. My eyes are clouded over for some reason, but it seems like I'm surrounded by leaves. Underneath me, pokey things stick up and dig into my legs. It feels like I'm sitting in a tree with branches and twigs prodding me.

My blurry vision gives me a headache, but I slowly begin to hear the sounds of voices. It seems like a crowd of people getting closer and closer. It horribly reminds me of the dream about my mom except this time the voices sound taunting rather than angry and wanting to hurt someone. I'm confused about what's happening and I can't think clearly.

I hear someone, a voice that sounds young, yell, "There!"

I turn towards the sound, disoriented, and then a hard pebble knocks into my forehead. It catches me off guard and I lose my balance, snatching at the branches I can hardly see. Still, I feel the branches drop out from under me and I yell out as I fall through the air.

Just before I hit the ground, my eyes fly open.

"Carter, what happened?" Marina demands.

"Strange dream," I mutter, shaking my head. "I was in a tree, but I couldn't see well, and people were looking for me. It seemed like they were teasing me and then someone threw a rock at me. I fell…and that's all I remember."

Marina's eyebrows knit together. "That's strange. It's like we're getting messages or something."

"I don't know if everything's related. But even if it is, it could be a trick. Kairo might eventually lead us to our death."

"That's why I wanted to stay here. We know so little that anything we do might end up with us dead."

As confused voices began to rise above us, Marina's eyes widen. "You yelled out in your sleep! Quick, there's a closet under the staircase!"

She forces the door open and shoves me inside, closing the closet just as light floods into the basement.

"Mom, Dad, you're being ridiculous!" Rain insists desperately. "There's obviously nobody here. It was a dream!"

"It wasn't a dream, I'm sure of it!" her mom replies surely.

"Well, maybe it was someone down the street, but it definitely wasn't in our house! That doesn't even make sense!"

"I think you might be overreacting a bit," her dad says.

"You heard it, too!"

"Maybe, but it was probably just some kids messing around outside."

"Exactly!" Rain exclaims in exasperation.

"I'm still looking around!" her mom replies stubbornly. "It never hurts to be on the safe side."

Footsteps on the creaking wooden floorboards make me shrink into the corner of the closet. Marina and I huddle close, worried that Rain's parents will open the door. I hold my breath as they get closer and closer…but then they walk in the other direction.

"See, nobody here," Rain says calmly.

"I guess you were right," her mom agrees reluctantly as they walk up the stairs. "But it just sounded so close."

The door swings shut and Marina and I cautiously walk out of the closet.

"Okay, so you think this dream was a message or something?" Marina asks immediately.

"I'm really not sure. It could be from the same girl, but I don't know."

"What was that?" Rain whispers furiously from the top of the stairs. "I thought you two were going to at least *try* to be quiet!"

"Bad dream," I say guiltily.

"Do you mean just a regular bad dream or some strange Serion bad dream?" she questions, walking down so we can see her.

"We're not sure," Marina speaks for me.

"Okay, well, you should probably try to stay away from the house during the day and just come here at night. That way it's less time that we have to worry about my parents finding you. And I'm sure that there's lots of places you miss going to, Marina."

"The ocean!" she suggests instantaneously.

"There's a risk that somebody might see you," Rain warns.

"I don't care."

"Well, it's early anyway, so you should go now."

"Do you want to come? Meet you there." Marina is already practically skipping up the stairs before Rain can even answer.

"I will just be a minute," Rain says.

I nod and run after Marina, careful to keep my footsteps quiet. I catch up with her down the sidewalk as she runs down to the beach. The sand is cool beneath our feet as we step off the path. The sky is still gray blue with only a pale glow on the horizon since the sun hasn't risen yet. The only reason I'm not shivering in the morning wind, is because I'm running, which generates heat.

"I've really missed the ocean," Marina says breathlessly.

"Yeah, I can tell," I say with a laugh.

161

We stop by the water's edge, right where its foam makes a line on the wet sand. There are no rocks here, but it still reminds me of the shipwreck. I've always been scared of the water; always been a terrible swimmer. It's only gotten worse since I discovered I could control fire. Now every time I see water bigger than a little kid's miniature pool, I get nervous. The only time I was alright was when I was forced to leave the island, or when I was saving Marina. Her life is much more important than my fear of swimming.

"I'm guessing you're not coming," say states.

I shake my head. "You go without me."

Marina nods and splashes into the waves. When she's about three feet deep, she dives into the water, nearly a perfect arc with her hair flying up above her. I watch as the ripples she makes die down and her reflection under the water disappears, even though the surface is still and clear. Marina could be far away by now; I saw how far she could get that day she nearly died.

Even after that, she's still never scared of water. I came close to death twice because of the water and it's made me even more scared of it. It's ironic that I'm terrified of the ocean, but I love Marina, who basically symbolizes water and ice.

"Where did she go?" Rain runs up behind me.

"Probably far away by now."

Rain nods and starts swimming farther out to sea. Even after several minutes I still see her blonde hair streaming out, unlike how Marina immediately vanished. I grin, thinking how Rain will never catch up to Marina.

Chapter Nineteen

Marina

I speed so quickly through the water that everything is a blur. I can hardly even see the clear blue color all around me and the fish that dart between my toes look nonexistent. But it doesn't matter, because I feel the exhilaration of finally being able to swim in the ocean again.

The only thing in existence is the cold water rushing against my skin. I'm oblivious to everything else; my soaked clothes don't weigh me down at all and my fast pace doesn't even give me a pressurized headache. All that registers in my brain is that I'm finally able to be in the sea again; finally. Then the entire moment shifts, and all the happiness is sucked away.

I stop in confusion just as Rain screams, the sound distorted by the water. I jet up to the surface and look around frantically, swimming to shore as fast as I can.

"It's a body!" Rain yells.

She bobs a few yards away with an expression of disgust and terror, pointing at something below the surface. Carter stands on the sand, looking at her in worry and bewilderment. I catch up to Rain and plunge beneath the water to see what she's screaming about.

I gasp at the horrific sight. Lying on the sandy seafloor is what I can vaguely make out as a body. It's bloated and disfigured with wrinkled, pasty skin that seems to be barely attached to the chalky bones. It must have been destroyed by water damage. Gulping, I look closely at the face.

Looking past the water-induced wrinkles, I can see a face wrinkled by age with a calm and determined expression. The eyes are closed and the short silvery gray hair is tangled and in one spot matted with the slightest bit of blood. I now notice the wound on the person's side which looks like multiple gunshots all in the same general area. I take one more look at the face and realize who the body belonged to.

"It's the librarian!" I exclaim, but the words rise to the surface as bubbles. I swim up and to the shore, running to Carter. "It's the librarian!"

"What?" he asks.

"Rain found a body and it's the librarian."

Carter's expression turns to disgust as he understands her fate. "Oh...should we bring her here?"

"I'll get her if you want."

I turn back to face the water and hurry to where Rain still floats. Just as my head submerges, I see the librarian's body shimmer and then slowly appear less substantial. Her swollen arm fades and the condition moves up her body until she turns completely invisible and vanishes.

"She turned invisible," I say as I surface.

"That's a relief," Rain says, letting out a breath.

Seeing a disfigured body underwater must've traumatized her, because the color is only just now returning to her face. I don't think she even realized the strength it was taking to keep afloat and she's not even breathing hard. Rain looks toward the shore without another word and starts doing some sort of limp doggy-paddle back to land with her light hair hanging in her face.

"What happened?" Carter asks as Rain and I step onto land.

"She turned invisible," I answer.

I notice that through the whole ordeal Carter never took a step closer to the ocean. Looking down at his feet, I can see that he was always careful to stand a foot away from the line the water drew on the sand. I feel bad that I can never share my love of the ocean with him, but what can I expect? It's only brought him bad memories. Carter nearly drowned twice and watched me almost drown. The ocean kept him trapped on the island and his powers revolve around heat, the opposite of water and ice.

Which is why it's so surprising that me, ice, and Carter, fire, are so close when we're exact opposites.

"Oh, that was her power, wasn't it?" Carter says, remembering.

"How are neither of you even surprised?" Rain demands. "We just found a dead body underwater that looks disgusting, and you knew her, but Carter, you never even moved and Marina, I don't know…you're just so calm!"

"I'm kind of scared of the ocean," Carter mumbles.

"We've been through a lot," I attempt to explain.

Suddenly I feel long fingers reach up around my foot and claw at my ankle. I scream, one long nonstop sound, and watch the hand rise up from the ground.

"It's a zombie!" Rain screeches, jumping back.

Carter immediately takes action and raises his foot above the hand which has now risen to show an arm encased in black cloth. As the fingers try to pull me down, I falter and fall backwards. I'm scrambling away on the ground while Carter stomps his foot down on the hand.

It bends down in an unnatural way with a damaging-sounding crunch. Then, it just shrinks back into the sand. All three of us stand still, staring at the spot where the hand disappeared. I'm breathing hard and just trying to stay calm. *A hand just rose out of the ground and grabbed me.*

"It was the living dead," Rain says again, only half question.

"No," Carter replies. "Just Kairo," he adds with disgust.

"But how...?" I whisper.

"We still don't know what all of his abilities are."

I just nod slowly. "It's almost like he can transport parts of his body. Wait, if Kairo was able to transport his hand here...then he knows where we are!"

Carter and I both freeze, our eyes wide in panic. We've tried so hard to prevent this, but still, somehow, he's found a way to locate us. And with this newfound power, he could appear any second. Attack any minute. Now it's not just Carter and I who are in danger, but since Rain is here, she's just as much a target as we are.

"We have to get out of here!" Carter yells.

"Rain has to come! If she stays Kairo will torture her until he gets more information!"

Rain's face is ashen, but she nods in comprehension. Carter takes my hand and pulls me down the beach with Rain taking off after us. I hear her stifle another scream and look over my shoulder, just in time to see several fingers bent at odd angles fade away.

"Just keep going!" I direct.

"What about your parents?" she inquires.

I stop dead in my tracks. Carter shuffles to a halt and Rain slows. I can't just leave again without ever saying a word to my parents. This might be the last time I come here; might even be close to my last moments alive. I can't just leave my entire family in question and depression forever. That would be cruel. And judging from how Carter hurt Kairo's hand, I think he bought us a little extra time.

"I have to see my mom and dad," I state. "I promise I'll be fast."

Carter looks about to object, but shuts his mouth and follows me to my house. I frantically ring the doorbell multiple times as we stand on the porch. I can hear the shuffle of footsteps inside and my stomach flips with guilt and anticipation. The metallic clicks of the lock opening seem to slow time down as the door slowly, slowly creaks open.

My mom sighs, looking ragged and tired, as she stares at the ground. She looks up and her face turns sheet white. It's like she's petrified.

"Mom," I whisper.

"Marina, is it really you?" she begs, reaching out to touch my shoulder.

"Yes."

"It's Marina! She's back!" my mom cheers.

My dad and brothers practically fly towards the doorway. My heart aches to see the drastic change in them since the last time I saw them. My mom is pale and too skinny with her hair messy and her eyes surrounded by purple smudges. My dad looks almost sickly and his teeth have a yellow tint. His eyes are sunken in so that if it was any worse, they might seem hollow. Even my little brothers look sad and tired, but luckily their physical appearance hasn't been greatly altered.

"What happened to you?" my dad questions desperately.

They all hug me so tightly that the air nearly drains out of me.

"I only have a few minutes. If you want the full story then you have to believe me. You can't question anything I say."

I can tell my family is repressing tears of joy. They try hard to obey, looking at me with full attention.

"I lived on an uncharted island. Carter showed up and we discovered we have powers. I can control water and ice and he can control fire. A man named Kairo started trying to murder us so we left and stayed with Dr. Corry at the lab. His son Luke helped us learn what was happening to us. Carter left to protect me from Kairo and eventually I decided to come home. I stayed in Rain's basement and then Carter found me," I gush the condensed version. "And, I'm Serion. I'm from another planet."

Their slack jaws hang open in stark shock. It's my dad who first sputters, "You're –you're from another planet?"

"Yes, you have to believe me. And I know I'm adopted."

"We believe you, honey," my mom promises. "Oh, I'm just so glad you're home!"

"I'm so sorry I left!" I exclaim.

Then the tears come. We all breakdown as we hug each other, hot tears streaming down our faces. I didn't realize how much I missed my family; how I possibly lived so long without them. Rain stands by, sniffling slightly, touched by the reuniting. Carter looks unsure of what to do, standing right next to me.

"Marina, we really should go," Carter says quietly after a few minutes.

"Is this your boyfriend?" my youngest brother pesters.

I laugh. "Yes, this is Carter."

"Nice to meet you," he says politely.

"I'm really sorry, but we all have to go before Kairo returns," I say urgently.

"What? You can't!" my mom cries.

"We have to or we'll be killed. I love you all!" I start running down the drive, choking back another bout of tears. It pains me to see my family so helpless after I've only just come back, but it's all I can do to save everyone I care about.

"Where can we go?" Rain shouts.

"Just keeping running," I respond.

"It seems like we're always running to nowhere," Carter says in spite of the stress.

"How did Kairo even know where to find us?"

"Someone must have told him, and I can't imagine any of the Corrys betraying us. I know Kairo did have spies looking for me though."

Suddenly an image flashes through my m[...]
the subway with purple hair. He'd seem[...]
interested in me since he'd kept staring at m[...]
thought it was just an attraction, but I wonder i[...]
to gather information to report to Kairo.

"There was a boy on the subway who kept st[...]
"Did you recognize him?"

"No, but he gave me the creeps. He had p[...]
this shirt with a bloody picture on it."

Carter shakes his head. "I don't know how he[...]
many people to work with him, but whatever h[...]
worked. I think they're mostly all just terrified [...]
them." Suddenly he gasps and stumbles to[...]
clutching his leg.

"Carter!" I yell. I peel back his pant leg and [...]
uneven, boiling skin. "I don't think that healed."

"It didn't," he says through gritted teeth.

"Then we should stop! You can't be running lik[...]
"No, no, I'll be fine," he mutters stubbornly.

When I pull him to his feet, his face is contorted[...]
but I know he won't rest no matter what I say. [...]
against my shoulder and signal for Rain to do the s[...]
other side. Carter looks like a limp puppet barely ha[...]
our shoulders, but he perseveres and doesn't comp[...]
haul him down the street.

After a while, I glance at Rain and see she's [...]
Carter's quite a bit taller than both of us and we wo[...]
to support him for much longer.

We've distanced into the forest-like areas a litt[...]
my house that we always seem to come to. M[...]
populated and busy, but a few miles out and it's defi[...]
one of the most bustling areas.

"What's that?" Rain asks, sniffing the air.

The breeze carries an acrid, smoky scent. I look c[...]
at the trees behind us and see small tendrils of [...]
smoke curling from the tops. I stare and suddenly[...]

to the ground as writhing orange flames leap

ask incredulously.

t me," he replies.

better?" He nods. "We have to go!"

Rain use all their strength to keep up with my
but the fire is faster. It consumes the dry wood
e pine branches as quickly as a swift animal
its predator. The woods around us give the fire
to flourish.

oke burns my lungs as I breathe it in. My eyes
rollably and I feel the sweltering heat through the
shirt. If we just run, we're not going to be able to
tire out, whereas fire just grows stronger.

we have to do something!" I yell over the
ar.

ly way I'm helpful is that I can stand in front of
rt me the least."

to put it out."

ding all my energy through my hands, I watch as the
ze into a line of icy sculptures, but I know it won't
. I feel the water just a mile or so away, the
nd rivers beneath me. It pulls towards my hands and
ear a crack and a wavering flame escapes, a geyser
ockets up from the earth.

es the fire until it vanishes, but something tells me
he end.

na!" Rain yelps.

and see fire racing at us from all three other
s. It starts to catch onto branches and closes in on our
side. It's moving impossibly fast, circling around us
aunting us to come closer. Its flames reach higher and
ntil they must tower at least ten feet. Soon we're
n a cage of fire that isn't going to back down.

r shoves me behind him, as close to the center as
We crouch down and he wraps his arms around me,

shielding my body from the fire. Rain cowers behind him –it's the best protection we're going to get.

The scorching fumes fill my throat and the burning is unbearable. The more air I breathe in, it seems like a fire is blazing inside of me and roasting my insides. I gasp for air, but it's thin and polluted by the inferno. Even if we don't get burned to death, I know that eventually I'll suffocate.

Carter seems to be holding up fine, but he looks terrified, probably for what will happen to me. Rain looks so beyond shock and fear that her ashen face is emotionless as she just watches in a trance with a stony expression on her face. The flames enclose and soon I feel that there's no escape. I could never summon enough water to extinguish all this fire, before it's too late. I'm positive that these are going to be our last moments alive.

"I'm sorry," I whisper, thinking of my family. "Bye, Rain." My voice comes out as a croak.

"I love you, Marina," Carter says with a small smile, looking over his shoulder.

My heart flips, but my voice seems to be lost.

After that, I just watch the golden orange flames mesmerizingly dance closer as my lungs tighten in pain. Eventually, I feel the blistering heat radiating just above me, but my thoughts are blurred and foggy. All I remember is an exasperated scream, Rain's scream of pure terror, before everything dissolves into blackness.

Chapter Twenty

Carter

"Marina, I have a plan," I rasp close to her ear. The heat doesn't affect me, but my lungs are still closing in and feel singed.

She stirs, having been passed out from inhaling too much smoke. "What?" Her voice comes out several octaves lower with a horrible tone that makes it sound painful just to speak.

"I think I can walk through the fire without being hurt. Maybe if you put ice around you and Rain and you both run quickly, we can all make it out."

"But we're not wet."

"Just focus on making the temperature colder, but try not to freeze your insides. I believe you can do it."

Marina gives me a forced smile and shakes Rain awake, muttering the plan. I watch as she stands straight and a shell of hard ice forms all around her, just frosty enough around the joints so she can move. Then she turns toward Rain, looking worried she might accidently hurt her. She takes a deep breath and slowly Rain's body becomes coated in an identical frozen layer.

They seem hesitant, their eyes watery and clouded from the lack of air.

I shove Marina through the fire, the ice bending at her joints, and she drags Rain along with her. I really hope they were fast enough before the ice melted away.

Just as I'm about to follow, a paper catches my eye. It lies in the center of the open area as if it had always been there, even though I never noticed it. Its edges are singed and crinkled, but other than that, it seems new and intact. I snatch it up and my jaw hangs open as my eyes dart over the page.

Across the top are big black typed letters reading 'found', like it was a flyer for some sort of convict. But right beneath that dooming heading is an unmistakable picture of my mother.

"Carter!" Marina's strained scream rings out.

I shove the paper in my pocket and put a hand protectively over it, running through the inferno. I feel the heat around me. It parches my throat and burns my eyes so water streams out of them, but it doesn't really hurt in a harmful way. Soon I emerge out the other side and gratefully gulp a mouthful of air, feeling it replenish my aching lungs.

The ice is gone, but Rain sits shivering on the ground with water pooling around her. She looks like she might be going into shock. Marina looks depleted and tired, but overall fine.

I throw my arms around her, but after a second she turns back to the fire.

"We need to put this out."

She again freezes the fire, but I notice the difference. Before it looked sheer, just like a layer on the outside. Now the flames are solidly frozen. They look strange, but beautiful, writhing up towards the sky in a ring. I know that soon the sun will melt them, which is good, because anyone who witnessed this would in the least have a lot of questions.

"Look what I found." I shove the flyer in her face.

She takes it and her eyes turn into circles. "But...how?" she stammers.

"I knew she was still alive!" I retort. "I just knew it!"

"Who?" Rain's mumble is barely audible.

"I thought the government killed my mom."

Her eyes widen in surprise. I guess there were a few parts of our story we forgot to tell her.

"Do you think that the fire was caused by her?" Marina asks incredulously, practically reading the thought that zooms into my mind.

"It makes sense, doesn't it?" I agree. "Even if Kairo set the forest on fire, he doesn't have the power to control it like that. Only someone with fire powers could do that. And my mom's abilities were identical to mine."

"But why would she try to put us in danger?"

It feels like I was soaring over the clouds and just suddenly plummeted to the ground, knocking all the wind out of me. That comment makes me wonder why my own mom would do that if she knew it could kill us. I'm tempted to say this was all staged by Kairo, but the evidence does seem to point to her.

"Have you realized that it's getting dark and we have nowhere to stay?" Rain points out.

"We could go back to the lab –" Marina begins.

I shake my head. "It's too far away."

"Is this near where you heard Kairo and his followers?"

"I'm really not sure."

She shrugs and we just keep walking further and further. I don't think any of us are in the condition for another long journey. Marina's coughing in dry fits like she's having a hard time breathing. Rain is shivering so violently that I wonder if she could get hypothermia. And even though I won't admit it, my leg throbs horribly.

I don't know if it'll ever be quite the same. I cauterized it so I wouldn't be poisoned, but there was definitely some damage done. My immunity to fire only lasts to a certain breaking point, just as Marina's breathing under water does. We learned that the terrible day she almost drowned.

We emerge into the busier city and Marina exclaims, "I see something!"

On the edge of the trees sits a small...I'm not sure what to call it. House? Cabin? Shack? It's a messiest, saddest excuse for a house I've ever seen. It hardly even has a shape, more like a lopsided box. The walls are a mix of wooden planks, fiberglass board, and sheets of metal. It's a mess and certainly looks abandoned. I've been tending to sneak into abandoned houses a lot lately.

"That's where we're staying for the night," I announce.

The door knob turns easily, but the door's jammed shut. I push on it, but it hardly budges. "Stand back," I tell the girls. I get a running start and kick out my good leg, which slams into the door with powerful force. It swings open and bangs against the wall.

"This must've been blocking it." Marina nods at a large chest and shoves it to the side. From the way she grunts, it must be heavy.

"There's probably supplies in it," Rain says thankfully.

"We'll check later," I reply. "First we have to make sure there's really nobody else here."

I walk in ahead of Marina and Rain, ready to attack. A quick search proves the house to be empty with a grimy bathroom, one bedroom containing only a bed, and the main room which seems to serve as both a living room and kitchen. A moth-eaten faded brown couch is pushed up against one of the walls.

"This place is disgusting," Rain remarks.

"Would you rather sleep in the forest?" I raise an eyebrow.

"No," she sighs, probably wishing she hadn't left home. She shivers again.

I start to ball my hand into a fist to generate heat, but I quickly retract it as I recall what occurred last time I carelessly used my powers. "I think there's some blankets in the bedroom."

Rain stands up to retrieve a blanket. "Thanks."

I nod and walk over to the chest, probably the nicest object in the ramshackle house. "Let's see what's in here." I flip the latch and open the lid to find…nothing. It's empty. I give it a test shove and realize it's much lighter than before, hardly weighing anything.

"Whatever was in it is gone," I state.

"But…how?" Marina wonders, pushing it with her foot. "You're right. It's a lot lighter."

"Maybe you're just imagining it," Rain suggests. "Maybe," we both agree, but it's just because we don't want to think of the possibilities.

That night Rain sleeps in the bedroom and Marina on the couch. I grab the one of the few blankets that was piled on top of the bed and lay on the floor beside the couch. The blanket is thin and holey, maybe even spotted with mold induced by the sea air, but it's better than nothing.

Just as I've gotten groggy and am barely awake, I realize I didn't pay attention to sounds coming from the other side when I tried to open it. The soft thumping and shuffling seemed like just objects moving in the chest, but now I realize it seemed more like a body being thrown around, a person heavy enough to weigh down the chest, who could've gotten up and left when we were searching the house.

***

"Carter, he found us!" Marina exclaims.

"What?" I mumble sleepily. Then I remember my last thoughts before I fell asleep and sit up, wide awake. "What?" I ask, more clearly.

"I can just…sense it," she tells me. "Kairo's coming. We have to leave fast."

The two of us burst into Rain's room. Marina shakes her awake and quickly explains what's going on.

"Let's get out of here!" she practically yells, eyes wide.

We race to the door, but when I try to open it, it's sealed shut. I kick, push, slam my body against it, but nothing works, even when we use all our strength together. We're trapped inside and there's nothing we can do about it.

I now see what Marina meant about sensing Kairo. I can tell he's near. And his influence is getting stronger.

His metallic voice seeps into my mind, whispering hypnotic words. "Stand away from the door. You will be weak. You will be safe. You want to help me."

Rain starts heavily walking backwards in a trance, her eyes glazed over. Marina snatches her arm and pulls her forward as we all resist against Kairo's powers. He's powerful, but we are too. We just have to withstand him if we value our lives.

I force myself to fill my head with my own thoughts. I am strong. I am brave. I can fight Kairo and I can win. But it's no use. The strong, forceful words slowly diminish until I can barely grasp their memory. Then all my attempts to stop Kairo melt away and I find myself moving in slow motion; stumbling, tripping backwards, falling through the air…

My head smacks the ground and pain racks my skull. My eyes open wide, awoken from the haze.

I bolt to my feet and create a small, controlled flame in the palm of my hand. If I can focus on the fire, only the fire, then maybe I'll be safe.

It burns boldly through the early morning. I study the wavering flames, the orange and golden color, and the heat that surrounds it. I find myself no longer hearing Kairo's words or falling under any trance. "Focus on the fire," I instruct.

For a moment we all stare unblinkingly at the fire and then a gust of air blows it out. The dim ceiling light flickers haphazardly and then plunges us into pitch darkness.

The door slams open violently and Kairo stands there angrily, his cloak billowing in the wind.

Chapter Twenty One

Marina

Kairo's menacing golden eyes pan the room. His predatory gaze falls on Rain, seeing her as a defenseless, easy target. She collapses to the ground and lets loose a scream of agony. She writhes pitifully, grimacing in pain. All the while Kairo just stares at her, not at all sorry.

Carter dives at him, but Kairo pushes him away with ease. Carter stumbles backwards, trying to set Kairo on fire, but he trips over a loose floorboard. I notice that he's staring at the scar on Kairo's cheek.

I look closer and analyze the bright white, taut skin. The lines look healed, but there's still hints of mottled red that look irreparable. It reminds me of Carter's leg. It was burned, maybe even by someone with fire powers. Maybe by Carter's mom.

With the other two lying on the floor, momentarily stunned, it's up to me. Kairo turns and I focus all my energy into making his cloak colder and colder...

I ignore the pain starting to stab through my bones and hear a subtle icy crackling noise. Sweat beads on my forehead. I block out the alien thoughts that try to penetrate my brain; the aching that's making my legs want to break. The only thing that matters is freezing Kairo...rendering him helpless at least for a while. I can do this. I have to save Carter and Rain.

Kairo's eyebrows knit together in a fierce glare. There's nothing he can really do against ice except attempt to distract me. But I'm focused. I'm determined.

I watch his cloak turn from black to solid, frozen white. His immobile expression is livid.

This is our chance to escape.

But before I can react, I feel something materialize in my right hand. I'm bewildered to see the gleaming blade of a smooth, sharp dagger. The silver blade looks like it can slice through anything. Engravings curl and twist across the hilt which has a large turquoise stone implanted in it. Right in the center is an *S* carved in some sort of fancy script with a detailed ocean wave arching over it.

There's a crunching noise and I see Kairo's freed his arm and shuffled to face Rain. His deadly silver gun is pointed directly at her heart.

"Rain!" I screech and launch myself at Kairo.

I raise my new dagger in the air and drive it through his hand. Blood spurts out as he gives a cry of pain and loses his grip on the gun, but not before a bullet shoots out in a puff of smoke. Rain rolls out of the way in panic and for a moment I think that it missed her.

But Kairo's too good.

She screams and blood seeps through the left sleeve of her shirt, dying the pale blue a bright red. Carter nods over to her, signaling that he'll hold off Kairo. I rush to Rain's side.

"It's just your arm, right?"

She nods silently.

"Don't worry. It'll be okay then."

I pull up her sleeve and gulp back the bile that fills my mouth. It's not as bad as Carter's burn, but her skin is raw and bloody. I work quickly, fishing the bullet out of Rain's wound and then chilling the temperature so she won't lose as much blood. I tear the clean part of her sleeve off and tie it around the bullet injury in a slightly sloppy tourniquet.

Looking up, I see Carter's giving the fight everything he's got. Kairo's broken free of my icy cage and is shooting death rays at Carter from his eyes. Carter is agile and dodges every actual bullet, but he can only withstand the pain and mind control for so long.

The flames he tries to create are weak and withering. He has no weapon to use against the gun.

"Carter!"

My dagger spins through the air and he catches the hilt. Moving quickly, he tosses it straight at Kairo. It doesn't quite reach his heart, but it impales his stomach and his gun slides across the floor, out of his reach. Kairo gasps and doubles over. I only now notice that both of his hands are in bad condition.

One is covered in drips of blood while the other is bruised and crunched-looking from Carter stepping on it.

Kairo takes a deep breath, and stands straight up, his malice masking the pain. He pulls the gore spattered dagger from his stomach and throws it down. "You think it's that easy do you? You may not know this, but we Serions have higher pain tolerance than humans. Sure it hurts, but it's a lot harder to kill us."

With that said, he turns to Carter and all in a split-second, his leg kicks out powerfully and Carter slumps against the wall.

I think we've all given up on powers momentarily. It's hard to focus when you're injured. And I'm the only one unharmed. So now it's just brute force.

Rain is helpless and trying to just recover herself. Carter has the wind knocked out of him for now. It's just me, a fifteen-year-old girl with no combat training against a powerful, strong man who must've fought many battles, who's an experienced killer.

His hands are clenched at his sides. His hands are nearly useless. They're hurt and weak. If I aim near his legs then he can't fling them out to kick me, and I might have a chance at leaving not fatally injured.

With what seems impossible speed, Kairo appears in front of me and immediately punches me square in the face. It aches and feels like thousands of knives are jutting into my jawline, but I squeeze my eyes shut and clench my jaw against the pain, even as the metallic taste of blood ebbs into my mouth.

Kairo prepares to punch again, but I'm faster. My lean, not-particularly-tall frame proves to be useful as I bend away from his strong arm. My right leg swings forward and knocks his legs out from beneath him. It think it's over. That was my mistake.

I underestimated Kairo. Just because he was weakened and injured, I let my guard down.

As I turn, preparing to leave, I hear a scraping sound against the floor. My eyes widen as I look, but it seems that I can only move in slow motion.

I feel the horrible pain blaze through my side. My thoughts mix together and my vision is blurred. The silver sheen of Kairo's gun is still across the room. But my dagger, I now realize, was in his reach. He stabbed me with my own dagger. Rain's cry of panic is muted and Carter's screams of rage run together. I hear him yelling out to me, but I can't make out the words.

My hazy vision is a great disadvantage as I try to see what's going on. Carter seems brimming with pure anger. Kairo's cloak almost is instantly engulfed in fire. He throws it down and stamps out the flames, but then fire starts crawling up his clothing. Kairo's physically stronger, but he has no defense against fire. As Carter corners him against the wall, he must realize his odds in winning this aren't likely and decides to leave before there's any real damage.

"This is not the end!" he hisses promisingly.

My sight just becomes more distorted to the point where I can barely make out more than a mix of colors. My head is pounding and my side throbs.

I see blonde hair above me as Rain scrambles to my side. Another figure moves closer and I recognize Carter's warm hand on my cheek.

They're both frantically shouting at me, but my hearing is as useless as if I were deaf. My senses lose purpose and the lights and color of the room slowly get darker and darker.

I remember when we were trapped in the fire, thinking we were going to die, and Carter said he loved me. I never got the chance to reply.

"I love you, too, Carter," I mumble as everything goes black.

***

The first thing that registers in my mind is bright lights and white all around me. My head is groggy, but slowly everything comes into focus. I'm lying on a couch, a pure white couch. The sterile mix of pure white and metal is familiar, but I can't quite place it.

A face with worried bright blue eyes appears in my peripheral view.

"Luke?" I ask incredulously.

"Hey, Marina," he replies.

"What happened?"

"You were out of it for two days. Carter called me, and we picked you up from that house." He grimaces. "You lost a lot of blood, but my dad cleaned and bandaged the injury. It should be okay, but you need a lot of rest."

"Thank you for helping us," I mumble.

"I told you to call if you were in danger," he accuses.

"It kind of all happened at once." I quickly fill Luke in on everything that occurred since I left. "Where are Carter and Rain now?"

"Sleeping. They were both exhausted. I'm supposed to make sure you're okay."

"Have you discovered anything important?"

Luke sighs heavily. "You know my dad. There's a lot he doesn't share with me, or even my mom. He'll seem either worried or pleased with something in his research, but then just shut himself away. Personally, I think he's at least on the verge of discovering *something*."

"I really hope so. It's tough not even really knowing who we are."

"The Serions' past is so mysterious. Dad was sure you, Carter, and Kairo were the last, but now there's no way of knowing. Carter thinks his mom's still alive and you've both been hearing that girl speak to you. Dad was certain you were the only ones left though, so maybe it's some sort of memory or…spirit?" He runs his hand through his hair in exasperation. "This is all so stressful."

"At least you're human," I say.

"But I'm so involved in this that it's almost like I'm not."

After a moment of silence, I carefully stagger to my feet. As soon as I lean weight on my left leg, it feels like stinging, liquid lead is traveling through my veins. I yelp and Luke quickly props me against his shoulder. I shift most of my weight against him as he drags me across the floor and all the way to the rooms of their house.

We come to a closed door, and Luke knocks on it. It's the room that Carter stayed in last time we were here. Sure enough, his weary face shows as the door opens. Immediately, color and alertness floods back into his features when he sees me.

"Marina! I was so worried! It was awful when you got stabbed," he rambles. "Then you passed out and I thought…I thought…"

I press my lips against his, and then pull away when I realize Luke is there.

Luke just gives a tired grin and clears his throat. "And that dagger just appeared, didn't it?"

I nod. "I'm not sure how, but I know it must be Serion. There's even an *S* on it."

"I have it right here," Carter says, reaching for something out of view.

As he hands me the dagger, the bright lights above glint off the metal. Carter must have cleaned off the blood and gore that previously stained the reflective surface. That blade impaled Kairo's stomach and drove into my side. And yet here it is, looking bright, new, and lethal.

"I saw it happen," Carter adds. "It was just suddenly there."

Luke takes the weapon and turns it over in his hands. "So much we don't know," he murmurs. "Ever since you left, we've been worried constantly. My dad's always locked away doing research. Now you're here, but Kairo does know that you were here before. He could return."

A sharp pain prickles through my jaw and I remember how Kairo punched me there. It had seemed insignificant because of my side, but now it's an annoyance that only causes more aching.

"Honestly, how much blood did I lose?" I wonder, since my head is still spinning.

Carter pales. "A lot."

"Can I lay down? I'm getting dizzy, and I think I just need some sleep."

A headache pounds in my temple and from there my vision goes fuzzy. I'm shaky on my legs as Carter and Luke guide me to the room down the hall that was mine from last time. I barely remember falling onto the bed and going to sleep as soon as my head hit the pillow.

But I do remember one thing crystal clear.

Just before I fell asleep, the silhouette of a girl shone in my mind followed by the words, "Please, can you find me? Help…!" The last word racks my brain as a booming echo.

***

I wake up to voices rising outside my door. I stay still and listen for a moment.

"It was like before, but louder and stronger," Carter explained. "And I saw her, but it was like a shadow, dark and I couldn't see the features."

"That's exactly what I saw," Luke agrees.

"I didn't get any strange dream," Rain remarks in slight disappointment.

"You're not Serion," Luke replies matter-of-factly.

"Neither are you!"

"I know. I feel like I'm missing something. It just somehow seemed familiar…well, not quite, it was more like I should remember something."

"I had the dream, too," I say, opening the door.

"You know, I'm going to see if Dad can scan the world for any trace of telepathy. I think he might have just advanced enough technology." He leaves with a purposeful expression.

The people I can trust and confide in, who I feel closest to, are all right here, right now. Carter, Rain, Luke, and I are all together, like a team. I never dreamed Rain would become a part of this, but here she is now, bravely fighting Kairo and sticking by my side no matter what she learns.

"So Kairo's tried to kill me, I've met Luke, and I've been to Dr. Corry's lab. All that's left is the island," Rain says.

I laugh. "I don't think we'll ever be going back."

But maybe we will. Carter and I share a knowing smile. It was nice back on the island, living in bliss ignorance. We were oblivious to the fact that we were Serion or that Kairo desperately wanted us dead. Sure, we knew there was something strange happening, but I should've believed that sometimes it's better to not know everything.

Carter and I both came close to death on that island multiple times. At first, I'd looked at him as an intruder in my private life. But as I saved him, I think a part of my heart leaped at the sight of him. And the island was where we fell in love.

The motions of the day are vague and unimportant. I feel much better and the dizzying headache has left, but my jaw is sore and pain will sometimes rocket through my side. Dr. Corry has taken Luke's suggestion and is so wrapped up in his work that I still haven't seen him since I arrived. Ellen is hospitable as usual and Carter, Rain, and I can finally get some safety and peaceful rest.

That night, just after dinner, when I'm walking to my room, I feel a hand that's warmer than most on my shoulder.

"Come on," he says with a grin.

"Where are we going?" I giggle as he takes my hand and pulls me along.

"I want to make sure this time at the lab is a lot better than the last."

A twinge of sadness pulls at my heart at the memory. His attempt at a fancy dinner had been sweet, but carelessness had given Kairo access to our whereabouts. Carter leaving as an act of selflessness was brave and caring. I should remember that instead of the despair and sorrow it left me with.

The night air is refreshing and cool. Even if it might make Carter shiver, I drink in the night's icy edge with pleasure. The multicolored lights of the city's buildings light up a skyline. The traffic is loud as cars skid over the road and angry drivers blare their horns. But Carter doesn't lead me into the city. We run alongside the road, always staying closer to the desolate side, home to Dr. Corry's lab.

"Where are we going?" I repeat.

"You'll see."

Finally, we stop at a platform and it feels good to be breathless. I scan the area and see it overlooks the ocean. It's hard to make out the waves, but bright lights reflect off the deep blue water. The chilling wind sends salty mist flying in my face. I stand with my arms back and my head tilted to the sky. I close my eyes and feel at home with the cold air caressing me and the ocean's roar calling to me.

"Do you like it?" Carter asks.

"It's perfect."

He helps me onto the ledge and we sit side by side with our feet dangling over emptiness. It's daring, but neither of us feels like we're going to fall and besides, the hills of sand beneath are soft. It's the best I've felt next to the ocean in a long time, leaning into Carter and knowing instinctively that Kairo will finally ambush us or leave traces of his murderous power.

"It's almost like being back on the island," he murmurs.

"Almost," I agree.

Our hands clasp together with an unbreakable bond, and I'm reminded of the first time we touched. It burned me, and he practically froze. I'm not sure if that no longer happens because we're in control, or because we care about each other so much that we ignore it. I think it's a combination of both.

"Marina, I'm never going to leave again," Carter promises. "It was so hard being without you. You're the only person I truly care about."

"What about your dad?" He doesn't talk about his dad often.

"Sometimes I'm mad because he didn't tell me so many things, but I forgive him. And I'm not worried that he's stressed I'm dead. He knew I was Serion, and he must've known that something would happen someday. Besides, we weren't close enough that I felt I could tell him anything."

"I know exactly how it feels," I whisper. "I trust you more than anyone."

I look up into his eyes, those eyes with bright golden sparks, and he stares into mine. The space between us closes and we kiss underneath the light of the moon. I feel safe and at home with Carter, with my arms around his neck and his hands twirling strands of my hair.

We're locked together as we kiss, and I don't want it to ever end. I'm happiest with Carter, and happier now than I've been in a long time.

Chapter Twenty Two

Carter

Last night really was perfect. I hope Marina realizes how much I care about her, and I hope I made up for deserting her. But everything I do is for her: for her safety, for her survival, for her happiness. Marina means the world to me.

But walking down the hall, my blissful thoughts are disrupted.

"So, Dad did a thorough search of the entire world for any trace of telepathy." Luke is suddenly at my side with Marina trailing along.

"And?" I prompt.

"There's not a single telepath in existence."

"What?" I ask in disbelief.

That makes absolutely no sense. We know that this girl speaks to us through her mind telepathy. I know she's a living, breathing person. Luke thought it could be a memory triggered, but how? How can that be possible when we all hear her, yet none of us remember her?

"That was exactly what I said," Marina speaks up.

"It really doesn't make sense. But what does?" Luke shrugs.

"Nothing," Marina and I answer simultaneously.

Swift footsteps signal someone walking towards us. It's Dr. Corry. He definitely looks changed since the last time I saw him, weeks ago. He looks thinner and his now sallow skin has paled. The skin under his eyes has bagged and is shaded in purple. Dr. Corry is clearly exhausted and doesn't look as lively as before. The excessive research hasn't at all been good for him.

He tries to smile, but it doesn't reach his eyes the way it used to. It's forced and exhausted.

"Maybe we need to stop trying so hard," Marina suggests gently. "We should let explanations come to us and just focus on not being killed."

"Well..." the scientist begins.

"That's a good idea, Marina," Luke speaks up. I can tell he's worried for his dad's health.

"I suppose you're right," Dr. Corry agrees. "Rest would be beneficial for all of us."

The day spans out slowly. Everything we do is aimless and full of boredom, but it's a nice change. It's not until that night when something significant happens. I wake up and instinctively feel someone's presence; eyes on my back.

The room's temperature rapidly rises, which feels comfortable to me, but I still recognize it as unnatural. Smoke wafts to my nose and the air has a hazier quality.

"Who's there?" I ask quietly.

But the answer is already there. As pale blue sparks grow into amber flames on my sleeve, fire I didn't cause, I know surely there is only one other person who can do this. Someone I was sure hadn't died. I'd been right. But I'd never ever dreamed this person would try to hurt me.

"Mom?"

A branch cracks outside my window as the person, the Serion, stumbles. The fire diminishes and the smoke lifts. I hear distinct footsteps trying to get away quickly, but quietly. I want to look out my window, but it crosses my mind that maybe I'm wrong. Maybe it's somebody else. I try to convince myself it's a stranger working with Kairo.

But I have to know the truth.

Just as I whip back the green curtains, a shadow vanishes behind the building and out of sight. I saw one other thing: a few strands of hair flying out behind the person, behind her. They were reddish blonde.

***

Nothing makes sense anymore.

I know how Marina feels when she needs to get away. I think about spending time with her, but right now I need to be alone.

Though I can't just escape into the ocean the way she can. It's too cold, too vigorous, too wet. For the first time I actually miss Arizona. I miss the sweltering heat that blazes all year long and the cactuses with prickles jutting out of their sides. I miss the dry, symmetrical hills of sand and the dust storms that make my eyes sting and my throat close.

It's fitting that I lived in Arizona just before I developed fire powers. It's one of the hottest states and Washington is just too chilly, but it's perfect for Marina. It seems that fate had a say in where we grew up.

For just a second I think about calling my dad, but decide against it.

Too risky. I don't know how he'll react. Instead I set off into the city, smiling as I pass the ledge where Marina and I sat the night before.

Having no idea where to go, I find myself walking into a small restaurant. Nearly all the wooden chairs and tables are occupied and the place smells like cheeseburgers. Pictures that look historical with their grainy quality cover the yellow walls and some seem to be barely hanging onto the bent nails holding them up. As soon as the bell attached to the door rings above me, everybody turns to stare.

A woman at the table closest to me gasps and pushes her children behind her. An old lady backs against the wall. I hear worried murmuring, but then all noise stops. There's no more spoons clattering or idle chatter. Instead all wide eyes are on me and nobody moves a muscle.

"Hello?" I say awkwardly.

The man behind the front desk slowly puts down the menus in his hand. "Everybody stay calm. What's your name, boy? Is it Carter?"

"What –why?"

"Don't worry, the police are on their way!" A lady triumphantly holds up her phone, but when I raise my eyebrows she cringes and slumps down like an injured dog.

"Don't worry, he's not armed," a burly man announces.

"What's going on?" I question in bewilderment.

"Oh, don't give me that crap!" the burly man exclaims. "We all know you're the wanted killer that the man warned us about a few minutes ago."

Wanted killer? "What man?"

"Give me a break."

A blaring siren shrieks in my ears and roving red lights circle over the windows as two black and white police cars race to the curb. I'm out the back door so fast that I nearly skid on the polished tile. I don't even stop for a second as the restaurant rises into chaos. The large man is chasing me and soon police sprint to catch up with him, horrifying guns in their hands.

I want to yell, "You've been tricked! I'm not a murderer," but if it was Kairo, he could convince the innocent humans of anything. I wonder briefly why he didn't come after me, but instead got regular people riled up to chase me. He must've known I was near. Right now that's my biggest concern.

The only solution to getting away is…a police man lets out an exclamation of pain before the thought is even fully formed. I can imagine the blistering, red-hot burns forming on each of their arms trailing wisps of smoke.

The distraction gives me just enough time to dart behind a building and launch myself off the ledge overlooking the sea. I brace myself for the impact and miraculously tuck my head down so that I roll down the sand. Then my leg gets caught in a small, damp hill and my speed bends it with an agonizing crunch. I sprawl out with my burned leg bent at an awkward angle. It provoked the healing injury, which now blazes.

I clench my jaw and wait for the pain to lessen. But it only gets worse.

This was a wound that never really healed. It just became a more bearable version of what it was before. Now the pain is worse than ever. My shorts reveal that it's starting to swell and bruise with purple spots. I'm sure it must be broken.

Needing to get away from the close-by police officers, I haul myself up and limp down the beach all the way to a staircase covered in sandy grime and salty splotches of green algae. Clutching the railing so hard I get splinters, I manage to pull myself to the top and all the way to the door of the lab. I wrench it open and feeling wobbly, collapse to the floor.

The sound echoes through the open room and two unfamiliar workers turn to stare at me in confusion. Dr. Corry quickly strides in. "I'll take care of him." He leaves for a moment and returns wheeling a black canvas stretcher.

I pull myself up and fall back into the stretcher. It seems to hurt much more than it should. The ache spreads up my leg until my whole body seems to throb. Something isn't right.

Next thing I know, my leg is stiff and set in a stiff plaster cast. It's propped in a sling dangling from the ceiling and I'm afraid to move it. Uniform beds line the white walls so that it resembles a hospital, but I'm the only occupant. There's nobody near and the walls are bare, even of windows, except for an open door. I lift my head and carefully keep my lower body still.

"Um, hello?" I call.

I half-expect Marina to rush in with relief or Luke to scientifically explain exactly what happened, but there's just stillness. I don't hear Marina, Luke, and Rain making random conversation just to pass time or Ellen hurrying around to finish the day's chores. I don't hear Dr. Corry working on an experiment or even his employees walking through the halls with clipboards.

Maybe it's late at night and everyone's in the house whereas I'm in the lab. But even if that's true, something doesn't seem right.

Suddenly, the room seems to morph into another place. Shadows falls across the rest of the room and loose restraints appear beside my wrists and ankles. The sling vanishes and my incased leg drops heavily onto the bed. I expect excruciating pain, but there's nothing. Cautiously, I stand up and it's like I was never even hurt. I find myself in a long hall.

Voices fill my head, but they are meaningless. I can't define the words, owners, or even tones, but somehow they bring panic. I run faster and faster, but I don't know where I'm going and darkness surrounds me. I don't seem to ever tire, but this trek seems to never end. Just when I think I'm about to get away, something pinches my back with a sharp sting.

My eyes fly open in realization that it was just a dream.

In this reality, Marina does anxiously stand over me with Luke close by.

Much to their surprise, I start genuinely laughing. "How is it that one of us always ends up passing out from being injured?"

Marina cracks a grin and starts laughing with me. Our loud laughter sounds nearly delirious and Luke looks concerned. It's all the stress and fear and anxiety finally pouring out of us as if it were just one, big ridiculous joke. It feels good to laugh as I haven't *really* laughed in a long time.

She reaches down, avoiding my elevated leg, and hugs me tightly. I hold onto her for a while until pain shoots through my thigh and she let's go.

"So was my leg all that bad?"

"Dad discovered something else about Serions," Luke informs. "Apparently broken bones are rare and much more dangerous than they are for humans."

"Why?" we both wonder.

"Human bones are filled with marrow so as long as they're quickly set in a cast, everything is fine. And it won't damage the rest of the body. Serion bones, I guess, flow with a substance that reflects their power. With broken bones, it could leak out and spread through the body, which, depending on what it is, could be fatal, even if they're generally immune to whatever it is."

I raise an eyebrow. "So right now fire is coursing through my bones?"

He nods. "That's why it hurt worse than you'd think. It's lucky you got here in time or you could've burned your insides."

"This just gets weirder and weirder every day," Marina mutters.

"Maybe you just get weirder every day." Luke's rare joke comes with a smile.

She lightly punches his arm.

"I'm probably bed-ridden for a few days," I sigh. This position couldn't possibly be more uncomfortable.

"Serions supposedly heal faster than humans, but I wouldn't take any chances," Luke replied.

"I think I dreamed about the girl again." Their wide-eyes launch me into a re-telling of my dream. "And it wasn't exactly her contacting me," I finish. "But it was a message, like she was trying to show me something, like that one in the tree."

"Who is this girl?" Marina wonders out loud.

"Not a living telepath," Luke remarks.

"But then who?" I shake my head. It's a mystery.

That question sticks in my mind for the rest of the day. Whoever, whatever, this is, it's persistent in contacting us all through every way possible. So far it's only by telepathically, but she pushes into our dreams, our consciousness, and finds ways to drop us into some sorts of simulations.

Then I'm distracted from that nagging question.

A buzzing starts in my fingertips and slowly spreads through my arms. It's a constant tingling that isn't as irritating as when your feet fall asleep, but is much more consistent than a small itch. The feeling spreads all over my body and makes me shiver. A memory is triggered at the back of my mind, something I'd forgotten long since.

On the island Marina and I woke up saying we both felt a tingling feeling. This is identical to that time. The chills dive down my spine and then slowly subside until I'm left with nothing but shaky hands. It was stronger than before, and I don't have the slightest clue what caused it.

"Buzzy feeling?" Marina asks shortly, peeking over the doorframe.

"Yep."

"Same as on the island?"

I just nod.

"Can we really just ignore this any longer? It's all related." She just stares at me for an answer, unblinkingly.

Embarrassment comes over me as she seems to study me. I must look pathetic laying helpless in a hospital bed with my leg set in a block of concrete, raised vulnerably. I wonder if she's pitying me for getting hurt so often lately. First I got shot with a poison arrow, which I had to burn out. That did enough scarring damage, but then I broke the same leg and nearly flooded with liquid fire? That's some ridiculously bad luck.

I don't want her to always have to be saving me or watching me be injured and as useless as paralyzed.

Her reaction is the complete opposite. "You're so brave, Carter," she comments. "If it wasn't for you, I'd definitely be dead by now. You're a much better fighter than me and you never question yourself."

"And you're the reason I keep trying so hard," I admit. "I know that I have to protect you. I'd sacrifice my life for yours."

"Aw, Carter, I'd do the same for you."

It looks like she's nearly tearing up with emotion. Marina comes to sit on the edge of my bed and takes my hand, twining her fingers around mine so they fit together. She leans down and lightly kisses my forehead. Her long hair brushes against my face as she sits up again.

I run my hand through her hair. It's soft and silky and actually reminds me of smooth, cool ocean waves as my hand passes through it. Our abilities don't just affect our personalities and life styles, but also our appearances. That only now really clicks into my mind.

Marina's long-lashed eyes are the beautiful turquoise color of the ocean and the texture of her hair seems to symbolize waves. I've only vacantly noticed before, that she smells faintly of the salty sea. I think the scent only recently became noticeable again, as it was on the island, like a nature-themed perfume. It fits her. Marina's true power may be classified as ice, but ice melts into water. I feel like she's more drawn to the water side, and that the ice would be harsher and colder.

Back when I first met her, she was sad and resolute. It was then she more often reflected the ice aspect of her powers. Now it's the ocean she longs for, with ice merely being a useful addition.

"I really hope your leg is better soon. It must be awful not moving all day," she sympathizes.

"Oh, don't worry, I can live with it."

"Well, I'm here for you whenever you need me."

"Thank you, and about what you said earlier, we can ignore this. Maybe if we don't talk about it or think about it, it'll leave."

"Even if that's true, Kairo won't leave."

"No, but we can't either. The police are after me."

"That still doesn't make sense." She furrows her brow in confusion. "If Kairo knew we were close by, why wouldn't he find us himself? What's the benefit in telling humans you're a murderer so they'll obviously set the police on you?"

"They never actually did say who the man was," I point out.

"It would at least have to be someone working for Kairo."

"True."

Marina frowns. "Let's stop there. Stop thinking about it and it *might* go away."

I envision a wall rising up around my brain and shielding my thoughts from being penetrated. It's figurative, but seems to work, at least for now.

When Marina's there, I don't notice the cold that is part of her, but when she leaves, the coldness of her presence remains. With her gone, it's just a freezing patch of air around me that makes goose bumps prickle on the surface of my skin.

It counteracts the heat that I try to radiate and cuts into me as if with a steely edge. I like Marina so much that when she's here, I'm oblivious to the chilling aura surrounding her. But there's nothing I like about the cold that trails behind her. It lingers around me and seems to never disappear, no matter what I do. So I stay huddled under the insufficiently thin covers, shaking and trying to get some sleep.

The darkened lights and workers locking the doors signal nightfall. I know that I'm in the lab all alone. All around me is stony silence. I imagine Marina, Luke, Rain, Dr. Corry, and Ellen all laughing over a steaming dinner and make a face at the packaged sandwich that a woman wordlessly dropped on the tray above me earlier. The meat looks suspiciously watery and old.

My stomach growls and jabs with hunger like a lion's trying to claw its way out, so I unwrap the thin plastic and take a bite. The bread is dry and crumbly and the meat odd-tasting like it's on the verge of expiration, but it's food, even if it's gross hospital food.

This isn't even a hospital, but scientists are doctors, so I assume they have some provisions in case of emergencies like mine.

After taking a swig of bottled water, the open door seems to stare at me. I now desperately wish they'd shut it. Even though it's creepy enough being alone in the white room at night, it's small and I can see everything, whereas an open door facing a long hall could welcome unwanted visitors. I turn myself away, but now it just seems that I'll turn around to find someone standing over me.

The only sound is the annoyingly repetitive ticking of the white clock mounted above me. I can't even see the time. Out of boredom, unwanted thoughts seep into my head. They're my own, but of the things I'm trying hard to forget: the mystery girl's voice, the flash of hair I think belongs to my mom, the searing pain as fire flowed through me, Kairo plunging that dagger into Marina's side.

In all these memories I was helpless. I stood by and watched tragedies unfold or unknown clues escape, just out of my grasp. It makes my stomach feel queasy.

And then somewhere, deep in the shadows of the hall outside, I think I hear a single noise. It's as if somebody lurched forward too quickly and their foot tapped against the polished floor. Panic leaps into my throat and I almost gag while my eyes bore into the doorway. I wait for something else to happen, but when nothing does, I finally summon the control to fall asleep.

Even in my subconscious, I can't shake the jumpy feeling. It's a feeling of fear that my throat will be slit when I'm helpless and asleep in the darkest hour of the night.

I awaken to the too-sanitary lab, lights just above me blinding my sleepy eyes. My hands immediately fly to my throat as I gain consciousness. Everything seems intact with me and the room around. There's no evidence of an intruder, despite what I thought I heard last night.

The open doorway had probably gotten me anxious and it had all just been a trick of the mind.

"Carter, I think we can try removing that cast." Dr. Corry strides into the room, looking rejuvenated since the last time I saw him. He's gained the needed healthy amount of weight and the shadows under his eyes have lightened.

"Oh, thank God." My leg is so stiff that I can hardly feel my toes.

I tense while the saw's serrated blade whirs. He brings it down on my cast and it reverberates through my leg, but luckily the cast falls apart quickly and my fear of it slicing through my flesh leaves. I shake out my foot and the color returns to my pale leg. My skin's wrinkled from being molded to the indentions of the cast.

"So how does it feel?"

Only a small twinge stings my leg as I stand up and lean all my weight on it, which wasn't really that smart. "Fine."

"Okay, then, you're good to go. Just try not to do anymore damage to that same leg."

"I can't really make any promises."

He chuckles. "Well, I think Marina will be happy to see you and I have work to do."

"Okay, thanks."

He nods and walks back down the hall. I almost tell him to not research the Serions any longer, but bite my lip before the words come out. Maybe he really has stopped thinking about my long-gone planet and I wouldn't want to remind him.

I hear voices raising when I'm standing outside the back door. It only gets louder and louder the closer I get to the living room.

"Did you really live like this?" Rain complains. "How can you be so isolated?"

"It's for all of our safety!" Marina answers. "I'd rather not be dead!"

"Sometimes I feel dead," she mutters under her breath.

"What?" Marina narrows her eyes.

"I'm sorry, but I need to get out! Maybe I can't go home or to school now. Maybe I can't see my parents for a while, but can't we at least go to the beach or the mall?"

"We need to stick together! I thought we were best friends!"

"We are! But I'm not one of you!"

Marina looks as if she's been slapped and Rain's face turns to shock as she realizes the damage of her words.

"What do you think I am?" Marina says with quiet anger. "Some sort of freakish, abnormal monster?"

"No, no, Marina, that's not what I meant," Rain stammers.

"You know, maybe you're right!" Marina cries. "Maybe I should be locked away and kept separate from humanity because I'm dangerous and weird and not normal! Maybe you should just leave because you belong with normal humans!"

"Marina!" I plant myself in between them, acting as a barrier. "I thought we've been over this. I thought *you* were over this."

She cringes. "Oh, you're right. I'm sorry, Rain."

"No, I'm sorry," Rain corrects. "It's hard never leaving one building, but you *are* my best friend and I'll stay here if it means you're safe."

They reach around me and into an emotional hug. They both look so desperate and depleted that the drop of a hat could set them into a fit of tears. I'm careful to not move a muscle in case it would somehow trigger a weeping girl drama, which I certainly don't want to be caught in the middle of.

"Carter!" Marina brightens like she's seeing me for the first time. "You got your cast off!"

"Yep, good as new."

"You sure have bad luck with that leg," Rain comments.

"I really hope that was the end of it."

"You know, we can switch around everything," Marina says in determination. "If we really want something, we can make it happen. And we will. Kairo can't hurt us and we won't let him win! We can stand up against anything that comes our way because we will work together!"

She links arms with Rain and I and a heaviness lifts at her inspirational words. If either of them sense the trouble hanging in the air, they don't let on, so I force myself to ignore it. That may have been a mistake.

Chapter Twenty Three

Marina

Late in the night, my ears ring with music and laughter as figures dance across my dreams. When my eyes open to the guest room, the same noise sounds from down the hall.

Curiously, I pad down the hall and peak over the threshold to the living room. Carter, Rain, and Luke are all dancing haphazardly around the room while the music's upbeat pace rises in volume. I raise my eyebrows at their strange behavior.

Then new, unfamiliar dancers materialize like they've all been dropped down from the sky. I find myself wondering if I just didn't notice them before. The walls roll and blur like they're caught in a heat mirage. Nausea clouds my head and suddenly it switches to a giddy feeling.

I blink.

The setting has completely changed. The walls dotted with framed pictures now resemble a large, dimmed gym strung with strings of colored lights and bouquets of balloons. A table is strewn with long-stemmed glasses next to a glass bowl of cherry red punch. The music is blaring and a spinning disco ball throws silver patches across the floor. Girls in party dresses dance beside cute boys, giggling and flirting.

It bears so much resemblance to my high school dances, so many of which I missed.

I feel naked in my pajamas when everyone else is wearing silk and chiffon. Hanging my head, I watch in awe as the warm, loose pants change into a poufy skirt that hits the middle of my thighs. I'm wearing a silky, shimmering dress that's the same color as my eyes. Reaching up, I feel that my hair's been coiled and sprayed into perfect curls.

The thing is that none of this strikes me as odd. Excitement gets the best of me and I feel woozy, like I'm floating on clouds. It's like I'm drunk, even though the only time I've touched alcohol was when I was ten and mistook it for root beer.

"Marina, let's dance!" Carter calls. His normally calm tone is enthusiastic, and he's dressed up in a tuxedo.

I skip over and twirl into him. Carter swings me around and my head pounds. Rain flashes me a smile from where she's dancing with a tall, dark eyed guy whose bright orange tie looks cutely off-center. A girl with a fancy black hairdo and a long red dress whirls into Luke's arms. All of us are happy and any traces of confused worry is pushed away.

Carter and I dance through the fast songs, and I laugh as he badly mimics the words. When a melodic slow song flows through the speakers he wraps his arms around my waist and my hands are on his shoulders. We sway to the soft beat and my head is rested against his chest. He presses his lips to the top of my head, and my grasp around his neck tightens.

As another quick song comes on, I start to perspire.

"Care for a drink?" Carter asks.

I nod and we stroll to the beverage table holding hands. Rain playfully waves at the guy she was talking to as she meets up with us. Luke is near and I hear him offer to get the girl a drink. She smiles and watches him walk over to the table.

"This is fun!" Rain laughs.

"It really is!" Luke exclaims uncharacteristically.

Carter hands us all glasses. "A toast to good times?"

"To good times!" I chorus and our glasses clink together.

The sweet fruity taste fills my mouth and it's addictive. I drain my cup and reach down for another, but Carter holds onto my wrist. "Just in case somebody tampered with these, it's not a good idea to have too much."

"Oh, they taste fine!" Rain waves him away and takes another.

Luke shrugs and does the same. Soon, we've all chugged down two full cups of the sugary punch. I grin at the red staining Carter's upper lip and wipe it off for him.

"Is it just me or is it getting hot in here?" Rain whines.

She's right. Heat rises into my cheeks and Carter and Luke's faces are flushing. Rain fans herself and my legs start to feel unstable.

"Whoa, I'm flying!" Rain hoots feverishly.

I stare at her and an alarm ringing through my mind seems to tell me I'm missing something, but Carter flings me into a dance and that questioning is gone. We hold hands and jump around. Rain and Luke are dancing and seem to have ditched whoever they were talking to before.

"Is the room spinning?" I wonder out loud.

"Yep," Carter confirms.

"Do you think it's special effects?" I say brainlessly.

"If they are, they're pretty good."

"So we're supposed to be dizzy?"

"I guess."

Carter falters and nearly trips over his own feet. I stabilize him, but then my own legs start to quiver like noodles. Luke and Rain fall beside us and we all end up in a heap. Luke gags and Rain's eyes seem to bulge. Carter looks ashen and I groan with a feeling of sickness.

"Special effects?" Rain stammers.

"No," I whisper angrily.

A glass goblet rolls beside me, a missing piece shattered in an array of shards. The red liquid leaks out like blood. That's the last thing that my sight captures just when the weight of what really happened sinks in. And then a fog blurs the room into darkness.

When light comes into focus, I feel drained. Before my eyes are even fully open, my stomach lurches and my throat is stung raw as I throw up. It makes a putrid, poisonous green puddle in front of me.

Poison.

That's what this was.

Carter regains consciousness, shortly followed by Luke. We're a mess. They're throwing up, and I cough and gag at the foul taste that won't leave my mouth. Even after all the poison comes up, Luke can't stop a fit of retching that looks painful. Carter looks like he's choking on his own spit.

The floor is a mix of green, spreading and blending together. We all take a step back from the awful smell. Everything has gone back to the old way it was. My pretty dress has left behind sweat-soaked pajamas and my hair is tangled from sleep. The decorations, music, and dancers are all gone and have merely left us sick and weak. The memory of the dance seems like a dream or something we all desperately fantasized to escape the danger we're always in.

Rain is still knocked out on the floor, her fingertips almost touching the poison.

"Did we all go crazy?" Luke asks in disbelief.

"No," Carter says, his eyes flicking over the room. "Look at the glass."

"Poison," we all agree.

"But how?" Luke wonders.

"More importantly, why is Rain still not waking up?" I ask frantically. I bend down and poke her arm. "Rain, Rain!" I pick up her arm and it limply flops back down. I gasp and my fingers fly to check her pulse. It pounds through her wrist, faintly, but still holding on. "What's wrong with her?" I cry.

"She should be awake," Carter says. Then his eyes widen. "That glass is hers. She drank more than any of us."

Pieces of the dance fill my mind and Rain seemed the most out of it. Where Carter and Luke still showed some traces of sense and reason, she was simply ready to party and have a good time, all logic gone. She'd gulped down the 'punch' like it was going to disappear any second, drinking every last drop of as many glasses as she could get her hands on.

"What should we do?" My voice gets higher and higher. "What if…what if she…?"

Carter puts his arm around me. "Shh, it'll be okay. Luke, shouldn't we take her to your dad?"

"Right." Luke flings Rain's drooping body over his shoulder like she weighs nothing.

For a moment, I think I see a disco ball forming on the ceiling, but when I blink, it's gone. I'm still not sure what happened. Kairo may be able to influence our decisions, but there's no way he could implant a whole realistic event in our heads. Especially since we've been able to resist his less obvious manipulations.

I'm doing what feels like a sprint, but it's really more of a clumsy jog. My stomach gurgles and I try to gulp it down. Still, a leftover stream of green poison finds its way out of my system. Carter looks back and stops to check on me. My legs shake and I fall to my knees while retches rack my feeble body. It burns my lungs and stomach and feels much worse than the actual throwing up.

Carter scoops me into his arms, and I huddle close to his chest. He's the only thing stabilizing me.

"We need to make sure the poison didn't do any real damage to you, either." His words are barely audible.

I drank more of the lethal concoction than Carter or Luke. Luke downed more than Carter. We all had two, but the fuzziness after that is only now clearing.

Two glasses didn't seem to do more than knocking the drinker unconscious and causing them to throw up, but who knows what more can do? Rain is unconscious and I feel a mess. Luke falters ahead of us and pauses to take a deep breath before continuing his fast stride.

"Are you okay?" I whisper into Carter's ear.

"Mostly, for now anyway."

Luke is tracking red footprints that change to an oozing bright green. I shake my head and the hallucinations vanish. "No!" My croaking voice is firm.

"Huh?"

"Nothing."

Dr. Corry's voice shouts a few commands at Luke and next thing I know, I'm lying in the room that Carter was in just days before.

Thin tubes pierce into blue veins in my arms and a screen beeps above me, just within my view. I know I must be on pain killers because nothing hurts the way it did before. This feels like a surreal dream. Wavering lines trace patterns across the machine. It's a line, rising and falling with the rate of my heart. It arches up unexpectedly and then climbs down into small hills.

The indications of my breathing just get smaller and smaller. My lungs aren't constricting, but I can feel my heart slowing by the minute.

It fills me with terror to watch my own life recede right before my eyes.

Just as the line is barely more than a straight plane running across the screen, I clench my fists and run a pep talk through my head.

I am brave.

I am strong.

I am Serion.

I can live.

I will *live.*

It's as if the stark determination struck my heart and restarted it. I feel its bold beat in my chest and my dull vision slowly returns to normal. The wavering line is still on the very low side, but it's trailing higher with every increasing heartbeat. The muck that was packed into my brain melts and leaves my senses sharp and clear. I was able to beat the poison.

"I'm okay!" I exclaim.

Carter chuckles from where he sits in the hospital bed next to me. IV's hang loosely from his inner elbows. His wilted face shows he's depleted, but he recovered faster than I did. Luke is at an unconscious state that makes me worry, but his heart is beating fairly steadily and his fingers stir with minimal movements.

Wires and IV's are hooked up to Rain from all angles as her machine beeps alarmingly. Dr. Corry and Ellen are clustered around her, and I glimpse that the streak on the lit-up screen above her is barely peaking. She's been my best friend forever, and it's even worse watching her come close to death than seeing myself dying.

"Rain, Rain," I panic.

"They're doing everything they can," Carter says tensely.

I sit bolt-straight, my fingers digging into my palms until the skin is torn up. Sweat rolls down the back of my neck. The endless track of high beeps now seem to belong in my ears. Eventually, I can't take watching Rain's vague life line lessen.

"Can't the poison be drawn out of her system?" I demand.

"No," Dr. Corry says regretfully, wiping his brow. "That would require a surgery and removing some flesh."

"Is that possible?"

"It moved too quickly. By the time Luke brought her by, it had already spread into her veins. If I try to remove the poison, she'll be dead in minutes."

"She might already be." But I can't bear to say it as a loud comeback like I meant to. It's a small huff under my breath. The words *can't* be true.

Carter may be the person I care about most, ev
I've only know him recently. But Rain's been there
whole life, and she'll always be my best friend. I
give up on her now. I can't just let her die right in fr

"Maybe I'll be able to do something," I declare.

As I cross the room, the high sounds accelerate,
faster. I quicken my pace, surging with panic, bu
come to a stop beside Rain's unconscious form, th
the screen go dead. One long line runs the len
machine, over and over, with an endless, uniform ri

It's over.

I wasn't fast enough.

It tears through my soul like a knife, but the pai
I stand in immobilized shock. My eyes widen into h
and my mouth hangs open in utter disbelief. The
crumples and I start bawling, wailing as fat tears st
my cheeks.

Any other time I'd be embarrassed to cry in fror
like this, but not now. I can't hold it back.

My best friend is dead.

I grab her wrist, limp and cold, absent of move
and squeeze tightly. As the world swims before n
tighter and tighter. I feel Carter's grip on my sho
comes to console me, but it's not helping. I know
close, but I don't even glance up. I'm not st
crying, but I know Rain's death didn't hurt the
me. It didn't cut into their hearts.

Rain is the only thing that my vision allows m
it's an awful image. Rain, so full of life, pasty
helpless, her hair splayed around her face in a pal
features are calm and peaceful, as if warring wi
convulsing through me.

My nails bite into her flesh just as they did
before. I don't even feel bad for making marks;
to any piece of her still attached to Earth, even
lifeless body.

can't be dead," I murmur. "You just can't be!"

…p over her, my head hung in despair. The cold
…rush of ice flows through my fingertips even though
…ntentional. I don't stop it, both because I don't have
…th to figure out how and because it gives me a little
…e iciness flows from my fingers into her skin. I can
…ead through her wrist and continue its way up her

…rdrops roll down my face and one drops onto her
…rt, a wet splotch in the fabric. I hardly know what's
…ny longer.
…s happening?" Luke asks curiously.
…t sure," Dr. Corry remarks incredulously.
…, what are you doing?" Carter's whisper tickles my
…on't respond.
…n I doing? Then I hear a pause in the long stream of
…ore it starts again. It's like music to my ears. It was
…fast, probably unnoticed by the others, but it gave
…d that's all I need.
…er I am doing, I pore all my energy into it. My eyes
…hut, my hands practically turning her wrist black
…t I can feel powerful adrenaline coursing through
…d running into hers as my hand acts as the link

…king!" Luke says incredulously.
…s on the monitor space out and fall into a rhythmic
…y fall back into a normal heart rate.
…the pulse pounding in Rain's wrist and warmth
…er fingertips. I would give a shout of joy, but I
…ocused. If this is going to work, I have to stay

…fe flows into her right before my eyes, I can't
…he one bringing her back to life. This isn't a
…. I'm sure of that. No matter how extraordinary
…erions may be, I just know we can't raise the

dead. But maybe we can transfer some of our power into dying humans clinging onto a last fraying thread of life.

Kairo said himself that we Serions are hard to kill. In all my grief, I must've found the unknown ability to give some of that excess, pain-tolerating energy to Rain.

She must have had a small spark of life left deep inside her.

My unblinking eyes are dry and sting as I keep them trained on Rain's face. Her eyelids flutter and open to reveal lively blue.

I throw myself at her and hug her so hard it's like I'm never going to let go.

"Marina...can't breathe," she chokes.

"Sorry!" I give her some space.

"Why are you all looking at me like you've seen a ghost?"

It's true. Carter, Luke, Dr. Corry, and Ellen's eyes are as round as a startled cat caught in headlights. Their gaze shifts from me, who revived a dead body, to Rain, who came back to life from death. I'm almost amused by their faces, but I swallow down the laughter.

"You were...dead," Carter answers slowly, breaking down the words like he doesn't understand them.

"Dead?" Rain's eyes bulge out of her head. "That's not even possible! How am I...?"

"Marina brought you back to life." Luke's voice is mono-tone, like he's reading from a textbook. It's a cover for the shock.

"You did what?"

"Brought you back to life," I repeat. It does sound insane, even in my own ears.

Dr. Corry clears his throat. "Serions are much harder to kill than humans. She must have passed some of that on to you." Finally, someone is saying something logical.

"That's...amazing," she stammers. "Last thing I remember is the dance..." Visions swim in my eyes. I see flashes of shimmering dresses under a disco ball. I hear the roar of too-loud music and the DJ calling out inaudible words. I see a couple kissing in the corner...feel the heat of Carter's hand on my waist. The shattered cup with drops of green poison dripping off the jagged edge stands out prominently. It's a splotch of blue that doesn't belong in a field of green grass.

It sinks into me that the whole ordeal had a strange feel to it. I should've sensed it before the rush clouded my reasoning.

"It was a hallucination." Carter suddenly looks exhausted.

"Nothing about our lives makes sense anymore," Rain sighs.

And we all just start laughing. It's like when Carter was in the hospital, but now we all join in, even Dr. Corry. It's a happy chorus that combines into one, musical sound. It's reminds me that we're united, that we can overcome anything. We've been through so much, together.

A stab in the side, a leg broken down with three infectious injuries, an actual poisoned death.

Any other three teenagers would have long since been corpses, but we persevered through it with each other's support.

It's moments like this when Kairo seems like a little puny fly I could easily smash under my shoe.

It only really dawns on me now, that things are changing and in more ways than just mine and Carter's lives. We're simply small puzzle pieces who have a role to play in a much bigger event. I'm not sure if it's something Kairo set into motion, or something transferred from Serion that was destined to happen, but I know it's coming.

The air buzzes with powerful electricity and I can almost feel the Earth shifting under my feet. Something is shifting and the only thing I can't predict is what it will improve and what it'll be the downfall of. It feels like a new era is awakening.

Chapter Twenty Four

Carter

Now that everything is as under control as it can be, now that we're all healed, the cold of Washington really hits me. Every time I so much as crack open the window, I'm hit with an icy front. It's a blade cutting through me that makes my whole body shudder.

I don't know how they stand this every day. I don't know how people can actually live here for years. But I can tell the difference. The normal residents of Aberdeen know how to dress warmly, sometimes shivering, but get used to their home city. The cold is magnified several times for me, but I assume that to Marina, the freezing air feels better.

The longer I stay in the lab, the more I miss Arizona. My fingers hover over the phone's keypad daily as I wonder if I should call my dad. Every time all ten digits of the number are typed in, I wait until the screen dims and end up pressing 'off'.

I make up my mind that today I will force myself to press 'call', to wait while it rings, and to talk without ending before he answers. I'm not really sure why I'm so nervous to speak to my dad again. He knew that I was Serion. I didn't run away leaving my parents devastated and clueless. A shipwreck washed me far away without my approval.

Thoughts whirl through my mind, things I can't believe I was idiotic enough to not think of before.

My dad doesn't know I survived. He never saw me make it to the island. For all he knows, I could've drowned, and I would've if Marina hadn't saved me. Worse, I never saw my dad make it back to the shore. Somehow, I'd always assumed he'd survived, but I never really knew, and I still don't. At least he was headed in the right direction, but the waves were brutal and he didn't have a boat.

My body makes the decision before my brain and the dial tone rings in my left ear. I'm desperate for him to answer. If it comes down to necessity, I can survive with just Marina by my side, but he is my father and I haven't seen him in weeks.

"Who is this?" His familiar voice is tired with a yawn.

"Carter." My answer is short and emotionless. I'm not sure how to react.

"Carter?" he exclaims. "What happened? I've been so worried...!"

"Before anything, let's get one thing straight." It's hard to keep the anger laced into my voice, but then I remember all the years of deceit. "I know I'm Serion. And I know you lied to me."

"It was for your own good! I was trying to protect you, and I wanted you to have as normal of a life as you could. I was going to tell you on that trip to Washington. You were sixteen and old enough to handle it, but then the storm came."

I sigh deeply. "I forgive you. I get it. There's something you should know, though. I think Mom's alive."

"What?" Dad is so stunned that he sputters on the words, choking and coughing. He clears his throat, getting past the initial shock. "Um, go on."

"There's been strange fires forming, one's I don't cause, and a poster with her picture that said 'found'. I thought at first it might've been Kairo messing with me, but I saw someone sneak around the building, with hair just like hers."

"Katrina would never try to kill you," he says hoarsely.

"I don't know if it's her fault, but I'm pretty sure it's her."

"What do you mean, not her fault?"

"Kairo could be behind it."

"Kairo," he murmurs. "That was who Katrina said we had to hide from. It's ironic that in the end it was the government who got her."

"That's what we *thought* anyway."

"I can't believe she's alive. This is crazy! Where are you, anyway?"

"Aberdeen, in Dr. Corry's lab. I'm here with Marina, Luke, and Rain."

"I think your mom knew Dr. Corry. I met Katrina up near Aberdeen, and we lived in Washington for a while. I remember her mentioning the lab before. But who are the others?"

"Luke's Dr. Corry's son, Rain's Marina's best friend, and Marina's...well...I guess she's my girlfriend." My mouth curves into a grin at the word. I've never officially called her my girlfriend, but it sounds so right. We fell in love in a different way than normal teenagers asking each other out to the movies.

"You've got a girlfriend?"

"Yeah..." I'm suddenly embarrassed. "You know Dad, I should go. I'll call you when I can, alright?"

"Wait, Carter –" he protests.

But I press the 'end' button and flip the phone shut with a slap before he finishes the sentence.

Hearing from Dad wasn't heartfelt the way Marina was reunited with her parents. There was a tension that had never been there before. It makes sense now, though. How could he tell a kid growing up with a somewhat normal life that he was an alien?

It would've destroyed my childhood. I would've been like Luke, but it would've been worse.

Maybe if I'd suspected something, it would've been more obvious. I might have noticed the strangeness in how we constantly moved when he held a steady, likeable job. He even periodically changed his careers. I was often homeschooled and when I wasn't, the longest I stayed in one school was a year. Threads of the lives I'd made in various cities fell apart.

My friends fell out of touch when we never kept in contact other than a few phone calls. Girls I had liked moved on and got new boyfriends. Still, I always coped with it because it was what I'd always known.

Dad had always thought the government killed Mom and knew Kairo had been tracking her. He feared that they could somehow link her to me and I'd meet the same fate.

Maybe she wasn't murdered by the government, but clearly it was an attempt. You can tell just from the report that was leaked onto the internet. They knew something was up, even if it was hidden from most of society. The disappearance I'd previously interpreted as her death might have actually been her stealthily hiding away where they couldn't find her.

The door clicks open and Marina smiles at me sympathetically. "Decide not to call again?"

"No, I talked to him."

"You – you did what? Really? Well, is everything alright?"

"Yeah, I told him I think my mom's alive. And I told him that you're my girlfriend."

"Girlfriend, huh?" She takes my hand and runs her other hand gently along my cheek.

I tilt my head down and kiss her, holding her against me with my hand on her back. She twists her hand into my hair and kisses back. I think that for once we won't be interrupted by danger or terror, but then I hear Rain's voice.

"You know, I'm here, too, lovebirds," she teases.

Marina leans back, with my arm still around her, and gives Rain an irritated look. "Great timing."

"So what's so important?" I ask. A sigh covers up the annoyance.

"Luke is missing."

"What?"

"He's gone. Don't you think we should find him?"

"Yes, obviously!" Marina says.

"Why would he just leave?" I wonder while we follow her to his room.

Nothing seems out of place. The sports posters from years ago plastering the walls are straight and his navy bedspread is sloppily tucked in. As usual, clothes are strewn in the corner. Then, I see a single crumpled paper sitting in a ball on his desk.

I unfold the creases and stare at the inked words. *That wasn't the end of the poison. I said I'd be back. One of you better meet me or everyone dies. 6 PM in the forest. –K*

"Everyone will die anyway," I mutter, holding up the note for them to read.

K: It could stand for Kairo, it could stand for *Katrina*. No, that's ridiculous. Kairo plainly told us he'd be back, whereas Katrina hasn't spoken to me since I was a baby. It's obviously Kairo, and any other suggestion would be crazy.

"It's five forty-five now," Rain tells us. "We don't have much time left." *Before Luke is killed.*

219

Chapter Twenty Five

Marina

"I don't know, but we need to look for him, now!" Carter commands.

"He sacrificed his life for *all* of us," I say softly.

This act showed true friendship, bravery, and commitment. Even when Kairo surely hoped Carter or I would show up, Luke took our place in attempt to prevent our deaths. We are people he's only met in the past month or two, but I realize that we are his only friends. Aside from his parents, we are all he's got and the only ones he cares about. He's proven his true loyalty.

But this is what we've all become. Aside from each of our parents and siblings, away in safety, the four of us are each other's only family.

Maybe Rain still holds onto friends from school. We both have distant relatives living in other states, but those relationships are fading away. They are not the people who cry with us, who fight with us, who endure torture and pain with us. They are not the people who are constantly by our sides in this crazy ordeal, risking their lives every day.

We are family. And that is why we must save Luke.

I'm out the door step before Carter and Rain, luck somehow interfering and guiding me into the forest less than a mile from Dr. Corry's lab. I weave my way through the trees and plead to myself that I'm taking the right path.

My feet prickle, not sore, but anxious to keep moving. So I twist through the plants, only now realizing my feet are bare. A sharp twig pokes through the sole of my left heel and I'm sure it drew blood. It's a minor injury. I can ignore it.

Finally, when I know Rain is about to suggest we change course, I hear a voice rise above the wind.

Just a little farther, I tell myself. When the voices rise and I glimpse figures just ahead, I shove Carter and Rain behind a massive tree trunk and press against Carter, only my eyes peeking out.

Kairo's cloak is singed and shredded at the hem so it gives the appearance of the grim reaper. He never even bothered to repair it. He's ringed by his cronies, all dressed in their uniform black. None of them wear cloaks similar to his, but many have black jackets zipped up to their necks with overly concealing hoods tugged over their heads. They look like shadows silhouetted against the dusky sky.

Luke is hanging from a sturdy tree branch, his arms stretched above his head. His ankles and wrists are tightly bound with ragged rope. His eyelids droop heavily and his bare arms are scattered with scratches and red cuts.

Kairo flicks his hand up impatiently and Luke lets out a scream that makes my ears sore, his eyes flying open in agony. He flails around, but the binds hold him in place. It's a horrific sight. Carter puts his arms around me in a steely grip before I try to run out and save him.

"Can't you just kill me?" Luke pleads. "That was the bargain! I didn't come here to be tortured!"

I've never seen him look so helpless or pitiful. Luke is the oldest out of us, always calm and mature, brave and level-headed. Watching him be brought down like this terrifies me, not only for Luke's sake, but for what Kairo will do to me.

He lets out a cackle. "What fun would that be?"

It's unbearable to watch Luke be tortured further as pain repeatedly racks his body. I feel that it would've been enough to kill anyone else, but maybe it's really just a feeling, not physically damaging. I turn my face into Carter's shoulder, no longer wanting to watch. Then I realize how dead my brain has gone from the worry. I don't have to just sit back and watch; I can fight without moving a muscle.

The coast is all around me. The ocean distantly washes into my hearing and I know that water streams beneath my feet. It's like it was in the forest where fire burned around us, but it's even stronger. I can summon the water into the veins of the earth; it will answer my call. I can almost hear it filling in cracks in the dirt under my feet, feel a slight rumble as the ground ripples with the sloshing movement.

"Shouldn't you be more injured by now?" Kairo tries to use mockery to cover confusion.

It's true –I'm glad he's not –but logically, *shouldn't* Luke have more injuries?

"Okay, I give up. Lias, hand me my gun. All of you, aim your weapons."

A man who towers above even Kairo hands over the all-too-familiar silver gun. His face is completely unseen behind darkness. *Lias.*

"If only you'd been more efficient with your so-called poison then I wouldn't have to go through this extra trouble!" Kairo says angrily. "And I don't care how thorough your little 'illusion' was. The poison was the important part!"

"I did my best," a deceitful voice filled with cunning answers back.

His little illusion, his poison. That means…

"Get ready to fire," Kairo commands bluntly. "Three…"
I regain my control on the water I gravitated to me, and now I can even hear it rushing towards the people in black. The land becomes porous as little spouts of water spray into their faces. I hear gagging and choking as it catches them off guard. A particularly strong blast punches Kairo's face.

"What the hell is this?"

His gun is still trained on Luke, his finger on the trigger. Just as his scowl turns venomous and his eyes began to dart from tree to tree, water floods everywhere.

It seems to be pouring everywhere, from geysers blasting their feet out from beneath them, from splashes that arch above their heads, and from tree trunks that it seems to ricochet off of. It's a deluge so powerful that water inches higher, creeping up to their ankles.

People in black are knocked off their feet and swept away by the tidal wave. They snort and gag in attempt to fight the water that fills their noses and spurts into their eyes so they can't see. Kairo stands his ground, but looks ridiculous as he haphazardly shoots at anything moving, driven by madness. His black hair is plastered to his forehead and he spits out a stream of water.

One of his hooded followers stumbles to the ground as a bullet shoots their stomach. Lying vulnerable and unprotected, the current pulls the dying body onto its chest, water filling its lungs and red puffs ballooning around it as it's washed away.

"Kairo, you're shooting our people!" Lias accuses.

"Don't tell me what to do!"

My flood dies down and the rushing stream drains away down the hill, carrying flailing bodies with it. It leaves Kairo's group looking disoriented and absurd, similar to drowned rats. Half of them are sprawled in pools, water spraying from their mouths as they cough it out of their lungs. Some have tumbled down the hill and lie in a similar state. Only Kairo and Lias still stand, angry, but off-guard.

"Now's our chance," Carter signals.

I'd forgotten I was carrying it, but I find my fingers curling around my dagger's hilt and pulling it from my pocket. Rain picks up a particularly sharp branch as a makeshift weapon, but Carter walks forward confidently, unarmed.

My eyes drift to Luke, who without a second glance could pass for dead. His body is motionlessly suspended in the air like he's given up on trying any longer. His waterlogged clothes cling to his body and his hair hangs in his downcast eyes. He hasn't spotted us and even with his normally alert mind, he doesn't seem to have pieced everything together.

Carter creeps up behind Kairo and Lias. It's pure luck that none of the others are yet aware of anything besides spitting up water. Rain holds her stick like a spear, stepping in a circle as guard. I scale the tree, quietly hoisting myself from branch to branch and finding stable footholds. Eventually I balance onto Luke's branch and lean as far as stability will allow.

Luke's head turns and his eyes revive with disbelief and sheer happiness. I hold a finger to my lips and saw off the binds on his wrists. The skin has been rubbed red and raw. It's almost impossible that nobody has turned around by now. Luke drops down with the smallest of thuds, but it's enough.

Suddenly, the entire group is at ready, on their feet, several weapons poised at each of us.

None of us move a muscle; still as statues.

"How stupid are you?" Kairo says sinisterly. "You're surrounded."

Taking everyone by surprise, Rain rams her stick-spear square into Kairo's back with enough force that it drives into his skin. At least an inch of the ragged wooden end disappears into his flesh. All of us are stunned that Rain, with her slim body and seemingly weak arms, could've accomplished this.

His delayed cry of pain and rage sends a barrage of arrows and spears flying straight at Rain. I let out a yelp and fall from the tree, my legs bending at awkward angles beneath me, but I barely notice the sprained pain. Carter and Luke jump to defense, but there's nothing they can do to stop dozens of weapons all aimed at the same target simultaneously.

And Rain can't jump out of the way in time.

Chapter Twenty Six

Carter

That's when something miraculous happens. Just when the points are inches away from Rain's face, the force of wind pushing away blonde strands, they freeze.

The deadly arrows and spears hang in the air, quivering as if they're itching to move, but something holds them back. I stare at everyone in awe, but Marina and Luke are just as stunned as I am. Some of the others still have their hoods somehow glued to their faces, but those who don't aren't sure how to react. Even Kairo is perplexed beyond understanding.

Rain is immobile, her eyes crossed as she watches an arrow tremble in front of her nose.

"Is it the girl?" Lias asks incredulously. "The *human* girl?"

Rain puts her hands up like she's surrendering. "No," she whispers. "It's not me."

Then the weapons stand still and move forward just a fraction. For an awful moment I think they're going to resume their flight, piercing her from all directions, but then they drop.

Whatever force shielded Rain is gone, but it saved her life. It's incredible. It's impossible. All of us are stunned by what just happened.

"What wretched power is this?" Kairo yells.

"It's impossible; there's no others," a woman with piercings trailing down her cheek states surely.

"No, no there's not." Kairo says the words like he's trying to convince himself.

It would've been foolish to believe that the fight would be over. This distraction just bought us a little bit of time to free Luke, but that doesn't mean anything's over. It never does.

The petrified moment speeds up until it seems rapid fire. Kairo tugs the 'spear' from his back and brings it down hard on his knee. It snaps in half, and he tosses it carelessly to the side. I'm aware of Luke nimbly untying the rope from his ankles and Marina boosting herself against the tree trunk to stand without falling. Her legs look shaky; that fall did damage.

They all surge forward to retrieve their weapons and that's when it begins.

But we are no match for Kairo's workers. Marina's legs are sprained, Luke is shaky and sore, and Rain and I are unarmed. My brain goes into fighting mode, my consciousness not even reacting to the blows. My body takes over, dodging, ducking, and jumping to the side. Small fires flash in the corner of my vision. Sparks ignite on the tips of flammable objects.

I'm only aware of my opponent when it's a hooded fighter.

Somehow the stance and movement seems familiar. I'm almost able to predict what will happen next; we have a similar fighting style.

The jacket is oversized, but as the figure moves I'm able to tell it's a woman. She's good, but this is getting nowhere. She clutches a knife, but it hasn't been used yet. It doesn't really make sense, but she uses it as a fear mechanism and instead punches and kicks at the right opportunity. The strangest part is that I don't use my strengths either.

My fire has abandoned me mentally and it's just force. The battle could've easily been a fight breaking out in the middle of a high school, void of weapons or powers.

Finally, when she's turning around, I catch her off guard. My strong leg swings out, knocking her off-balance and trips her. She lands on her back, her knuckles white with her grip on her shining, unused knife. Her legs are bent and her hood is wadded up behind her head.

I find myself staring into eyes that are mirrors of mine. Her jaw is set in determination, even as I tower over her, but my mouth hangs open with a gasp. Her hazel eyes narrow, this action unfamiliar against the laugh lines crinkled at the corners of her eyes. Her hair is like fire, glinting with shades of red and blonde. It's just too much to see her again at a moment like this.

"Mom," I whisper.

She was dead. She was gone. That is what Dad and I believed for sixteen years, yet she's alive and she's here right in front of me, working with Kairo.

"Carter," she addresses curtly.

"How could you?" I say in disbelief.

"Oh, Carter." Her voice is scornful and gives off the impression that I'm a little kid with so much to learn. "The Awakening is already in motion, and there's nothing you can do to stop it. No matter what you and your friends do, you stand no chance against this power. *So don't even try.*"

"What is the Awakening?" I've never heard it mentioned before.

"It will lead to the revolution against Earth and humanity. It's the rise of Serion power. It's when the gateway is finally opening."

"You married a human!" I say critically.

"Biggest mistake of my life!"

It's like a slap in the face. It takes me a moment to realize this isn't Katrina Pyric, not the woman we knew sixteen years ago, anyway. I've seen the pictures and heard the stories my dad tells with such adoration. Something has warped her brain and her eyes glint with the hardened stare of a killer, which was absent even in the smiling photograph on the internet.

It reassures me that this isn't truly my mom, but it also activates fear. Maybe she's been so tormented that there's no going back and now this is the real Katrina Pyric.

"Mom." The word feels foreign in my mouth when it's being directed at a living person. "What happened to you? This isn't who you are."

"Oh, Carter, this is who I always was. Remember, you didn't know me. Your head might've been filled with pictures of a supportive woman who died saving her child and husband, but that's far from reality. And now it's time to face the cold, hard truth."

"I know you weren't like this. Dad loved you…"

"And that's what blinded him."

It's so quick I almost miss it, but when I say 'Dad', emotion flickers in her eyes. It's something like sorrow, longing, *memory*, but then it's replaced with this newfound cruel sheen that seems all too similar to Kairo's maniacal stare.

"And Carter, you are not my son, but an enemy who needs to be taken down."

I expect it. For the first time, her knife comes soaring at my heart, but I wrap my fingers around it, my grip unbreakable, before it reaches its intended target. In one swift move I wretch the blade from her grasp and the metal waves with heat. I think about setting her into a blaze, but remember she'd be immune. It would be pointless; fire against fire.

Instead, I ram the blade into her right calf, something clicking inside me that envies her for an undamaged leg. I couldn't bring myself to do any fatal damage.

My mom's scream is guttural and makes my heart ache, but I force myself to turn and trudge away, leaving her lying injured. Marina's eyes pan the scene and everything sinks in within a second. I'm assuming what was confident victory, judging from the blood on her dagger, changes into incredulity and sympathy.

"It was your mom. And she –"

"Tried to murder me. She's not the same person."

"Hey, look out!" Luke calls. Marina fights off a stunted sword with her weapon. "You need to be focused!" he adds. "There's time for talking later!"

When I try to fight another attacker, my moves have turned sloppy and distracted. My head just isn't in the fight. I'm knocked flat on my back and a long, serrated knife glints at my throat and another hand pins my arms down at my sides. His hood still hangs down as if it's glued to his face with tar, but I recognize Lias' impossible height.

"Didn't think your stamina would last forever, did you?" he hisses.

Black spots of panic blink on the sides of my vision. I don't see any way out of this. The others are occupied and haven't noticed that I'm on the verge of being killed. I can imagine Lias' sneer somewhere in the shadows of his hood and grimace as the edge of the metal bites into my neck.

He's torturous, pressing the knife down slowly so I'll feel every ounce of pain. The last fading ray of sunlight shines against a sword that lies close to my free arm. I inch it closer and closer, my fingers stretching as far as they can. When it's so close, Lias' head turns.

The weapon I'm reaching for transforms into a writhing cobra, its fangs bared as it locks its eyes on me. A whisper inside my head tells me it's not real, so I shut my eyes to block out the image. My fingers close around the hilt and in a split second I swing it around so it slices through Lias' arm, hitting bone.

He doesn't scream, but the inhuman sound he lets loose sounds worse.

Kairo turns and sees his wounded warriors. He may well be the only one unharmed. "Lias? Katrina? You're all weak!" he spits in disgust. "Do you realize you're losing to four teenagers?"

"Who have powers," a young woman mutters in excuse.

"So what?" He lets out a battle cry that must be code because they all duck and flatten themselves against the ground.

It's an open fire.

Rain screeches as a bullet streaks past her ear. It slices off a strip of skin, turning her ear crimson with blood. A silver flash is headed straight for Luke's chest. His reflexes save his life, but he's still disoriented and it shoots straight through the palm of his hand. His mouth is open, silently screaming, as he clutches his left hand. I cringe at the shard of pearly white bone poking out.

I freeze in terror when my eyes turn to Marina. Several bullets are traveling speedily towards her. My nails cut into my palms with fearful anticipation, but somehow, she's not hit. Marina looks stunned at her luck, not even noticing that one ripped a gash in her jeans and brushed against her leg, tearing up the outer layer of skin. By some magnificent force of sheer luck, I haven't been hit in anyway, yet.

We should all be more damaged. We should all be dead.

With bullets flying everywhere, they can't all miss. Even in his blinding fury, Kairo has a dead-on aim and by now, at least two of us should be bleeding to death with our hearts barely beating.

The other fighters slash steely swords, shoot arrows, and throw yard-long spears, all with impeccable aim, but it's like someone invisible is knocking them off course. Only the bullets do minor damage and even that is nowhere near fatal. It's not as noticeable as before, but I suspect whatever held the weapons from reaching Rain before is activated again now.

Kairo takes a step closer to me, his eyes flashing like a madman.

"No," I protest in exasperation as his eyes dart to the almost healed wound in my leg.

He grins manically, the fact that he's losing a battle miserably, twisting his mind beyond reason. "Oh, yes."

Panic erupts inside me, and I know the barrier shielding me has fallen apart. The silver gun is aimed. The bullet clicks into the chamber. Kairo's finger pushes down and smoke puffs out with a booming explosive sound. My thoughts don't translate into actions quickly enough, but I have just enough time to stumble backwards. Searing pain agonizes my foot.

I can't hold back the scream. It feels like my foot is shattering.

"I've had enough of this!" Marina declares.

She plunges her strange dagger into Kairo's side, ironically in just the spot he stabbed her with the same weapon. As Luke and Rain hold off the others, she furiously twists the blade and drives it deeper. Kairo's cry of pain is a cross between a scream and a howl. He knocks Marina off her feet as easily as if he's flicking away a fly and hurls the dagger at her head, the hilt contacting with her skull.

"We have more important things to do right now," Katrina says calmly. "They're injured enough for now, but don't worry, there's always next time."

Kairo clenches his hands so tightly they turn pure white, but reluctantly retreats, sense returning into his warped features. The scar burned onto his face stands out more prominently than ever. Before they change their mind, I break into a limping run and drag the others with me. I was right. Kairo did change his mind. He can't keep his anger pent up that long.

The gun is hidden in his robe for now, but he looks powerful and threatening with an army charging behind him.

We trip over our own feet running through the forest. Marina's and my legs aren't in the best condition and Luke's left arm hangs uselessly limp at his side. Rain's face is contorted in a grimace and whenever we try to say something, she needs it repeated multiple times to understand.

I find Marina's hand and her shaky fingers clasp around mine. Our hands are a mess of sweat and blood, but neither of us bother to notice.

My foot throbs in pain and her odd limping run shows the bullet that grazed her thigh is affecting her. Our only advantage is the dark enveloping us. It makes it harder to run without tripping and falling, but the space we gained with our head start is filled with dark as black as ink.

A hand closes around my bicep and tugs Marina and me to the side. Luke whispers for us to follow a hidden trail zigzagging out for a ways and then looping back the way we came. It will certainly throw our enemies off track since we haven't once veered from the wide path straight ahead.

I make sure my footsteps are light and silent. My eyes strain into squinted slits when I try to see well enough to step around the dead leaves that pattern the forest floor. The direction we're taking seems new, even to Luke, and we'll undoubtedly get lost at some point, but that hardly matters when you have a choice of life or painful death.

The further we distance ourselves, the more the thundering footsteps and angry yelling fade, until they're no longer audible.

"Is it safe to stop?" Rain whispers.

"I think so, but we need to wait here for a while. Just stay quiet." He crouches down, but his squared shoulders and eyes that peer through the bushes show tense alertness.

I sit in the layer of leaves and twigs and Marina throws herself into my side. I hold her close and she shivers even though it's not cold, trembling because she's scared. "Don't worry, I'm here for you," I whisper in her ear.

Even though I can't see it, I feel the softness of her kissing my cheek. "This is like the island, when we first met Kairo," she says. "We've been through so much since then."

"I'm never letting you go," I say, holding her tighter.

"Are you still awake?" Luke asks quietly. "It's not safe to fall asleep."

"Yeah, we're awake," I answer.

His hand hangs motionless in his lap and his mouth twists in pain whenever so much as a leaf brushes against it.

"We should do something about the injuries," Marina suggests, reading my mind.

I stifle a yell as I yank my sneaker off my foot and peel back the sock. It's sticky and soaked with warm blood. In the pale light the moon provides us, I see not the color of flesh, but the dark color of blood. A gaping hole is opened right in the center. I can see the bullet buried halfway through my foot, revealing a sickening flash of exposed bone.

She gasps. "Carter, we have to do something! Do you know how to take the bullet out, Luke?"

"I can try," he offers, faltering.

I glance at his hand, where there's no need to remove the bullet. It shot straight through, making a clean hole that was surely agonizingly damaging. Luke reaches for my foot and I squeeze my eyes shut against the pain I know will follow.

"My hands are too big. One of the girls will have to do it."

"Marina," I instantly say.

"I'm not a doctor…I don't know…" she frets.

"You can do this, I trust you."

It hurts terribly, searing up to my ankle as her thumb and forefinger carefully draw out the bullet. I force myself to hold back even the groans building in my throat, not wanting her to feel bad. And it does feel better once the bullet is removed. "Thank you," I choke out.

"I should freeze the injuries. That might temporarily help."

She draws a small stream of water out of the ground and it looks beautiful translucently floating up to her cupped hand. She gently washes the gore from Luke's hand, my foot, Rain's ear, her own leg. Once only small drips of blood flow, she fills the wounds with a layer of ice to cleanse and slow blood loss.

The cold stings my skin, but I bear
otherwise infection could set in and l

"They've probably moved on," Ra

"Maybe, but we can't go back t
forlornly.

"What?" Rain turns her good ear c

"Kairo and the others expect us to
know where to find us."

"I think they've known where we
say. "The police are still after me,
attempt to catch me and later Kair
kidnap me."

"Well, none of us are in the condit
points out.

Luke looks up abruptly. "We can t

After the stealthy trek back to the l
returns carrying an armful of provisio
them into the backseat and jumps into
driving because her injuries are
avoiding a wreck. I ride shotgun with
the back. She pounds her foot down
surge out of the driveway.

The car flies down the gravelly ro
as a dizzying blur. Without our sea
bounce and jerk forward with each sw

"I don't have my driver's license!"

"It doesn't matter. The law is th
Luke reassures her.

I pull my seatbelt over my chest
and the others follow my lead. It's
narrow down the various ways of dea
my head.

We could get into a car accident.

We could get caught by the police,
being thought of as a murderer.

And of course, Kairo could easily tr

sten to the note?" Marina accuses.
t we'd come after you, and he'd try

ns. "But I was just trying to take
rything I could to save your lives. I
for. I don't have a girlfriend or go to
ould do fine without me."

We're all family now and *we* need

l and looks out of place in his pale,
ches his eyes. His bright blue eyes are
his blood-drained face, but they show
e again on the run, this time we're all
re better prepared and we will fight
ening my mom speaks of.

ing?" I wonder out loud. My question
l looks. "My mom talked about it," I
will lead to the rise of Serion power

silent, contemplating the newfound
ighs us down with lead-like dread.
e car's atmosphere like words and I
read them. The same thoughts race
nds: the same realizations, the same
was poured out in the fight and our
show no emotion to the conclusions.

as become a murderous villain.
e created the illusion that sent Rain to

al. It's something unknown, but it will
ructive. It's something we must stop.
to ask what we'll do, Marina gasps as
e. She screams, her eyes glued to the
on the breaks. I follow her gaze as the
y halt, the smell of burnt rubber filling

the air. Standing only inches from the hood, Kairo appeared out of thin air in the middle of the road with his army crowded menacingly behind him.

"Marina, just drive!" Luke commands.

She's petrified, her arms trembling. I notice the bump rising on her forehead caused by the impact of her dagger. She's probably nauseous, but I know the main reason is that she doesn't want to be responsible for another mass death.

"Drive," Rain pleads.

She closes her eyes tightly and surges forward. Most everyone lunges out of the way in time, but a solitary figure is caught in the headlights. The boy looks maybe thirteen or fourteen, panic in his wide eyes. From the side of the road, a woman with multiple piercings on her cheek screams in horror, probably his mother. I reach across Marina and slam the heel of my hand into the wheel so the horn blares.

The boy stays frozen, too scared to know how to move. His mother runs for him, yelling furiously, but it's too late.

The bump our wheels tread over churns my stomach. Beneath the engine's roar, I hear the crunch of bones being crushed beneath the weight. Marina's eyes fly open, again on the road, and she shrieks between a series of sobs.

"I –k –killed him," she cries. "They're all dead. I killed them all!"

She's having a flashback of when everyone drowned under her sheet of ice. I'd taught her to understand that everything was an accident and she wasn't a freak or a killer, but today's trauma has set her over the edge. She leans her head into my shoulder, tears staining the cloth. I grip the steering wheel and steer for her so we don't crash into a tree.

Looking back, I can see the crumpled lifeless body, the woman crying over it. I can guess the boy's story. He came from a broken family, his mom craving money or power. He was helplessly dragged into this mess. He was innocent, and it was just terrible luck he was the one to be killed.

"I killed them," Marina repeats in a whimper.

"No, Marina, it's not your fault," I tell her. It doesn't seem to work so I lean towards her, brushing a kiss against her jawline and say so softly the others can't hear it, "I love you."

That knocks her out of the trance. Tears shine on her cheeks and I wipe them off with my thumb. I kiss her softly, but Luke clears his throat.

"Sorry, guys, but you need to keep your eyes on the road."

She regains control of the wheel and I lean back into my seat. The headlights seem dull in the darkness, barely illuminating the dusty road. It's an old path twining through the forest, leading away from anything resembling city. There's no trace of Kairo, but it's clear he transported himself in front of our car. He was able to bring the others with him.

This Awakening is feeding him strength and power.

I can only hope that since we're Serion, it'll do the same for us. Otherwise, we're outmatched. He'll be our rival, but also our superior. Unless we develop new abilities, Kairo will easily be able to overpower us and he'll get everything he wants.

"Are we ever going to stop?" Rain questions.

I realize that I fell asleep, my neck sore from being turned at an awkward angle. Marina's eyes strain to keep open and stay focused on the road. They're shaded gray with exhaustion.

"I can drive," I offer, but the ache in my foot reminds me why I didn't in the first place.

"We should find a hotel soon," Luke suggests.

"You should've said that before I drove into the middle of nowhere," Marina mutters. "And Luke, I think your car's running out of gas."

"You've got to be kidding me!"

I can feel the car slowing as it reaches empty. The engine gives a few determined grunts and then it just stops. Marina twists the keys in the ignition, stamps on the gas pedal several times, but nothing revives the car. She sighs in exasperation.

"There might be a spare gallon of gasoline in the trunk," Luke says with his hand on the door.

"Well, is it safe to go out there?" Rain worries.

"Yeah." He adds in a barely audible whisper, "I hope." Luke lugs a gallon of gasoline from the trunk and sets it down on the road. "Carter, you and I will search the area and Marina and Rain can fill the tank."

"Be safe." Marina locked away the fear inside her, but her eyes show where it's trying to escape.

"I promise, I'll come back."

Luke and I walk a little further down the pot-hole filled road and then venture into the forest. The moon is a bright silvery circle in the sky, providing the only light in this deserted area. I'm not sure what we're looking for, or what we'll find, but I move tensely, my eyes boring into the shadows.

"Are we supposed to be finding a city?" I question.

"Maybe, but I've never been here before. We might just have to stay in the car if there's nothing around."

"So no going back, huh?"

"Not unless you feel like dying." Luke gives a short laugh at his own sarcasm, but it quickly silences.

These woods, under these circumstances, are not a place for laughter. We need to be on guard and aware of any attacks. I gulp back a yell every time a spiky pine branch brushes against my arm. I jump to my feet every time I stumble over the ragged, unexpected terrain. I constantly peer over my shoulder, just waiting for something to lunge from the darkness.

"This seems pointless," I sigh when we still haven't spotted a single city light.

"We'll just have to drive. There's no point in going in further."

We turn nearly in unison and I can hear that both of our footsteps sound heavy and exasperated. Falling leaves nest in my hair and a craggy branch scrapes across my cheek. It's far

239

too cold here at night, but the heat of determination, fear, and focus burns inside me. The wet ocean mist is absent and I harden against the biting wind, flicking it away from my face.

I can see the blurry light beaming from the car's headlights. It's blotchy through the trees, but I have to shield my eyes from the glare, unable to see Marina or Rain. We're only a few yards away when a sound prickles up my spine and my feet shuffle into a sprint.

There's a screech that sounds like nails digging into metal and then a horrified shriek cut short.

Chapter Twenty Seven

Marina

I pour the slimy gasoline into the tank and the unpleasantly strong stench fills the air. I pull the empty container away and shut the hatch, throwing it back into the trunk. Rain and I lean against the car, our eyes constantly searching the area.

"So was I missed when I left?"

"We were all worried about you, except Connie, who of course tried to convince everyone you were a lunatic. But forget about her; she's an idiot and a sleaze."

Connie's the girl who shoves down everyone to get whatever she wants. She's the backstabbing, bossy girl who tries to claw her way to the top, always trying to best me. Connie specifically despised me when the boy we both liked went on a couple brief dates with me.

"And of course, I missed all the parties, the surfing, and ironically, even the dances," I sigh.

"It's not like high school's over. When this is all through, you'll still have a couple years left."

"*If* this is ever over."

"It will be."

"I can't just pick up my old life again!" I exclaim. "I haven't spoken to my other friends in months and any relationships I had before are over. Carter's my boyfriend. Everyone will either think I'm some dangerous creature that wants to kill, or a delusional runaway who needs psychological help!"

"The best way to get over that is to face it head-on," Rain says gently.

"Facing it head-on can lead to misery," I scorn.

"That's a risk you need to take." She gives me a disapproving look. "You survived on an island for half a year with no provisions. You fought a crazy guy that can torture a person by simply looking at them and *won*, more than once! You can turn an inferno to ice without touching it. You can force water to shoot out of dry land. Come on, Marina, after all that you can handle anything!"

I hug her and it's like old times when we can share anything, our worst fears, her feelings for her boyfriend Hunter. Rain has always been like my sister, and I'm so glad I didn't leave her behind forever.

Drumming my fingers rhythmically on the car's hood, I strain my eyes to see into the forest. Carter and Luke are taking a long time, but nothing alarms me. Rain rubs her hands vigorously up and down her bare arms and her teeth chatter. The salty smell of the ocean doesn't linger in the air, but the cold still revives me and lifts my sleepy eyelids.

"What's that?" That tone, the one that comes just before you freak out, puts me on edge.

No more than fifty yards away, two luminous dots glow yellow. They're like a pair of eyes.

Slowly, the pin-pricks of reflected light move closer and I attach them to a dark shape. Another shape appears beside it, but without the glowing eyes it's harder to see. The headlights make it possible to eventually identify the creatures: a sleek gray wolf and a graceful deer.

It's so strange to see these two animals calmly walking beside each other as if they were friends that I'm taken off guard. The deer doesn't seem fearful and the wolf doesn't look to have any urge to attack. They prowl closer with such acute intelligence that I sense something isn't right. This behavior is abnormal for a deer, and it's even stranger for a wolf to leave the woods in solidary, unprovoked.

It's then I notice something foreign in both of their eyes: pain.

The deer gives me a pitiful look with wide brown eyes, but it's replaced by an odd sort of trance. It misses a step, its dappled brown and white leg faltering. The wolf's muscles ripple through its sleek gray and brown body with each step it takes. It's like they're both arrows strung back on a bow, just waiting for the string to be pulled so they can fly forward.

"This isn't natural," Rain breathes.

And then they lunge, bounding forward like they're on a mission. I know we won't be able to lock ourselves in the car in time, so Rain and I scramble onto the hood of the car and climb up the window shield. We dig our shoes in for traction and cling to each other, shrinking as far into the center as we can manage.

They come to a stop just before colliding with the vehicle. But of course, that's not the end of it.

Their claws scrape along the metal and make me cringe. The wolf pounces, flinging its agile body into the air over and over again. With unnatural ability, the deer follows, its branches of antlers colliding with the car as it bows its head. The next time the deer jumps, I stare into its eyes and see pain in its dilated pupils. I notice the repetitive nearly robotic way they move.

It's like they're being controlled and tortured.

The pain and anger thrives with the wolf's natural aggressive nature, but the gentle deer is merely being driven to madness. There's a glimpse of docile terror in its face.

This is cruel. Kairo shouldn't be abusing innocent animals to get to us.

"It's okay. We're not going to hurt you." I reach my hand out towards the deer, against the tip of its antler.

"Are you insane?" Rain shrieks.

The animal bows its brown head and lands softly on the ground, stopping its attack. Just when I've knocked the deer out of this craze, the wolf lunges onto the hood of the car and leaps up towards us. For one awful moment, it stands above us like an alpha with the wind lifting its gray fur, its eyes glinting like suns.

It looks almost beautiful.

Then it pounces, reaching out a paw armored with razor-like claws. Its claws rake down Rain's leg, drawing blood in four symmetrical lines. The other paw jabs into my arm and the talons press down until they're buried all the way into my flesh. The pain shoots down to my fingertips and throbs through my shoulder, making the world spin.

I'm aware of Rain being shoved off and the wolf's other paw is still raised, stained with fresh blood. Her scream sounds strained as she thumps onto the asphalt.

Its yellow eyes stare rabidly, and I scream as loud as I can. It's not out of pain or loss, but just pure terror. I'm not being held at knife point, burned alive with a raging inferno, or trapped in the sea as water fills my lungs, but this predatory animal seems scarier than anything I've ever faced.

It's because I can't reason with it or buy time. I just can't bring myself to kill it –it's one of Kairo's innocent pawns.

As it raises its paw, the fur sticking up in hardened bristles of red, I'm still yelling. When I feel four claws drive into my chest, I'm cut off mid-scream and all I feel is the horrible pain, spreading through me like burning acid.

Next thing I know, the weight of the wolf crashes off me. There's a thud on the ground and someone fumbles for the dagger in my pocket. When they've found it, they leap off the car, leaving me sprawled across the top. Another figure, only a dark blur in my vision, leans over me and pulls down the neck of my shirt. I'm too out of it to think of modesty as cloth is pressed to my chest in an attempt to mop up the blood.

The wolf gives an eerie howl at the white circle of moon and it's answered by several distant calls. It whimpers as if in pain, then growls as if it's fighting with someone.

I hear the bang of the window being shattered and see the stag's antlers covered in fragments of glass as it prances down the street and into the forest. I'm too weak to lift my head, but the sides of my vision begin to clear. Rain's perched on the open door with her arms hanging onto the car for balance. She picks at a shard of glass stubbornly imbedded in her hand.

Carter holds onto my hand and his eyes look almost watery. He lays his head against mine so our foreheads touch. My chest throbs, but it's become bearable.

"Carter." My voice is scratchy.

He lets out a loud breath of relief, throwing his arms around me. I yelp as his weight presses against my wound so he gives me some space. I take in the torn hem of his shirt and the cloth he clutches, soaked through with blood, my blood.

My shirt is spattered with crimson, but when I stare at the wound, my mouth drops open.

Right before my eyes, the cuts are closing. Only three claw marks are gashed into my skin. Within minutes, they've all gotten smaller and vanished all together, leaving only a lingering ache and splotches of gore. I'm dumbfounded by my miraculous recovery.

The fight playing out right below me jerks my surprise from the healing. The wolf stands triumphantly over Luke, whose face is pasty with terror. His blue eyes are wide and his breaths are ragged and cautious. At any moment, the wolf could strike and leave Luke, the closest thing I have to an older brother, dead.

My dagger is strewn a few feet away, just out of his reach. I trace the stained surface back to the bleeding injury in the wolf's side. It's deep, but not enough to kill.

Still, Luke stretches his long arm and the wolf jumps over it, jolting the car. In one pounce, the animal is again positioned over Luke with the dagger sliding far beyond hope. The shaking car falls back into place, but I'm slipping off the side. I scramble to regain balance, but it's to no avail. I fall helplessly beside Luke and Rain crawls next to me.

The three of us are as doomed as three hurt baby birds in a lion's den.

But the wolf is unaware of Carter.

He silently leaps off the car and sneaks down the road where he retrieves the dagger. Stealthily moving up behind the gray wolf, he raises the weapon. The moonlight glints off the silver and red of the blade and lights up Carter's features. His light brown hair is disheveled and his mouth pressed in a line, but his jaw is set with determination. His blazing eyes give way to a pained look, like he can't bring himself to kill the animal.

Then his eyes find mine, so full of pleading, and that's the deciding factor.

Carter brings down the Serion dagger and it stabs through the wolf's back. He pulls it out and drives it through the animal's skin several more times, maiming it past repair. The wolf's cry is sad and pitiful as it falls to its side and lays in a heap, writhing for an awful moment, and then freezing into a corpse.

Its yellow eyes are opened wide and seem to stare straight through me. Dark blood pools around its carcass from its teeth and paws, showing the damage it had done, and from its back and side, revealing the harm it had in turn received.

I tear my eyes from the destroyed creature and without a word, haul myself into the car, into the back seat. Carter sits beside me so there's not an inch of space between us. Rain volunteers to drive without speaking it, so Luke brushes glass off the passenger seat and slams the door shut. His window is a gaping hole framed by a jagged, glassy border. We don't say it, but the lack of protection is a hazard.

I feel something prodding into my side and recoil. Carter stares at his lap, stunned. A foreign weapon has appeared, right before his eyes. Narrow and lengthened, it's more of a knife than a dagger. The pure silver blade's edges have a slight rippling affect, like they're pulsating with heat. The lethal appearance and detailed hilt are very similar to my dagger.

The hilt of his knife is speckled with engravings, just as mine is. The familiar 'S' is there, along with an etched blaze of fire. An unblemished amber stone is implanted in the drawn flames.

Carter is in awe as he runs his hand lightly over the weapon. Luke and Rain take in the extraordinary weapon for a moment, but having experienced my dagger's unexpected appearance, they turn away, abandoned of the strength to form sensible words.

After a last admirable look at the knife, Carter carefully places it into his bag that sits on the car floor. Neither of us say a word, but it seems a great accomplishment for him. I know the weapons granted to us must symbolize something meaningful.

The engine revs and we continue our path, leaving the dead wolf behind.

It may be found in the morning, plastered on the newspaper as vets examine the body killed by man-made weapons. There may be detectives wondering about the killer or parents scared a criminal is on the loose, or maybe just a population thinking it was self-defense against a wild creature. That was the truth, but not the entire truth.

It was Kairo acting through the body of a wolf, torturing and controlling it to shape it into a vicious animal that would attack us.

"You healed," Carter says in awe.

"Maybe Serions heal in life-threatening situations," I guess.

We both look at his leg, which didn't mend itself naturally. "Or maybe you're just special."

He presses his mouth to mine and we kiss, not even caring that Luke and Rain are there, not even sure if they're noticing. His hands slide around my waist and mine reach under his tattered sleeves, resting on his bare shoulders. I catch sight of Rain's slight grin in the mirror and gently pull away. I feel Carter's warm breath on my face when he lightly kisses the tip of my nose.

"No more stops," Luke says.

"The tank is full so I don't see any reason to." Rain presses her foot down harder, racing well past the speed limit.

"Look, there's a light ahead!" Luke points forward.

Soon multiple lights come into view as we arrive in a small town. Our vehicle slows in front of a parking lot inhabited by only a few cars. There's a neon sign reading *Landon Motel*, with the '*a*' burned out and the '*l*' flickering. Behind it is two small buildings with dingy windows and doors with chipped paint facing the lot. Rain turns towards us with her nose crinkled in distaste.

"Do we really have to stay here?"

"Since there doesn't seem to be anywhere else, yes," Luke sighs.

We stomp into the motel like it's taking all our effort just to walk inside. We're so preoccupied that none of us thought this plan through.

A young woman with her hair piled in a messy bun is hunched over the front desk in boredom. Her eyes flick up as we shove open the door and she claps her hand to her mouth, stifling a scream. She backs a few feet away from us as if we're dangerous.

I curse myself for not remembering our condition. We must be an alarming sight: four teenagers with tattered clothing covered in blood. I brush off my own shirt, but the red pool is as stubborn as if it were sewn into the fabric. And just running a hand through the snarls of my hair, I know it's matted with gore by the way it comes back red.

"Costume party." Luke's so exhausted that his lie sounds bored, and he doesn't even stop to glance up.

"It's not Halloween," she stutters.

"Party after a play, I mean," he covers up, lighting up the elevator button.

"Excuse me, but you'll need to pay for a room."

He sighs, hastily whips out a credit card, and reserves a room just for the night. We're in a horrible state, miserable and throbbing with pain, as we stomp down the hall. The room is bland with plain tan and white décor, but it's clean and has two narrow beds and a pull-out couch. With everything that has happened, it appears as a palace.

Carter tugs open the bathroom cabinet and holds up a first aid kit triumphantly. "We have to be quick."

Fresh blood still flows from all of our injuries. While mine is clotting faster, Rain's pouring like a waterfall. So, we spend the next hour dressing our wounds –cringing, groaning, and talking about nothing in particular just to distract ourselves.

The warm cloth is soothing when Carter wipes off my leg. When he takes it away, my skin is finally visible, or what's left of it anyway. I'm faced with a mess of shredded skin and exposed tender pink flesh that shouldn't be showing. Every few seconds, new ruby beads form on the skin, growing until they expand and trickle down the sides of my leg.

"Well, now we're twins," I joke humorlessly.

"Not exactly," he says. "The bullet just hurt you on the outside."

He's right; the damage won't be long-lasting. I glance at his right leg, bandaged tightly from foot to knee, and the truth sinks in. Carter's never been the same after the first poison arrow, and since then our hardships have only done more damage. Even after years of healing, he'll never be able to run the same way. He'll never know when the pain could kick in and make him stumble and fall into the path of no return…

The thought of it makes me want to hold onto him for every second I can, so I grab his hand.

Carter tucks in the white bandage coiling around my leg and kisses my hand. "You're safe now."

As I smile, his face goes out of focus, and my temple pounds. "I'm dizzy," I murmur.

"Your head!" he remembers, and I remember, too.

Lias hurled the dagger straight at my forehead and luckily it wasn't aimed for a kill. The blade faced in the other direction, but the steel of the hilt was still solid enough to give me a concussion. My brain feels foggy and twisted, my head muddled with confusion.

"Just hold on," he instructs.

"I can't stay awake…"

***

If anyone stepped into a hospital room of weak, bedridden patients, they probably wouldn't notice the difference between them and us. In the bed opposite me, Rain is sound asleep with her head wrapped and the bandage tied in multiple knots around her ear. Carter is sprawled across the pull-out bed with his casted foot peeking out beneath the covers. Luke slumps in his seated guard position against the door, his bandaged hand motionless.

As he nods off to sleep, his eyes jolt open and he slams his head back against the metal door. He rubs the back of his head in irritation and forces his eyes to stay open. He notices me stirring, my head lifting, and seems surprised to see me awake.

"So the concussion's gone?"

"I don't even know."

"Look Marina, all this has done a lot of damage to us." He keeps his voice quiet as he crosses the room. "Sacrifices have to be made. You must have noticed Carter's leg will never be the same. You and I will eventually heal, but it will take time. As for Rain..." He takes a deep breath. "There's a good chance she could stay half deaf."

I'm momentarily stunned. "For –forever?"

He nods gravely. "But it could've been much worse. She still has one good ear and it doesn't physically disable her to move."

I drop my head into my hands, feeling the ridges of the bandage. "This is awful, all of it."

"It's not, not really. We're all alive."

"I shouldn't be."

"Don't say that!" Luke accuses. "You deserve to live more than any of us!"

"That's not what I mean. I'm just saying that it's not logical. Even with the way Serions have higher injury and survival tolerance, Carter's leg didn't heal naturally. We had to rush him to your dad before it killed him."

"Maybe it's only in fatal situations. What you think could lead to death might narrowly escape it."

I run my fingers over my chest where the wolf clawed at my heart. The contact only produces a faint ache, but I shudder as I recall lying helpless and seeing the animal's blood-stained paw aimed at me. A wound that would've been deadly left not even a single gouge, scar, or trail of blood just hours later. This goes far beyond luck or ability. This is pure species, pure power.

"You somewhat have resistance to injury." I raise an eyebrow curiously, just coming to the realization.

His face twists with bewilderment. "I know, but I just don't know why."

I know that after our conversation, it takes ages for both of us to fall asleep again. I toss and turn and ponder over that last thing he said. It's only when I imagine the rolling waves of a calm, crystal ocean rolling into shore that I'm able to relax. I drift out of consciousness with the rhythm of my imaginary waves, becoming one with each turn in their current.

"Can't we just stay one more night?" Rain pleads the next morning.

"It's not a good idea," Carter contradicts.

"Maybe it is," I say, smoothing the covers over the mattress.

"At least somebody has logic!" Rain exclaims. "Can't you see we're all in terrible condition? Leaving will almost inevitably lead to fighting, which we're in no position to do." She puts her hands on her hips and stares down Carter and Luke.

Luke isn't easily persuaded. "In here we're like sitting ducks."

She still doesn't free her steely gaze, arching her eyebrows, trying to make them reconsider. I know this look well. Rain has the ability to simply give you this look that'll persuade you into nearly whatever she wants. I grew up with this tactic convincing me to sneak out to that midnight movie premiere Mom said I couldn't see and letting her borrow my new magazines she ended up spilling purple nail polish on.

Often, I regret going along with what she wants, but a good percentage of the time, Rain tends to be right.

"Fine, one more night," Carter surrenders.

It feels like we're prison fugitives hiding out in a dingy motel and just praying the police won't catch us. Every time I order a snack from room service or step outside for fresh air, I hang my head low and avert my eyes. I fear that anyone could secretly be after us, even if right now they're playing innocent to fool us. At least the police no longer seem to be searching for Carter. I haven't heard a thing about it, so he must've by some miracle been deemed innocent.

By evening, the room still looks pristine. It's hardly noticeable anybody has been here. I wad up my old tattered clothes and toss them into a black plastic garbage bag. Rain and I went to the nearby general store earlier and purchased a new set of clothes for everyone. We're trying hard to blend into society and it's exhausting.

Because Carter and I are different; we're Serion. We have to hide our identities so the government doesn't catch on that there's more of us left alive.

During that entire epidemic where Serions escaped to Earth in an attempt for refuge, Kairo wasn't only after them, but the government wanted to rid Earth of potential dangers. I still don't know how or why Kairo caused the destruction of Serion, but I know anything involving our past has been sealed away. It's a miracle that Carter and I survived in a world where all odds are against us.

I can only wonder if protection and lies have concealed other survivors. Kairo, Katrina, and Lias all managed to make themselves invisible until it became necessary to come out of hiding. And I know that somewhere, even if it's in the past, a girl who I presume to be Serion was held hostage. And I bet she knew a life-changing secret.

Sometimes I feel that odd tingling nip at my arms or start to be pulled into a life-like scene. Sometimes I hear the rustle of whispers entering my brain, but I always push them away, staying true to our promise.

"Feel like a walk?" Carter suggests, looping his arm through my elbow casually.

"Sure," I exhale, not caring about possible danger.

He takes me to the expanse behind the hotel. It's like an alley, dark and drafty, with two metal garbage bins pushed against the wall, but behind that is a stretch of free forest. The fresh sent of pine adds chill to the air and I hear the soft squeaks of nocturnal animals. If I look past the alley I can see the beauty of this place, without dangerously being out in the open.

"I'm glad we're finally alone," I say. "I think…"

Carter spins me around to face him and pulls me against his chest, stopping me mid-sentence. He kisses me and I feel closer to him than ever. I don't want the kiss to end, so I pull closer, pressed tightly against him. I feel the strength of his arms as they wrap around me and his fingers twist locks of my hair. I smell his scent which is like a cozy cabin fire, just a hint of smoke.

His lips move against mine and I'm breathless. My fingers move down to the hem of his shirt and reach under it, resting against his sides. His skin is warm, but it doesn't burn me like it once did.

In the heat of the moment I feel loved and powerful. Together we are fire and ice, normally opposites and enemies, but we weld together so the other can flourish. We bring out the best in each other and combined, we are unstoppable.

"I love you, Marina," Carter says softly.

I smile and kiss him lightly. His hand caresses my face, his thumb rubbing against my cheek. His fingertips are callused and hard from what we've endured, but they're a part of him. And I love everything about him.

We find ourselves running into the forest, laughing as we race each other to a sturdy tree. I feel carefree and alive with the wind streaming back my hair and the burning stars pricking the sky above. It's times like this when I forget all my worries and all the danger and simply enjoy living. It's moments like these when I feel like a normal teenager, sneaking off on a secret date with her boyfriend.

He agilely leaps onto a low branch and grabs my hand to pull me up with him. We climb up a few boughs and sit in the center of the interlocking branches, like it's a cradle cocooning us. We're several yards off the ground, but I don't feel like I'm going to fall. Even if I do, I trust that Carter would catch me.

I lean into his side and he puts his arm around me, massaging my shoulder.

"I could stay here forever," I whisper.

"So could I," he murmurs.

I realize by the height of the glowing moon and the deep navy of the sky that it's late at night. I didn't see the clock when we left, but last I looked it was a little after eight. Rain had been showering and Luke had been throwing out the remains of dinner. I don't know how late it is, but I don't care. I would freeze this moment in time if I could, but I can't stay awake forever.

He kisses my neck and then trails up to my cheek. Carter puts his thumb under my chin and turns my face so he can kiss me.

I put my arms around him and my eyes flutter shut. My last thought before I fall asleep is that this is the perfect moment.

Chapter Twenty Eight

Carter

My stomach plummets as I teeter off the branch. I instinctively tighten my arms around Marina so she won't fall down. Then I realize how idiotic that is because she'd be pulled down with me.

I lock my legs around the tree and hoist myself up with my free arm, not allowing myself to tumble further down. The commotion makes Marina lift up her head and blink with confusion. She looks cute just waking up, her sparkling eyes already bright.

"Good morning," I say.

"Morning," she replies, stifling a yawn with the back of her hand. "How did we not fall out of this tree?"

"I almost just did," I laugh.

Gray sunlight shines through the hazy openings in the early morning Washington clouds and meets my eyes through the leaves. The lush leaves are beaded with crystalline dew that fell onto the top of my head when I disturbed them.

"It's only just after sunrise," she observes.

"You know, this probably wasn't the smartest thing to do. Stay outside, in the open, in a tree, all night long. And on top of that we were asleep for several hours."

"Well, we got lucky. Nothing happened."

"Don't jinx it."

I lay my hand on top of hers, my fingers stretching past hers. Sparks prickle on my skin and they're not the bewildering kind that periodically taunt me. This is what I felt when we first touched. It's what convinced me even more of my feelings for her. I know it's a reaction we share, and Marina turns her palm against mine and holds my hand.

She shifts her weight on the prodding branch and the outermost one finally gives out. It crackles in warning and then the wood snaps and clatters to the ground. It leaves behind a jagged circle of the soft white inner wood.

She yelps and latches onto me, clinging on so she doesn't fall off the few flimsy branches supporting her weight. I pull her into my lap with an iron grip so she won't fall. I have a brief flashback of my life-like dream, the one where I was pelted with stones and woke up just as I was falling from the heights of a tree. I still don't understand it, though I know it was a foreign thought implanted inside of me.

"Thank you," she says quietly.

"This is nothing after we've saved each other from drowning, burning, and bleeding to death," I say in amusement.

"That's true." She unexpectedly gives a short laugh. "Our lives are like fictional stories. It's almost like I'm watching a sci-fi action movie and seeing my favorite character win over and over again. I just hope it has a good ending."

"So your favorite character is you?" I try to keep things light.

"Maybe it would be you."

I find myself kissing her again with the joy of last night still fresh. The soft waves of her hair smell like the sea when I run my fingers through it. Her long, dark eyelashes brush my eyelids as her face is close to mine. I feel a surge in my chest like strength and passion.

When we separate I take her face in my hands and she flashes her white teeth in a bright smile. She moves her head to rest just underneath my chin and I cradle her in my arms.

"I'm just imagining what Rain will say when she and Luke wake up and see we're still gone," she says.

"Was she always one to jump to conclusions?" I say.

"She always wanted to jump to conclusions. She likes being dramatic."

I picture Rain's mouth falling slightly open as she gets a sly look in her eyes, ridiculous thoughts forming in her head. It makes me laugh out loud and I can already see her trying to convince Luke of whatever her newest idea was. Rain is generally sensible, but like Marina agreed, she has that dramatic side that takes over in situations like this.

Her expression becomes thoughtful as she gazes at the sky. It fades from pale pink to a gray blue with the yellow circle of sun just peeking up over a grove of trees. The world is a palette of pastels, but it feels fresh and invigorating. For once the chill to the atmosphere feels good against my face.

"Do you ever wonder what's attached with being Serion?" she says distantly.

"I guess we'll just have to wait and see."

"I'm just worried that something will change and we won't be prepared for it."

"Change isn't always bad."

"I don't want to lose you." Her lip quivers.

"Marina, we're surrounded with change. Each day brings new things to focus on and we're in the middle of the 'Awakening', but that doesn't mean you're ever going to lose me. I'm never going to leave you. Anything that happens, we'll make it through."

"I'm not ready for anything else to worry about," she sighs.

"You're the strongest person I know," I tell her truthfully. "Look what you've overcome. You can do anything and I know that no matter what, you'll survive it."

Her eyes glitter bright as jewels with inspiration. She leans into me so her hip presses against my stomach and I dip my head down to kiss her collarbone. Her eyes close and her face is framed by windblown hair. Her lips curve up and she looks so serene that it pains me to know that this could be shattered at any moment. We never know when danger will strike like a viper.

But it's Marina who giggles as she swings down and lands on the ground as gracefully as a dancer. She tilts her chin up at me like she's taunting me to follow her.

Soon my feet touch the ground and she takes my hand and drags me into a run. We move through the trees and the light sunrays that highlight her hair with gold make me feel safe and carefree, like all I have to think about is spending the day with my girlfriend. Like I'm a normal teenager caught up in the excitement of sneaking out of school and running off with the girl I love.

The alley behind the motel doesn't look as impending in the daylight, just dirty with traces of a foul smell from the garbage bins. I hold her to a stop and say, "As much as I'd like to stay here, it's probably mean to make Luke and Rain wonder if we got hurt."

"Well, I'm sure Rain will be full of questions," Marina replies. "Do you really want to face that?"

"I think I can handle a few questions."

We mount the stairs covered in thin brown carpet, and it sounds like we're stomping down the soundless hallways. I wonder if the closed olive green doors just hide empty rooms, if we're the only four guests at the Landon Motel. Delicate spider webs laced across a light in the ceiling remind me that this place sits in a remote area where only desperate people like us would resort to staying.

They must be incredibly starved for money to allow four teenagers covered in blood and grime to stay here without questioning our lame, I now realize, cover-up story.

Luke is the only legal adult among us. His presence probably kept them from stopping us. Besides, I can tell we startled the secretary by the apprehensive look in her eyes every time we ask her for assistance.

"I just noticed, our injuries seem better," she points out.

My bandaged leg didn't feel a single stab of pain all through the night, through the run, the climb. Marina stubbornly yanked off the wrap wound around her head yesterday and opted for a small Band-Aid, which disappeared shortly after. Now there's just a raised bump bruised light gray ebbing into her hairline. Clearly, the concussion is long gone.

"I guess high pain tolerance can mean faster healing. See, being Serion has benefits, too."

She raps on our door and Luke appears seconds later with Marina's dagger held close to his body, pointed outwards.

"Whoa." I take a few steps back, taken back by the weapon.

"Sorry," he sighs, the creases of worry fading. "You can never be too careful."

I step over the threshold expecting to see a room packed and ready to vacate, but instead it morphs before my eyes. At first it's like viewing a movie taking place on an entire wall, but then we float in another place. Our feet aren't connected to any ground, though I don't feel like falling. None of us move a muscle, stunned by the sudden shift.

A woman's silhouette is visible and she seems terrified, clutching her head as if what she sees is horrifying. The vision focuses down on her hand, which is furiously scrawling down words on a scroll of paper.

Leaving her crying, I see a planet with a surface of mottled oranges and blues explode in a column of fire, a flash of light. Heavy rocky pieces of its ground drop down through the emptiness of space and many tumble to nowhere. As a familiar globe comes into view, a few of the remnants of Serion intrude Earth's atmosphere. The largest rock embeds itself in the sea and grows into an island I know all too well.

The sloped hill of sand and cliff of killer rocks bring about a powerful punch of memories. In a dizzying whirl, the sky repeatedly changes from night to day. Implying it to be years later, small ripples wave through the air around the island and travel outwards. They're as unnoticeable as heat waves, but I sense the power radiating off them and the change they will bring.

I know in my bones that harnessed correctly, it can strengthen and bring about new abilities. I'm shown faceless figures pouring from the mouth of a cave, sensing the change and erupting out of hiding.

The scroll fills the space all around us, but all but two words are blurred out. *The Awakening.* Then the fog lifts and reveals another handwritten script near the bottom of the page. *Destruction, oblivion, extinction of the human race.*

My heart plunges into my stomach at the last phrase.

This is the Awakening. It is the prophecy that drove Kairo and his band of followers to come into power. It's what took a shock and made it into a threat. It's what took a trauma and turned it into a life-risking, half oblivious war.

The Awakening is the beginning of a treacherous time that may have no escape. It's the start of the Serion fate set in stone.

We burdened humanity with our presence and our perilous future. If the plans succeed and all the humans are killed off in one bloody, gruesome war, it will be entirely our fault. There's no way of dodging the complete truth in that, no matter how ashamed of it I am.

The images fade back into the motel room, but those handwritten words are engraved inside me. I see the black ink forming curls and loops of letters every time I blink. My heart is heavy and my stomach churns with the knowledge of what we're up against, who we have to fight. I never imagined that torture I thought aimed only at Marina and I could be directed worldwide.

Marina curls and uncurls her long fingers into fists. Rain lightly taps her foot on the carpet, her eyes spaced out like black holes of nothing. Luke taps the flat of Marina's dagger into the cup of his palm over and over again.

We're all in some sort of shock. None of us know what to say.

The air is suddenly humid and I feel claustrophobic even in the open space. I clear my throat and suck in a large breath to keep from the possibility of hyperventilating. My temple pounds with the overwhelming thoughts warring to take over my consciousness. I don't know what to think or how to react. And the others are all as stunned as I am.

Then, the tingling begins as a prickle on the inside of my wrist. It spreads through my arm and becomes stronger as it moves through my body. It seeps into my bones and makes me shudder. It's like lead and liquid metal leaking into the cracks of my insides.

This time, instead of a strange sensation that confuses me, I can sense the disaster arriving. I know that trouble is on the way.

I can feel myself strengthening, my muscles hardening and my confidence in fighting a battle rising. I can sense myself getting a hold of control over my fire power. It's developing into more than ever before with new abilities and powers that I can train myself to use correctly. My mind opens and lets in knowledge, as if lost memories are zipping through the air and just waiting to be implanted inside.

Everything is falling into place.

This vision awakened something inside of me. I no longer float between two worlds, a human boy cursed with explosive powers, a shocking past, and a pack of killers determined to track me down. I'm now the true Serion I was born to be.

And with these new abilities comes the alarming realization that we're on the brink of elimination.

"We have to leave, right now!" I command.

They're startled out of the stupor by my authoritative voice and stumble behind me. We sling any necessary supply bags over our shoulders and I pocket the room's first aid kit. We leave behind the bag filled with our old, torn-up clothes. I feel a stab of sympathy for the maids who will find shirts and pants ripped to shreds, hardened with patterns of dried blood.

Deep inside me, I find the knowledge that taking the main route down the elevator and through the front doors will end badly. Instead, I spin on my heel and dart back into the room, confusing them all.

Marina catches on first when I throw open the window and within a minute we're all climbing down the fire escape. The black coat spray painted on the bars has chipped away and reveals iron stained with rust. We're able to cling to the ladder and swing ourselves down. Only Rain has to scramble for a hold when her hand starts sliding off the slippery metal.

I feel like a fugitive running from the law, and in a way I am a fugitive.

The second my feet connect with the concrete, I'm off running. Marina falls into step with me, our feet surging forward at the same pace. She reaches for my hand and as I take hers I can feel the energy coursing through both of us. We're combined, stronger together.

Whatever clicked inside me happened to her at the same moment. The Awakening that brought about new powers in Kairo has found its way into us.

Now we have all the potential to be equals.

Not just as a group, but one on one. Each of us should eventually be able to singly be Kairo's rival and equivalent.

Ultimately, the Awakening will lead to possible destruction and devastation, but it's also what enables us to put an end to that, with our heightened abilities. I'm not yet sure if the positives outweigh the negatives.

"What happened back there?" Luke squints as he scrutinizes me, the run not even affecting him. "You seem...different."

"The Awakening is what happened," Marina answers for me. "Can't you feel it? It's all around us."

"The Awakening." It's like Rain is testing the shape of the words in her mouth.

Behind us, far behind us, I hear the explosion of a gun. The shot doesn't collide with anything, but the sound is just as startling. I can picture Kairo angrily shooting his weapon at the sky when he finds that we've come and gone. Again, we've outsmarted him and now it's a whole other path he must track to find us.

"Here, this is yours." Luke passes the dagger to Marina.

"And this is yours."

I didn't even notice Rain was armed with my knife. I've had little time to study my personal weapon, but I find myself looking over every detail as I sprint through the forest. Marina's weapon may look more solid, but mine is thinner and longer. The blade gives the illusion of being wavy-edged like a burning flame. I can imagine it being heated, the blade radiating white-hot sparks.

The amber stone glows against the smooth silver. The fire etched around it almost seems to dance and flicker.

But when I blink away the glaze forming over my eyes, I see that it was just a trick of the light. The carvings are immobile and solid. What is engraved in steel can never be erased or manipulated unless it's burned or dented away. I have a hunch my sword is fairly immune to most damage.

"They're following us," Marina informs.

The hair on the back of my neck stands straight up in anticipation as I scour the open forest for any place to hide. In open daylight sneaking behind a tree would be pathetic, but we're in the heart of a dense forest with nowhere to go.

"Climb the trees," Luke directs.

"What? Isn't that vulnerable and–?" Rain begins. "Just do it," he says tirelessly.

He and I branch off into two plush trees side by side and boost up the girls until they get a steady hold on the branches. Then we swing ourselves up and climb as high as the sturdier branches will allow.

I tighten my grip on the branch, but the wood crumbles beneath my fingers. I'm left staring in awe at a blackened stump and sifting ash through my fingers. My hand brushes against Marina's and we both recoil. She rubs her red finger like she'd been burned and I shiver at the iciness that spreads through my hand. The branch supporting her is coated with patterns of frost.

"Our new powers –we've lost control," she gasps.

I cringe, not knowing how long this will last. With Kairo close, we're on the brink of a battle, so this is horrible timing. The images were sent by the girl who was speaking to us. When we shut her out, she used all of her strength to prepare this, to let us know what we are up against.

The awful timing was our own doing.

"Just focus, we can do this," I reassure her.

But there's another downside to this new loss of control. It's too dangerous to touch Marina, to be in physical contact with anybody. While the chill I feel at her touch is unpleasant, she could be burned just by me holding her hand. I imagine traumatizing her skin the way I was forced to permanently damage my leg just by hugging her.

The Awakening is a blessing and curse.

We may be Kairo's equals, but the one thing that drew us both to feel at peace with who we were has been snatched away. Even if this impediment is only temporary, our relationship was at a time all we had.

I know the same thing dawns on her by the melancholy smile she bravely gives me. And startlingly I'm reminded of another miserable reality I was recently faced with. My own mother basically told me I was the biggest mistake of her life.

Marina, reading my pain, says gently, "Carter, I'm here for you. And you still have your father."

"But she wasn't always like this," I say, certain of it.

"Kairo can twist even the best people's minds." She shakes her head sadly.

An arrow cuts through the air just centimeters from my face and imbeds itself in the wood beside me. My hand brushes against my forehead where the rush of air still prickles. I gulp down the foul taste of bile that stings my throat.

Whether it coincidently hit this tree, or they've tracked down our location, they're close. And this time I don't know if my powers will fail me.

Through a tangle of dense leaves, I can glimpse into the closest tree. Rain looks like a koala clinging on as if her life depends on it, which, I realize, it does. Luke is agilely balanced with his feet spread on different branches and his hands gripping higher ones. He's in a stance prepared to jump. He cranes his neck to look through gaps in the foliage.

"Jump," he whispers through gritted teeth.

"What?" Marina says like he's insane.

"Just jump," he pleads. He looks scared of the idea himself, but forces himself to stay level-headed as he shuts his eyes and springs to the next tree for demonstration.

Marina trembles, but together we brace ourselves as far as the tree will allow and then launch off into the next tree. There's a moment when I see the ground rushing beneath me that I imagine hitting the dirt at the wrong angle, snapping my neck, but then my feet collide with solid wood and I latch on. For an awful moment, she stumbles, but quickly regains her balance.

Rain is left in her starting point with a sheet-white face. We all look at her as a prompt to jump, but are only met with her vigorously, defiantly shaking her head.

"Please, Rain, please," Marina begs. "You can do it."

Taking a shaky breath, I see Rain's face light with a glimmer of hope. She crawls to the edge of her branch and as lightly as a bird, leaps through the air. With all her grace, I think she's going to make it.

Chapter Twenty Nine

Marina

Rain's hands close around bark and her left foot nestles itself into a notch, but when she tries to lock down the foot she rests most of her weight on, it hits a branch. A branch that's smooth and slick and narrow. Her eyes fill with horror as she yelps and staggers. She knows it's too late to catch her balance.

I gasp in horror as my eyes scan the long drop.

Rain's arms flail desperately as she falls backwards. Luke and Carter have pained expressions, but a scream bubbles in my chest. Luke claps his hand over my mouth so I don't give us away. His face tightens as we watch helplessly, unable to do anything.

Then, with a crunch that makes my stomach churn, she slams into the ground at a painful angle. She's sprawled on her back with her arms twisted above her.

Rain's face is pinched and vacant. She gags and then coughs up a spurt of bright red blood. It dribbles down her chin and drips into her hair, streaking the vibrant blonde with dark red. Her agonized eyes search through the trees and scan our faces, finally locking on mine. She gives a tiny smile that closely resembles a grimace like a sad farewell.

Her eyes roll back into her head and close. The ragged rise and fall of her chest becomes more and more subtle until it reaches a point where if she's still breathing, it's so shallow I can't tell.

I can't bear to stare at her body any longer so I bury my face into Luke's shoulder and silent tears roll from my eyes. He rubs my back in attempt to console me. I want to feel the comfort of Carter's hand in mine or his arms around me, but I know he can't touch me right now.

"Marina, we're here for you," he says instead.

A voice raises from the edge of the forest, but I'm not ready to move on. Pain gnaws at my heart and I feel rubbed raw. I can't believe what I just witnessed. It doesn't seem real. It doesn't seem possible. It seems too horrid to be real.

This is the girl who has been my best friend for my entire life.

Rain.

Now she's…

"She gone," Luke says tenderly. "You can't give up yourself because of this. You can't sacrifice yourself. Don't do that to Carter and me."

"Stay strong, Marina. We need you." Carter's voice is so gentle, so caring.

I give a tiny nod and suck in a deep breath to fill my aching lungs. We catapult ourselves through the tops of two more trees, landing perfectly. It's almost cruel irony when this is the exact way Rain fell…to her death.

We don't even pause for a second when we return to the ground. I take their advice and don't let anything hold me back from fighting for my life, but not long after, the forest lights up with the roving red lights and deafening sirens of police cars.

They speed over the unpaved ground and two black and white cars plant themselves on either side of us. Six policemen in total jump out and form a ring around us, all with their hands latched on guns. Guns that are focused on our foreheads.

"There he is, with his accomplices!" one man shouts.

"What do we do?" I hiss.

"Hands where I can see them!" the officer commands.

We freeze to the spot and raise our hands above our heads. I don't see any way out of this that won't get us in worse trouble with the law. The shackles they lock around my wrists are tight and restricting. I'm roughly pushed into the backseat of a car and Carter slams into my side. I grimace at the pain that flares through my arm at him just brushing against me. Luke is shoved into the other car and for just a moment we're left alone.

"Who would've thought it would be the police when we were running from Kairo," Carter says.

"How can we get out of this?"

The chief officer sticks his head in and drawls with a western twang, "You're not gonna."

I glare sharply as I imagine weeks in captivity, false trials for murder, and countless loose ends discovered as pieces of what-ever cover-up story I fabricate don't seem to add up. The one bonus is that it might save us from being killed.

With us, I doubt there is any true safe haven. We may fool ourselves into thinking we're off the hook, or temporarily find peace and tranquility, but it will never last. Prison may be the only thing that can shield us from death and disorder with its steel bars and advanced security systems. Still, with the Awakening taking place, I'm not going to get my hopes up.

The policeman is about to shut the door when he slouches over and grasps the handle for support. His back is to me, but I see beads of sweat dripping down his neck as he hunches over. I think it may be a heart attack, but then he collapses onto my feet.

His dead eyes stare at me like glass. His badge is marred black with the darkness seeping from the arrow piercing into his heart. This is it.

This is the Awakening when innocent human lives will be sacrificed, and not just to knock them out of the way. They will be targeted just as frequently as the Serions in Kairo's mission to take over. It may start slow, with mass deaths played off as freak accidents, but I can see the gruesome war that's on its way. And if things don't stop, it'll be inevitable.

A gunshot rings loud and clear and another officer falls dead before my eyes.

The Awakening; the Awakening of death and destruction.

"I have a plan," Carter says quietly, close to my face. "I might be able to melt the handcuffs."

He rests his hand on the seat so there's a space between his wrist and the metal, and I watch the steel sizzle as it heats up. Sweat sheens on his brow from the focus, but I see drops of the metal turning to liquid and smoking as they trickle onto the upholstery. When the shackles look flimsy, he fluidly pushes his arm through the metal and wipes the residue on the back of the car seat.

It oozes down to the floor like molten lava. Carter's wrist is red, but it isn't burned. He isn't in pain. Obviously, that doesn't reassure me.

He licks his lips like his mouth has gone dry. "Are you sure you trust me to do this?" he asks shakily.

"Y –yes," I stammer.

My eyes lock on him and the metal begins to simmer. The process is identical to how he freed his own hands a moment ago. Then, I feel a prickle in my wrist which soon turns into a scorching agony. Instinctively, I thrust my hand up, and it passes through the liquid metal, searing my skin.

The pain is so strong that I can only let out a breathy gasp.

Carter looks horrified. "Freeze it, Marina! Freeze it!" he commands. I listen, but my attempts come to no avail. The pain tears away my focus. "You can do it!" he encourages.

271

My wrist still blazes, but it seems slightly soothed, slightly more subdued. I'm shocked to see my wrist encased in a chunky block of ice when all I hoped to do was freeze a path of frost over the burn. I can feel water absorbing into my skin and repairing, but the damage has been done. The angry red screams at me through the blue tint of the ice.

"I'm so sorry," he whispers. He looks close to crying.

"It's fine…" I murmur, trembling. "We're not stable."

"I burned you…" He stares at the molten metal like he's going into shock. His lips are parted like he's about to speak, but can't find the right words to say. The gold flecks in his eyes shine brighter than ever, but now with unbearable self-disappointment. "*I hurt you.*"

"Carter, *Carter*, it's fine," I repeat.

"This is going to keep happening, but next time it could be worse. I'm dangerous."

"You promised me you wouldn't leave again!" I say fiercely. "I'd rather die than have you abandon me again! It's just a little burn, it'll heal."

"I promise I'll never hurt you again."

"You can't make promises like that. It was an accident. You don't have control –"

"Exactly. How can we live like this? Our best self-defense mechanism could result in hurting each other! Let me rephrase that, I can survive a little ice, but my fire could literally kill you!"

"A little ice? So I'm not as good as you!"

"No, that's not what I mean!" He claps his hand to his forehead in exasperation. "You've done a lot of amazing things and saved us countless times, but I'm more destructive. I can't help it. Water and ice preserve and clean, but fire burns and *destroys*."

"We will find a way to live."

"I can't live knowing that any day I could be the cause of your death!"

"We have more important things to do right now!" I hiss.

It's a miracle that our uprising hasn't been heard by now. All but one of the policemen have been struck dead. Just as the thought passes through me, I see an explosive bullet shoot straight through his chest and send him to the ground. The booming sound is delayed and follows a second later.

"We don't have much time," I say, not looking at Carter.

Before consulting with him, I make the sprint for the other car. From practice, I keep a light, soundless spring in my step and then throw myself into the open door. Luke gives me a questioning look as I scour the bag strapped to my back. My hands close around the hilt of my dagger.

The handcuffs will remain, but I may be able to separate the chain linking them together. If only I'd thought of this before.

Just as I raise the dagger, Luke says, "Wait."

I falter and respond, "I understand, you don't trust me to do this."

He swallows. "No, I do. Aim well."

The blade strays dangerously close to his left hand, but it hacks through the metal cleanly. He swings his arms as if the restraint already made him restless.

"They're almost here," I tell him.

He gives a swift nod and we both jump to the ground, heading further into the trees. I look over my shoulder and see that Carter's taken the cue and is right behind us. I can hear the rustle in trees as Kairo and the others burst into the clearing where we just stood, but we've covered ground quickly and are out of their sight. All they'll find is a destructed scene of their handiwork: dead officers and empty cars.

We run and run, and I wonder where there is to go. The answer is clear. There is nowhere to go. Our only escape is to keep running.

Because wherever we go, they will find us. We are never truly safe. We must stay on the move and then we'll have a chance at survival, but there will always be a chance of death.

Even if we slip out of Kairo's clutches, there's danger in the risks we must take.

I saw that with Rain.

She died with bravery and consideration beaming from her. She took a leap of faith to support me and leave her life behind: her parents, her home, her boyfriend. Still, I feel she didn't live her life to the fullest. She had a radiance full of potential and dreams for the future. All that enthusiasm and bright talent was wasted in one misperception...

I force the thought of her away. It's a distraction that will slow me down, a thought that will bring tears.

We run until darkness falls, hardly stopping. We run until my legs are numb and my lungs feel raw and burned. I stumble, but catch myself just before I go sprawling face-first into the dirt. Carter isn't so lucky.

His damaged leg gives out and he falls to the ground with a muffled cry of pain. He looks deteriorated and beat-up so I gratefully come to a stop and lean over him. His face is glossy with a layer of sweat and his mouth twisted into a grimace.

"Are you okay?" Luke asks. He's tired and breathless, but seems urgent to keep going.

"We can take a rest," I speak up firmly. He reluctantly crouches beside me.

"I'm –I'm okay," Carter assures. Even his voice is strained and scratchy and he stammers out the words.

"No, you're not okay. You can't keep running on that leg right now." I reach out to touch him, but he recoils, and I remember why.

Instead, Luke props him into a sitting position and he catches his breath. Carter's hair is spiked and waved in disarray and he's hunched over in pain. It kills me to see him like this and not be able to squeeze his hand to tell him everything will be alright.

"I think we should rest for the night," I tell Luke.

We sling Carter's arms over our shoulders and he limps between us. The only place remotely sheltered is the space surrounded by a tree trunk, shielded by dense leaves overhead. Carter slouches over with his back rested against the trunk and his eyes closed, sleep instantly overtaking him.

I'm restless and only sit beside him after pacing back and forth for several minutes. I resort to mindlessly drumming my fingers on the soft soil.

I yearn to lay my head on Carter's shoulder, to place my hand on his, to kiss his cheek.

Luke sees the longing in my eyes and says, "There's heartbreak in every love story. You're just lucky yours doesn't come from one of you not feeling the same way."

There's a note in his voice that makes me think he speaks from personal experience. "Were you in love once?" I ask quietly.

"Yes." His blue eyes fill with reminiscence. "She was beautiful and I thought we were in love, but I don't think I ever noticed that she wasn't as sincere as I thought. I found out she'd been dating another guy and she broke up with me. I always hoped that maybe one day I'd see her again, and he'd be out of her life. Maybe she'd feel the same way about me as I felt about her, but after high school I saw something in the paper. She'd been killed in a car crash."

"Luke, I'm so sorry."

His head hung low, he replies, "There's no need to be sorry. That was the past."

The more I learn about Luke, the more I understand the broken, bruised demeanor that used to sometimes surface. His entire life was traumatic and full of tragedy, with anything seemingly good turning out to be a lie. At least I got close to fifteen years of blissful ignorance, whereas he got none.

"You and Carter are lucky. It's obvious that you two are in love. Nothing can break you apart."

I sigh heavily. "I'd love to think that, but you never know. I don't know what tomorrow will bring. There was more written in that letter shown to us. What the words say are what I'm scared of. The Awakening made it so that we can't touch

275

each other, for now anyway, and this is only the beginning. I know that there's worse to come."

"Maybe not."

I can't think of a response, so I just study the patch of red scarring my wrist. Then a question crosses my mind. "How did we not think to take the car?"

"It would've been pointless anyway. Kairo would've caught us if we'd gone back."

"Isn't your dad going to be mad that we left his car?" I mumble sleepily.

"Nah, I doubt that's what he'll be worried about."

I find myself abruptly exhausted and my head falls to rest on my hands. My eyes close and the last thing I take in is the fresh pine smell of the dark forest all around me.

***

"What is this?" Luke exclaims angrily.

His shout shakes me from peaceful sleep and my eyes focus on the arm he holds up to our faces. A jagged *S* is sliced into his wrist, red with dried blood. It's carved in the same script as the letter on Carter's and my daggers. The sight startles me wide awake.

"What is this?" Carter cries in disgust.

An identical mark is tattooed onto his wrist. My gaze trails down to my own wrist, and to my horror, I discover that the same disturbing mark is etched into my skin. It's the Serion symbol, but it's been written in blood and revenge. It is a symbol of our weakness and our oblivion to their power in the few moments we rest to regroup and recharge.

"It's meant to threaten us," I say with rage.

"How did they even get away with this?" Luke clenches his fist tightly.

"Maybe they drugged us," Carter suggests.

He's right. It would explain the drowsy, light-headed way I feel now and how we slept through the torturous letters being carved. The mark cut into my flesh seers with pain, flaring a bright red that twists my head with anger.

"Why didn't he just kill us?" I wonder in bewilderment.

Before either of them can answer, a high, beeping ring fills the clear air. It's a sound that I've been isolated from for months: the ring of a cell phone. Luke shuffles through his front pocket and slides his finger up on the glassy screen. We wait attentively as he holds it up to his ear.

"Hello?" He seems to have second thoughts as he presses speaker and holds it out for us to hear.

Dr. Corry's voice crackles to life. "I have news." It's a tone I can't read, but I know it must be urgent. It so consumed his mind that he didn't ask if we were okay. Truth be told: we're not.

"What sort of news?" Luke questions.

"I've been able to develop my research methods into more advanced categories, and I've discovered something new. I've told you things in the past that I was so sure of, but this research has proved me unmistakably wrong." I brace myself for what he'll say, almost trembling with apprehension. "There are two other Serions living on Earth."

"We know," Carter responds.

"What?" Dr. Corry exclaims in shock.

"Katrina and Lias," I say dryly.

"Katrina and Lias?" he murmurs, recognition somewhat clicking. I can imagine his eyebrows knitting together in confusion. "No, I discovered two people with Serion lineage."

Luke looks ready to contradict his father, saying that's what Carter and I just explained, but then the shock that I'd originally prepared for jolts through us as he elaborates, "Two teenagers. They're just like you."

Chapter Thirty

Carter

Teenagers. Not Katrina or Lias. Two people we've been oblivious to all along.

The initial wave of astonishment settles and I stammer, "Who are they?"

"I haven't been able to find out much yet," he answers matter-of-factly. "But I have been able to conclude that one of them is a girl who lives in Colorado."

When he says it's a girl, a retained memory of the mystery girl's voice sounds through my mind. I recall her silhouette, the visions she placed me into, and the cries for help she pleaded. The forest-set dream was vivid, and Colorado is covered in many beautiful forests. This Serion girl must be the one who spoke to us. She must be the telepath.

"And we need to find her," Luke states, but his uncertainty makes it sound like a question.

"I think that would be a good idea," Dr. Corry answers.

"Do you know anything about the Awakening?" Marina says.

"The Awakening?"

"Never mind," Luke interrupts. "Thank you for telling us that, Dad."

"You four stick together and I know you'll be alright."

A hush falls over us and Marina bites her lips and shuts her eyes to hold in any welling tears. Luke stares at the phone intensely, but instead of rattling off a sad explanation, he just concludes, "Bye, Dad, I'll talk to you later," and presses the off button hard.

"Why didn't you tell him?" I wonder.

"I'm his only son, and you two are the next closest people he's got to children. We're all basically on a death mission. He doesn't need anything else to worry about. He doesn't need to know that one of us actually... died." His last word is barely spoken under his breath, so faint that the wind seems to carry it away.

"Death mission," I say. "That isn't what this is."

"That's what anyone else would see it as."

Marina clears her throat. "What now? We can't walk as far as Colorado."

"Maybe we should just wait a little while before setting off and see what happens," I suggest, and neither of them object.

That's when I see the dagger stuck into the bark just above where our heads were. I creep around it, analyzing without touching, as if it'll hurt me if I do. It bares close resemblance to Marina's in make, but looks sterile and unused. The Serion 'S' is etched into the hilt beneath a black opal stone, but in a way neither seem to belong.

The stone is small and unperfected with a rough spot like a drop of ink clouding the surface. The S has been written with a talented, careful hand, but there's a shakiness that doesn't match the symbol on our weapons. The row of carved people walking forward in unison perplexes me.

279

They're like a row of toy army men lined up, their feet raised in a walk at identical heights. Their arms are synchronized in a subtle swing. Then, I notice the dead look that image somehow conveys in their eyes. And beneath that is a small grimace, like suppressed pain.

It's that observation that leads me to be certain: This is Kairo's weapon, but it was handcrafted, by *him*. Our weapons materialized in battle like gifts from the sky. That's when everything clicks into place.

By some great Serion all-knowing power, a weapon is given to each Serion at the right time. It's a time when they prove their bravery and ability, but also their compassion and willingness to sacrifice themselves. And those are character traits Kairo is near impossible of displaying.

I feel a twinge of guilt for him, pitying the fact that he had to forge his own Serion weapon just to feel self-worth. Though instantly, the understanding vanishes.

It's pathetic that he imitated our weapons just to feel powerful, to feel as good as we are. It thrusts him down to a new lowly level. Before he was cruel-hearted, but this basically kicks away all his cocky self-confidence, even if he'd never admit it. I'm sure he never thought I would figure all this out.

As usual, Kairo has underestimated me.

Marina breaks out of her conversation with Luke and notices what I've been so wrapped up in. Her head tilts inquiringly as she tries to understand the realization beaming from my face.

"It's Kairo's," I began, and quickly explain my theory.

When I'm finished, Luke chuckles, "I knew he couldn't be as powerful as he thinks he is."

"That's not the point." Marina narrows her eyes at the dagger. "He's just as dangerous as we thought, just not as self-confident. We may be a step-up when it comes to messing with his mind, but he's just as strong as ever. This doesn't change that at all."

Luke's thoughtful silence becomes a slow nod of agreement. "We should leave it here. It could be rigged or poisoned."

"Good thinking," I say.

"Danger always seems to follow us," Marina sighs.

"We can't help it. Serions have a link that Kairo seems to have learned how to follow."

"I feel bad for always dragging you along, Luke. Without us, you'd be back in Aberdeen with your parents."

"Like I said, this has always been a part of my life," Luke says.

"But we've only made it worse."

A low whistle rings through the tops of the trees and my head darts up. My eyes focus on trees, but their leaves conceal what's sitting inside. My first thought is that it could be a bird singing. Then another whistle sounds shrilly and I know that it's human.

None of us have time to react. I hear rustles in the trees and within minutes people have dropped from each and form a ring around us. Their steps are slow, but their expressions menacing, as they surround us on all sides.

Each of them is armed and the few gaps in the closing circle are so narrow that I'd inevitably get a bullet in the shoulder. We form our own ring, though it's pathetic in comparison. Our backs press against each other and each of us faces outward so we won't be caught off-guard from any direction. I feel the buzz between Marina's and my shoulders that only the thin material of our shirts block.

"Oh, and now there's three," Katrina says in mock pity. *My own mother.*

I can feel Marina tremble at the mention of Rain's death, and it takes all my strength to stop myself from shaking, too. Something has twisted my mom into a wicked, vile being that it hurts me to be near. Anything she does drives deeper and stings harder than even Kairo's ruthless attacks, because of who she is.

281

"And then there were two," Lias grumbles.

I know what's coming. My arm instinctively flexes up and catches the spear aimed at Marina's neck. I stab it into the ground next to me so it juts up like a pole.

"No, there are five of them," Kairo says with a poisonous glare. His jaw clenches and his cloak billows like a black cloud. The scar marring his face stands out like a beacon, making his look more threatening than ever.

They were here all along. They heard everything we said. Any plans we could have made are as good as burned to ashes. I feel terrible for the poor girl in Colorado who will now have Kairo unleashed on her. And we're either going to be rendered useless or in even more danger than before.

For a moment it's a stare down. I find my eyes locked with Katrina's –Katrina. In my head I call her by her first name, like she's someone I barely know; like she's just an enemy I'm barely acquainted with, but know I should fear. But calling her Katrina is fitting, because the woman she is now is not my mother. That pains me, but it's the cold, hard truth.

Then Kairo surges forward and I point my knife in his direction, but instead he passes us and yanks his dagger from the tree it was lodged into. He taps it into his palm and a flicker of self-consciousness glows in his yellowy eyes as he looks at me. He knows what I realized. I match his stare with narrowed eyes and a set jaw of determination. Kairo feigns a sly grin to appear invincible and rejoins the circle, poised for the attack.

In the calm before the rage, we are still. We are a circle ringed by another, small in comparison to the buried history of a planet we do not remember. My eyes scan over their faces, some hardened with coldness, but others shaky and unsure. I can predict who will strike first, so I swallow to rid myself of the thickness wadding in my mouth like cotton.

I can do this.

Something triggers inside me and my arm moves up fluidly to aim. I pull back my arm in a single motion and hurl the knife at its target. It collides with the exact spot I'd been betting on and I know that unintentionally, I spread heat over the blade before I let it fly, making it even more deadly.

Kairo shoots lasers from his eyes, strangling back a scream of pain. The knife drove into the side of his face, right in the middle of the burn. Thick blood slowly drips down the side of his face. It's so dark it's almost black.

He stoops to pick my knife up off the ground and launches it with such strength that it lands far away in the mix of trees, farther than I can see. He tilts his head up to the sky and lets loose a bloodcurdling cry of rage that's almost like a battle call. I prepare for his workers to strike, but then he looks back at me. His face is more intimidating than I've ever seen it, the blood making it look gaunt and ghastly.

"I knew that you were just like your mother. You hit me in the same spot she burned my face all those years ago, but look what she's become. For one day when you realize your true loyalty, I will welcome you, Carter Pyric. Your talent will be…valuable."

That sets me off. I fling my arm out in an arc, and everywhere my fingers point, sparks ignite. Fire flares high and thrives on the dead leaves and dry sticks strewn across the forest floor. It blocks the ring of our enemies, forming a blazing barrier.

"I will never be one of you!" I exclaim spitefully.

Kairo's next move takes me off guard. In a split second my hands are twisted behind my back and I feel the very tip of his dagger digging into my neck. The Awakening has strengthened him the way it did to us, but the difference is that he *is* in control. He's not consumed by raging powers that rarely agree to cooperate. He has figured out how to transport his entire body over distances without walking a step.

In my distraction, the fire dies down and soon what's left of it is pathetic. Even the stick-thin girl with a terrified expression could hop over it with ease.

They flood over the sparking blackened circle and rush at us in an avalanche. Any move and I'll end up with a blade pushed straight through my neck. Luke is unarmed and Marina is feeble with her powers taking control over her. I feel terrible rendering them almost defenseless.

But somehow Marina seems to shine in a moment of greatness, just as I did.

She knows summoning a flood would take too long and be too risky, so she decides on ice. I hear the crackling of limbs cementing into place and the outbursts of protest, but nobody gets far. The area becomes a field of glistening, pale blue sculptures with hints of color underneath. Mouths hang open in exclamation and some weapons are raised to the sky, mid-attack. One man was lunging forward and teeters slowly before toppling over.

The iciness at my neck stinging, I see that even Kairo's sneer is frozen into place. Other than Marina, Luke, and I, every person is immobile in a shell of thick, hard ice. Ice melts, but we are safe for the moment.

Then, I see something shift amongst the frozen people. The figure rises and steps forward with a haughty stride. She shakes ash and chips of ice from her sleek red hair and tosses it over her shoulder. She looks pointedly at Marina. "Fire is stronger than ice."

"Not always," Marina holds the stare and doesn't back down.

"Maybe not," Katrina inquires. "But then they are at least an equal match. That's why it would be so...*interesting* to see you two against each other.

"That will *never* happen," I say.

Marina and I instinctively reach for each other's hands to show our loyalty. Our fingertips touch and there's a sizzle of electricity, but it's painful and searing. We both uneasily pull away, and much to my dismay, my mother chuckles.

"Look at you. You can't even touch each other! You're destined to be rivals."

"We make

"Oh, think

the vision.

"I doubt it sa

"Maybe not in plain

intentional. I did know the woman who wrote that."

"Who was she?"

"And why would I tell *you*."

I see a flinch of movement past her left shoulder and suddenly I understand her dragged out conversation is just a distraction. Beneath the ice crusted over him, I see Lias' eyes staring through me alertly. His burly hand twitches and the stagnant field of ice mutates into a terrifying scene.

The ice shatters like glass, but the people revealed transform into grotesque, mutilated monsters. Their images are so horrific that it's past anything in my worst nightmares. Then, they turn on each other, tearing their former comrades apart. Their features are so disfigured and unnatural that I can't even use their most distinguishing features to tell them apart.

A severed arm flies through the air in slow motion. It's bloated with bulging blue veins and the fingers still twitch, clawing for my face as if it were alive. Marina screams and I find myself screaming too, with the images beyond reason.

I force the terror pounding through me to slow. I dig my nails into my palms until they draw blood. I slow the rapid pace of my mind and focus on what is real.

The melodic chirp of birds calling from the trees. The pinecone that falls from the tree and scratches against my leg. The creaking of the ice, the relentless dripping of water as it melts into puddles.

Then, the gruesome illusion lifts, just in time for me to see a man hurling himself through the air with a sword raised above his head and a snarl across his face.

I must have broken the awful illusion's power, because Marina and Luke seem very aware of the man speeding

...mbles for her
...ere is little we
... —so close to

... in front of us. He yells, "No!" at the top of his lungs, as if the word can freeze time into place. He thrusts out his hand and turns his head away from the impact, and my mouth falls open with awe.

The attacker is thrown through the air and into a looming tree where a pointed branch pierces his throat. The forceful wave reverberates through the area and knocks everyone opposite us to the ground, some sliding backwards or colliding into each other. They cover their ears as if the boom is a deafening sound, though it does nothing to save them from the blast pounding them into the ground.

My eyes grow wide as I turn to Luke's outstretched hand and realize that the immensely powerful blast came from *him*.

The aftermath is chaotic, a tangle of limbs and our enemies are battered and groaning.

Marina's stunned face is the picture of pure shock. "Luke...what did you do?" she stammers.

Luke finally lifts his head and the grimace that must've been expecting someone to be terribly hurt turns into astonishment. He points to his chest innocently, like we're accusing him of a crime. "Me?"

"Yes," she breathes. "It was you."

His vibrant blue eyes take in the incident he caused. His features wipe blank. He looks beyond understanding, his mind refusing to comprehend what he did. It won't let in the truth of what this means, what we're all silently thinking.

"It was me. I did this," Luke says. He blinks, the impact hitting him. "That's impossible."

"But it happened," I say. "And we've learned that next to nothing is impossible."

Kairo and the others are still too disoriented to have gotten much further then pushing themselves into a shaky stance and mumbling inaudible words to each other as they grip each other's arms for balance. It buys us time, but the three of us just stare at each other, oblivious to the world around us. We stare at Luke, seeing him differently.

We don't see him just as the boy who was kind enough to give up any traces of his former life to help us on a dangerous mission. We see him as someone else entirely, and what we see goes against everything we believed.

"Luke," Marina says slowly. "What you did was Serion."

Chapter Thirty One

Marina

"**B**ut...I'm not," Luke says in shock. "I'm just...not."

"Serion powers develop between the ages of twelve and eighteen," Katrina states. She's the only one alert enough to respond. "He's nineteen, making this impossible."

"Impossible," I chorus.

But it's not, because it happened. Luke bowled down an entire army by just slamming his hand into the air, not even intentionally willing it to happen. Not only did hidden power surface, but it proved potential to be stronger than all of us, including Kairo.

"He must be killed!" Kairo hisses softly.

"That could destroy everything," Lias says. "That boy makes five. Without him, she may never rise."

"There will be others!"

"There are not others!"

I see what is happening crystal clear. The knowledge that someone who is only just showing signs of Serion lineage and is already greater than him, is driving him to insanity. He simply can't stand to exist in a world where he doesn't rule. And his only solution is to kill, because to him, that is the only way to eliminate the problem.

"Go, Luke, go," I say just loud enough for him to hear.

He takes a few unnoticeable steps to edge away and then bolts into a run. With just the right timing and coordination, he swoops down to snatch a fallen black pistol from the ground, but hardly misses a step. Still, Kairo is determined to shoot him down. He gets a glint in his cat-like eyes and I know exactly how he plans to kill him.

My feet are flying over the dirt before my mind carries out the decision to run, and Carter is at my side. The army pours forward just behind us, but to our advantage, they stumble and slur their threats in a jumble of disorder. Luke is already far ahead, so I can barely see the back of his head disappearing over the curve of the hill. I don't see how we could possibly catch up to him in time.

Kairo sets his plan into motion and for the first time I see him transport from his starting point.

It's not completely instant –traces of him linger for a second, and even when he's gone, I squint and make out what I never noticed before. A faint black haziness that remains. It's like smoke in the way that it travels in a misty, camouflaged cloud through the air, catapulting straight towards Luke.

I take a chance and planting my left foot on the ground, throw my dagger right at it. I clasp my hands together in hope and motion for Carter to keep going. The haze falls and takes the shape of a man, gradually growing darker in color. To my surprise, my almost blind shot was perfect. The blade is lodged into his stomach, just below his rib cage.

It's a wound that could easily be fatal. He doubles over and clutches at his stomach. He gags with an awful sound and spits up mucus mixed with a string of red. This is undoubtedly enough to stop him. But this time I've underestimated Kairo.

He yanks out the dagger with a muffled cry of pain and jumps to his feet. His run is a stumbling limp, but somehow he manages to gain almost as fast of speed as us.

I focus on the horizon and sprint faster than I ever have before. My feet pound into the dirt and my arms pump at my sides. Kairo can't kill one of my best friends.

It makes it worse that the weapon is my own Serion dagger, and that the blade is already covered from the tip to the base of the hilt in Kairo's blood. It seems like we have lost so much already. Carter's mom is as good as dead, and Rain actually died. I can't allow Luke to come to the same fate.

The ground becomes rocky and I have to watch where I step so I don't trip. My feet scramble for traction as I realize where I halted just in time. The rocky ledge stops at a cliff and plummets into a steep drop. The bottom is masked in a veil of dense, gray fog, so I can't estimate the damage a fall would cause. I knock loose clods of dirt that spiral into the gray and for an awful moment I think I'm going to fall. Then, I jump backwards and land on my backside with unforgiving rocks poking at me.

Then, all too quickly, Luke takes the drastic measure. He glances over his shoulder at the army charging towards us and springs off the cliff. His rushed command, "Jump!" is lost in the wind.

"No!" I screech, but it's too late.

I look over the ledge, but he's been lost in the fog. It eats away at me that I don't know what happened to him. He took a risk and maybe it paid off, but I won't know unless I follow his footsteps.

Carter, who was standing a few yards away, comes to my side. He's takes a look at the army that's quickly gaining ground and says uncertainly, "Should we jump?"

I don't answer for a few moments. I take in the towering green trees and my gaze falls to the vengeful troop ruining the tranquility of the beautiful forest. The dreadful image of Rain dying repeats itself in my head, and I realize that if we jump, we could fall to our death just the way she did. Even if the height isn't treacherous enough, it just takes one wrong landing…

Still, the word I speak is confident. "Yes."

Because sometimes it's a risk worth taking.

Carter nods and I'm filled with an overwhelming urge to hold his hand. This time I can't fight it. I grab his hand and he doesn't object. I feel his fire and my ice intermixing and burning acidly all the way to my bones. The pain symbolizes all the loss, sorrow, terror, and heartache we've been through, but it also reminds me of the love, victory, and survival. It fills me with adrenaline and fuels me to take a risk.

Right now the pain is exactly what I need, but somewhere underneath it, I feel the loving tenderness of Carter's grip that won't let go.

We stand there for a moment with our hands clasped between us. Then we look at each other in silent agreement and the last thing I see before we jump is the twinkle in Carter's beautiful eyes. And then we're falling.

Our hands stay locked together as we tumble through the air. My stomach feels hollow, and the wind carries away my erratic puffs of breath. The wind rushes against my face with such intensity that it feels like it holds the strength to rip off my skin. It stings my eyes, so I shut them reluctantly, wanting to see what's coming ahead, even if it's the opposite of what I want to see.

Next thing I know, I'm plunging into icy cold water. My eyes fly open, and I see rippling blue surrounding us. It strengthens me, seeming to wash away pain in any injuries I was too distracted to notice before. The floor is rocky and we would've been impaled if we'd sank just a few feet further.

Carter's and my hands have been forced apart, and I see his panicky face through the curtain of my hair floating around me. Not only is he running out of air, but the current is rapid and unpredictable.

I just realize that as the perfection of being underwater is crushed. The array of rocks speed up as we're tossed above them. Carter and I are like rag dolls being thrown around, but I don't see Luke anywhere. I whip my head from side to side, but he's nowhere in sight.

I turn my head back just in time to see the river's winding path turn sharply. The riverbed's sides are crusted with rocks and Carter's head is bashed against one. I scream, but the sound is lost in a stream of bubbles. His eyes roll back into his head and the water washes red from his hair. I latch onto him, still feeling a pulse, and kick up to the surface.

I ignore the fire that blazes through me where I touch him, because anything is worth it to save his life.

Our heads break the surface, but I'm sputtering out water as his weight and the current tries to drag me down. I pull together every ounce of strength in my body and find it in me to stroke to the shore and hang onto the solid ground. I hoist his body onto the grass and then pull myself up, where I collapse in defeat.

But there's no time to rest. His life is now a question, and the answer is up to me.

I pound my hands against his chest and water caught in his lungs streams from his mouth. Still, it's not enough to revive him. My palms are bumpy with painful blisters, and I fear that any more contact could do unrepairable damage to me. I can already feel heat traveling through my system and making me feel nauseous.

So, I position my mouth above his and breath all my air into him as a feeble attempt at mouth-to-mouth. There's less than a centimeter between our lips and the urge to kiss him consumes me.

It's almost impossible to ignore, but I'm distracted when Carter gives a hacking cough. His lids lift to reveal slits of eye, which soon open all the way. He rubs his head, and I know the hit will result in a nasty bump beneath his hair.

"It's official. Rocks hate me," he mutters and cracks a weary grin.

I can help but burst out laughing and he chuckles along with me. "That might be true," I say.

"So where's Luke?" he groans and staggers to his feet.

I shrug helplessly. "I don't see him anywhere."

Kairo and the others clearly haven't yet found the courage to gamble with the chance we took. Our hushed tones haven't yet revealed if we've survived, and no matter what he says, I doubt Kairo would give up anything that could result in his own death.

We trudge along the riverbed once Carter catches his balance. The weight of my soaked clothes tugs at me, and my hair is as tangled as a bundle of slick, wet seaweed. I run my fingers over the ends and realize how dead and frayed they are. The strands reach to my hips, but their tips are straggly and feel like burned straw from not being trimmed for months.

Carter wipes away the droplets dripping into his eyes. Though, his clothes are barely damp, and only the tips of his hair are peaked into points with water.

My soggy socks chafe my feet, and I'm worried that they'll end up covered in blisters. To me, water itself is fantastic, but wet, itchy clothes plastered against my skin are not.

A bitter argument rises from somewhere high above us. The hostile voices shout to be heard over each other and I can tell they're debating about the worth of taking the plunge. As they contemplate other strategies, they must not realize they're lagging further behind, even with the little effort we put into getting away.

When we've walked a good hundred yards up the river and there's still no sign of Luke, I start to worry. If the current dragged him much further and we haven't heard any yells of a struggle, he must have fallen unconscious.

Then, just upstream, I spot a dark shape that looks out of place among the racing white foam. There's enough distance between us that I can't tell a single detail as to what it is. It's merely a shadow that could be body-sized. A surge of hope fills me and I'm racing towards the shape.

I'm sure it's going to be Luke, but when I arrive at the riverbank, I deflate.

A misshaped and torn black, plastic bag floats along the surface. It's anchored down by a boulder, but it definitely doesn't provide any information to where Luke is.

"It's a plastic bag, isn't it?" Carter calls in defeat as he joins me.

My shoulders slump as I nod glumly. I'm about to give up hope. The situation that's becoming more and more probable is too painful to be possible. Rain. Luke. Gone, in just two days. I refuse to believe it. But no matter what, my mind falls prey and I feel like throwing up at the mere idea. My stomach is queasy as I imagine how we may one day return home: a duo that left with four members.

And Carter will always be by my side, because I refuse to let him go, no matter what.

"I was beginning to think you'd deserted me."

My head swivels around and my stomach unties itself. "Luke?" I exclaim.

"Who else?" he says. "Where have you been?" He looks worried, like he was in a deep search for us.

"We thought you might have died!" Carter says. "Where have *you* been?"

"The current carried me upstream and when I finally got away, I went back downstream to find you. You were gone, so I looped around. We must have been on opposite sides of the trees."

He gestures to the expanse of trees on our right side and I want to slap myself. How could I not stop to think that he could be somewhere in the trees? But he was clearly stuck in the river as long as we were because his clothes and hair drip as often as mine.

I glance from Carter to Luke and notice that their hair has grown longer and shaggier. When I met each of them, it was short and neat, but this journey has done a number on all of us. I know we must look rough around the edges.

I can only imagine others' impressions of us when we cut through bustling towns. Runaways who made violent escapes from juvie. Vagrants who will snatch away your purse if your attention strays for only a second.

"So we're going to Colorado?" Luke says plainly.

"We can't!" I exclaim incredulously. "They know that's where we're planning to go! It would be *pointless*!"

"No," he counters. "If we're fast then we can find the girl and discover what Kairo wants with all of us. She must know something!"

"That's hardly worth risking our lives for!"

"Well, she'll be dead before us if we don't warn her!"

That stops me and I ponder over his words with a frown. It's heartless to not save someone oblivious to the turmoil headed their way when we can help them. It's merciless to shove others in front of you to save yourself, but that's not what I'm doing. But when I speak my debate out loud, I realize it's just as selfish. "I can't risk losing either one of you." Because *I* wouldn't be able to handle it.

"My dad expects us to find her and he expects us to live," Luke says firmly. "I'm not going to let him down."

"I think I have a way around this," Carter says calmly. We both train our eyes on him anxiously. "They expect us to travel together, so if we split up, we're not in as much danger. We might have gotten some peace for now, because Kairo is out to get that girl. Luke, you can go to Colorado, if you don't mind being on your own."

He shrugs in compliance. "I'm fine with that."

"What? He'll be killed! Kairo wants him dead more than either of us right now!" I say.

"They track us by sensing our powers. If we show that we're headed somewhere entirely different than Colorado, they'll probably wait before attacking us to see if we're tricking them. They'll assume Luke is with us." Carter's face is stoic, but his tone lets on uncertainty. "And Luke, if you are Serion, then just make sure nothing sets you off. I doubt you're in control yet."

His face tightens at the mention of what astonished us all. "Yeah, okay," he chokes out.

I bite my lip and ask Carter, "So...we split up, too?"

"No, we can go back to your home, here in Washington." It comes out as more of a question.

I don't react for a moment, but then I give way to a slow nod. "And this is all betting on that Kairo will wait to make sure this isn't a trap; that we're really staying in Port Angeles?"

Carter takes a deep breath and replies, "I think it's the best chance for all of our survival."

The air seems heavy with the weight of our decision. The humidity presses against my face like a wet cloth threatening to suffocate me. This plan leaves us no room for error. One flaw will end in a broken neck.

I can't allow the weight of another death to burden us, so I must think through my every move. I must use common sense and ask myself each time: *What will it result in?* I realize, the girl does have some sort of forewarning that danger is coming. She pleaded for help, even though it's clearly not Kairo who's terrorizing her. We didn't aid her then, but she provided us with knowledge, and we owe her.

"Luke, you're brave to do this," I say admiringly.

"Thank you, Marina," he replies and hugs me in good bye, breaking away shivering. His electric blue eyes blaze with determination. He reaches forward to shake Carter's hand, but pulls away at the second of contact and rubs his hand furiously on his worn jeans. "God, that hurts!"

Carter just gives him a tired smile, "Sorry, I can't really help it."

Luke retrieves a long, curved stick from the ground and throws it far, so it's lost in the shroud of fog. It won't have come close to connecting with anyone, but it's a small act of defiance. It shows that we're still fighting, and no matter what they force us to endure, who they turn against us, who they slaughter, we're not going to give up.

The future may be a treacherous time of spilled blood and loss, but it holds promise. The silver ray of hope still glimmers, and I'm not going to let it go.

So as we say goodbye and part, I know it won't be forever. I watch Luke's retreating form grow smaller and smaller as mist spins across his path. When even squinting, I can't see a trace of him through the fog, I turn my back and face the direction that will point me to an entirely new fate.

"You know, we still have a chance," Carter says. "We always do."

"I know," I say.

It's the little things that remind me that we are united: the memory of our first kiss, the throbbing of my lungs as he saved me from drowning on the island, the face that I fall in love with every time I see it. Our strides match as we venture back into the forest, and I can't help but let a smile shine through my face.

Because I feel the Awakening coursing through my veins. I feel everything that makes me Serion pulsating through me. It shows beginnings, not endings. It shows life, not death. It proves that we're worth more than sacrifices or strange creatures to be taunted. It proves that every moment we spend on Earth has a purpose, and it proves that we are important.

I realize, with Carter by my side, that we can conquer anything.

And for once, I feel like I belong.

<u>Acknowledgements</u>

First of all, thank you to everyone who's read my first published novel. I'm incredibly grateful to you for reading it and helping my writing career become a success.

Thank you to my Mom for being the first to read my book. You did a great job editing and had nothing but positive things to say about each of my plotlines. I appreciate greatly that you were able to keep up with my insane pace and deadlines, while holding your role as a supportive mother at the same time.

To my Dad, thank you for volunteering to format my novel for me. I could never match your digital software skills on the computer. You've done an amazing job making each page look neat and uniform, finding the time to work on formatting when you weren't supporting our family with your hardworking job.

A.J., I chose to dedicate this book to you because you've always been fascinated with the scientific world and been the best little brother I could hope for. Pieces of your personality have inspired characters later to appear. Thank you for reminding me to take breaks and have fun and not get too caught up in my time-consuming writing.

I'm incredibly thankful to these three members of my immediate family listed above. They have been loving and supportive through all my hard work, and I love them immensely for never failing to be there for me.

And to my puppy Sierra, who's smile and wagging tail always brings me happiness. Your playful, loving personality can bring a smile to anyone's face.

Also, in memory of my Nana, whose Italian accent and crocheted blankets are greatly missed, and my kitten, Winter, who we all miss cuddling up against our legs. Even now that you're both in Heaven, you will never be forgotten.

Thank you to my Grandma Joan, for all the generosity you pour into helping raise all your grandchildren, and endlessly being loving and selfless.

And to my Grandpa Ernie and Grandpa Julian, who I never got the chance to meet, but I know your loving and watching over me from Heaven.

To my aunts, uncles, and cousins for enthusiastically anticipating when you'll get the chance to read my completed novel. I'm grateful for all of the support and love. All the laughter at our family get-togethers and the knowledge you will always be there for me means a lot.

Thank you to all of my friends, who have been excited to read my finished book for a long time. You mean so much to me for always sticking by my side and being people who I have countless memories with of all the fun times we shared.

Thank you to my third grade teacher, Mrs. Sanchez, for saying and believing that one day I would become a published author. Also, thanks to each of my other teachers for complementing my writing and encouraging my work.

To Rachel of Littera Designs, I'm so happy with the gorgeous cover you created. You're an extremely talented cover artist, and I am so grateful for the time you put into bringing my vision to life.

Lastly, thank you to the "what ifs" in every creative persons' imagination that keep the possibilities for far away planets and inhuman powers –even if they're only brought to existence in a world printed on paper –alive.

Coming Soon, Book Two of the Fire and Ice Series

CPSIA information can be obtained at www.ICGtesting.com
Printed in the USA
LVOW08s1542160615

442681LV00001B/140/P